DATE DUE

3/26			

GAYLORD   PRINTED IN U.S.A.

THE HUNT BALL

**Center Point
Large Print**

**This Large Print Book carries the
Seal of Approval of N.A.V.H.**

THE HUNT BALL

RITA MAE BROWN

CENTER POINT PUBLISHING
THORNDIKE, MAINE

This Center Point Large Print edition
is published in the year 2005 by arrangement with
Ballantine Books, an imprint of Random House Publishing
Group, a division of Random House, Inc.

The text of this Large Print edition is unabridged.
In other aspects, this book may vary from the original edition.
Printed in the United States of America.
Set in 16-point Times New Roman type.

ISBN 1-58547-666-8

Library of Congress Cataloging-in-Publication Data

Brown, Rita Mae.
    The hunt ball / Rita Mae Brown.--Center Point large print ed.
        p. cm.
    ISBN 1-58547-666-8 (lib. bdg. : alk. paper)
    1. Arnold, Jane (Fictitious character)--Fiction. 2. School administrators--Crimes
against--Fiction. 3. Women detectives--Virginia--Fiction. 4. Women hunters--Fiction.
5. Older women--Fiction. 6. Virginia--Fiction. 7. Large type books. I. Title.

PS3552.R698H86 2005b
813'.6--dc22
                                                                    2005015895

Grab mane and kick on!

Dedicated to Mrs. Mary Tattersall O'Brien, M.D.
Honorary Whipper-in
Oak Ridge Foxhunt Club

CAST OF CHARACTERS

HUMAN

Jane Arnold, "Sister," is the master of foxhounds of the Jefferson Hunt Club in central Virginia. She loves her hounds, her horses, her house pets. Occasionally, she finds humans lovable. Strong, healthy, vibrant at seventy-two, she's proof of the benefits of the outdoor life.

Shaker Crown is the huntsman. He's acquired the discipline of holding his tongue and his temper most times. He's wonderful with hounds. In his early forties, he's finding his way back to love.

Crawford Howard, a self-made man, moved to Virginia from Indiana. He's egotistical, ambitious, and thinks he knows more than he does about foxhunting. But he's also generous, intelligent, and fond of young people. His great disappointment is not being a father, but he never speaks of this, especially to his wife.

Marty Howard loves her husband. They've had their ups and downs but they understand each other. She is accustomed to sweeping up after him but she does this less than in the past. He's got to learn sometime. She's a better rider than her husband, which spurs him on.

Charlotte Norton is the young headmistress of Custis Hall, a prestigious prep school for young ladies. Dedicated to education, she's cool in a crisis.

Anne Harris, "Tootie," is one of the brightest students Charlotte Norton has ever known. Taciturn, observant, yet capable of delivering a stinging barb, this senior shines with promise. She's beautiful, petite, African American, and a strong rider.

Valentina Smith is the class president. Blonde, tall, lean, and drop-dead gorgeous, the kid is a natural politician. She and Tootie can clash at times but they are friends. She loves foxhunting.

Felicity Porter seems overshadowed by Tootie and Val but she is highly intelligent and has a sturdy self-regard. She's the kind of person who is quietly competent. She, too, is a good rider.

Pamela Rene seems burdened by being African American, whereas for Tootie it's a given. Pamela can't stand Val and feels tremendously competitive with Tootie, whom she accuses of being an Oreo cookie. Her family substituted money for love, which makes Pamela poor. Underneath it all, she's basically a good person, but that can be hard to appreciate.

Betty Franklin is the long-serving honorary whipper-in at the Jefferson Hunt Club. Her judgment, way with hounds, knowledge of territory, and ability to ride make her a standout. Many is the huntsman who would kill to have a Betty Franklin whip in to him or her. She's in her mid-forties, a mother, happily married, and a dear, dear friend to Sister.

Dr. Walter Lungrun, joint master of foxhounds of the Jefferson Hunt Club, has only held this position for a year. He's learning all he can. He adores Sister and the feeling is mutual. Their only complaint is that there's so much work to do, they rarely have time for a good talk. Walter is in his late thirties. He is the result of an affair Raymond Arnold Sr. had with Walter's mother. Mr. Lungrun never knew or pretended he didn't, and Sister didn't know until a year ago.

The Bancroft Family. Edward Bancroft, in his seventies, ran a large corporation founded by his family in the mid-nineteenth century. His wife, Tedi, is one of Sister's oldest friends. Tedi rides splendid Thoroughbreds and is always impeccably turned out, as is her surviving daughter, Sybil, who is in her second year as an honorary whipper-in. The Bancrofts are true givers in terms of money, time, and genuine caring.

Knute Nilsson is the treasurer of Custis Hall so he's forever obsessing about the budget. He's efficient, has kept the school in the black, and works well with Charlotte.

Al Perez combines two functions that dovetail, director of alumnae affairs and fund-raising. He's well liked by everyone and a natural for the job. Others attribute his warmth and good nature to his Hispanic background.

Bill Wheatley nears retirement as head of Custis Hall's theater department. The theater department (along with the riding program) is one of the best in the country for secondary schools. Bill has drive, imagination, and humor. But he's seen education change drastically and he's not sorry to be leaving.

Ben Sidel has been sheriff of the county for two years. Originally from Ohio, he sometimes needs help in the labyrinthine ways of the South. He relies on Sister's knowledge and discretion.

THE AMERICAN FOXHOUNDS

Sister and Shaker have carefully bred a balanced pack. The American foxhound blends English, French, and Irish blood, the first identifiable pack being brought here in 1650 by Robert de la Brooke of Maryland. Before that, individual hounds were shipped over, but de la Brooke brought an entire pack. In 1785, General Lafayette sent his mentor and hero, George Washington, a pack of French hounds whose voices were said to sound like "the bells of Moscow."

Whatever the strain, the American foxhound is highly intelligent, beautifully built with a strong sloping shoulder, powerful hips and thighs, and a nice tight foot. The whole aspect of the hound in motion is one of grace, power, and effortless covering of ground. They are "racier" than the English hound and stand perhaps two feet at the shoulder, although size is not nearly as important as nose, drive, cry, biddability. The American hound is sensitive, extremely loving, and has eyes that range from softest brown to gold to sky blue, although one doesn't often see the sky-blue eye. The hound lives to please its master and to chase foxes.

Cora is the strike hound, which means she often

finds the scent first. She's the dominant female in the pack and is in her sixth season.

Diana is the anchor hound and she's in her fourth season. All the other hounds trust her and if they need direction, she'll give it.

Dragon is her littermate. He possesses tremendous drive, a fabulous nose, but he's arrogant. He wants to be the strike hound. Cora hates him.

Dasher is also Diana and Dragon's littermate. He lacks his brother's brilliance but he's steady and smart.

Asa is in his seventh season and is invaluable in teaching the younger hounds, which are the second "D" litter and the "T" litter. A hound's name usually begins with the first letter of his mother's name. So the "D" hounds are out of Delia.

THE HORSES

Sister's horses are: **Keepsake,** a Thoroughbred/quarter horse cross, written TB/QH by horsemen. He's an intelligent gelding of eight years.

Lafayette, a gray Thoroughbred, is eleven now, fabulously athletic, talented, and wants to go.

Rickyroo is a seven-year-old Thoroughbred gelding who shows great promise.

Aztec is a six-year-old Thoroughbred gelding who is learning the ropes. He's also very athletic with great stamina. He has a good mind.

Shaker's horses come from the steeplechase circuit so they are all Thoroughbreds. **Showboat, HoJo,** and **Gunpowder** can all jump the moon, as you might expect.

Betty's two horses are: **Outlaw,** a tough quarter horse who has seen it all and can do it all.

Magellan, a Thoroughbred given to her by Sorrel Buruss, is bigger and rangier than Betty is accustomed to riding, but she's getting used to him.

Czpaka, a warm-blood owned by Crawford Howard, can't stand the man. He's quite handsome, not as quick as the Thoroughbreds, and when he's had it, he's had it. He's not above dumping Crawford.

THE FOXES

The reds can reach a height of sixteen inches, a length of forty-one inches, and they can weigh up to fifteen pounds. Obviously, since these are wild animals who do not willingly come forth to be measured and weighed, there's more variation than the standard cited above. **Target,** his spouse, **Charlene,** his **aunt Netty** and his **uncle Yancy** are the reds. They can be haughty.

A red fox has a white tip on the luxurious brush, except for Aunt Netty, who has a wisp of a white tip as her brush is tatty.

The grays may reach fifteen inches in height, be forty-four inches in length, and weigh up to fourteen pounds. The common wisdom is that grays are smaller than reds, but there are some big ones out there. Sometimes people call them slab-sided grays because they can be reddish. They do not have a white tip on their tail but they may have a black one as well as a black-tipped "mane." Some grays are so dark as to be black.

The grays are **Comet, Inky,** and **Georgia.**

Their dens are a bit more modest than those of the red fox, who likes to announce his abode with a prominent pile of dirt and bones outside. Perhaps not all grays are modest nor all reds full of themselves but as a rule of thumb, it's so.

THE BIRDS

Athena is a great horned owl. Horned owls can stand two and a half feet in height with a wingspread of four feet. They can weigh up to five pounds.

Bitsy is a screech owl and she is eight and a half inches high with a twenty-inch wingspread. She weighs a whopping six ounces and she's reddish brown. Her considerable lungs make up for her stature.

St. Just, a crow, is a foot and a half in height, his wingspread is a surprising three feet, and he weighs one pound.

Raleigh is a Doberman who likes to be with Sister.

Rooster is a harrier and was willed to Sister by her old lover, Peter Wheeler.

Golliwog, "Golly," is a large calico and would hate being included with the dogs as a pet. She is the Queen of All She Surveys.

CHAPTER 1

A shining silver shroud covered the lowlands along Broad Creek, deep and swift-running. The notes of the huntsman's horn, muffled, made his direction difficult to determine. Three young women, students at prestigious Custis Hall, followed the creek bed that bordered a cut hayfield. A gnarled tree, bending toward the clear water as if to bathe its branches, startled them.

"Looks like a giant witch," Valentina Smith blurted out.

They stopped to listen for hounds and the horn. Smooth gray stones jutted out of the creek, the water swirling and splashing around.

"Can you hear anything?" Felicity Porter, slender, serious, inquired.

"If we move away from the creek, we'll hear better." Valentina, as senior class president, was accustomed to taking charge.

Anne "Tootie" Harris, one of the best students at Custis Hall, was just as accustomed to resisting Valentina's assumed authority. "We'll get even more lost. Broad Creek runs south. It divides the Prescott land from Sister Jane's land. If we keep going we'll eventually reach the big old hog's back jump in the fence line. If we turn right at that jump we'll find the farm road back to the kennels."

Angry that she hadn't paid attention at the jump to where the rest of the riders disappeared into the fog, and now angry that she hadn't paid attention to the flow of Broad Creek, Valentina growled, "Well, shit, Tootie, we could go into menopause before we reach the hog's back jump!"

"One dollar, potty mouth." Felicity held out her hand with grim satisfaction.

"Felicity, how can you think of the kitty at a time like this? We could be lost for days. Why, we could die of thirst and—"

"Val, we're next to Broad Creek," Tootie dead-panned.

"You two are ganging up on me." Val tossed her head; her blonde ponytail, in a snood for riding, swayed slightly.

"No, we're not." Felicity rarely ran off the rails, her focus intense. "The deal when we started hunting with Jefferson Hunt was that each time one of us swore, one dollar to the kitty. I'm the bank."

Valentina fished in her tweed jacket. "You'll probably end up being a banker, F. I can see it now when you make your first million. You'll count the money, put it in a vault, and not even smile." She did, however, hand over her dollar.

Felicity leaned over to reach for the dollar, their horses side by side. She folded it in half, neatly sticking it in her inside jacket pocket. Felicity knew she wasn't quick-witted. No point in firing back at Valentina.

With Felicity and Valentina it was the tortoise and the hare. With Tootie and Valentina it was the hawk and the hare, two swift-moving creatures with opposing points of view.

"Come on, I'll get us back to the kennels," Tootie promised.

In the far distance the hounds sang, voices ranging from soprano to basso profundo, from tenor to darkest alto. The heavy moisture in the air accounted for the variation in clarity. The girls would hear the hounds moving toward them, then it would sound as though the hounds were turning.

"Coach will tear us a new one." Valentina did not reply to Tootie's suggestion, speaking about the coach's wrath instead.

"Coach? What about Mrs. Norton?" Felicity thought the headmistress's disapproval would be more severe than Bunny Taliaferro's, the riding coach, although Bunny naturally leaned toward censure.

"Wonder if they know we're not with the field? I mean, it's possible they're still in the fog, too. Sister Jane would get really upset if she thought we were in trouble." Valentina inhaled deeply. "If they don't know, let's swear never to tell."

"The Three Musketeers." Tootie half-smiled.

"All for one and one for all." Valentina beamed.

"But you always manage to be first among equals, Val. It's not exactly all for one and one for all. It's all for Valentina and then maybe Val for all," Tootie said, shooting a barb.

"Tootie, you can really be the African queen when you're in a mood. You know?" Valentina raised an eyebrow.

"Yeah, right." Tootie, an exceptionally beautiful green-eyed African American, shrugged it off.

"Will you two get over yourselves? If we don't find our way back, we're in deep doo-doo. If we do find the field, we're still in deep doo-doo but maybe not as deep."

"Felicity, say shit and be done with it." Val took out some of her discomfort on her sober classmate.

"One dollar."

"I could learn to hate you." Valentina fetched another crinkled dollar, fuming as Tootie hid a smile behind her gloved hand.

"Thank you." This time Felicity snatched the money.

Hounds sounded as if they were swinging toward them; the notes on the horn played one long note followed by a series of doubled and even tripled notes, one long note, and the process was repeated.

"All on," Tootie remarked.

Bunny Taliaferro drummed the basics of foxhunting into those students she selected as proficient enough to ride hard over big fences and uneven ground. The show-ring riders who panicked outside of a flat ring where they counted strides could never join the chosen few. This caused tensions because often the show-ring girls looked much prettier on a horse. Unfortunately, flying down a steep hill usually meant they popped off their horses like toast. The sound of "ooff" and "ohh" punctuated the hoofbeats on those occasions.

Valentina, Tootie, and Felicity performed well in the show ring—they'd made the school team—but they excelled over terrain, so had earned the privilege to hunt. Each girl could handle sudden situations calling for split-second decisions, and each girl could usually keep a horse between her legs even when the footing was slick as an eel. What Bunny prized most about them was they were bold, keen, go-forward girls.

"All on and heading our way." Felicity recognized the horn call, straining to make sure her ears weren't playing tricks on her.

"Christ, they'll all see us!" Valentina worried more about saving face than getting chewed out.

"One dollar."

"Christ isn't swearing."

"Christ isn't swearing. You are." Felicity in a rare moment of dry humor held out her hand.

"Not fair." Valentina bit her lip.

"Oh, pay up. You've got more money than God anyway," Tootie half-laughed.

"Sure," Valentina said sarcastically.

All of the girls came from wealthy families, but Valentina received the largest allowance and was the envy of the other students. To her credit she was generous.

She forked over the dollar bill.

"Look, they really are coming this way. Let's slip

back into the mists. We can bring up the rear right after they cross Broad Creek," Tootie suggested.

"Fox could turn." Felicity considered the gamble.

"Yes, but if he doesn't, the crossing is up past the trees. We'll hear them. If they turn, we'll keep going until we find the hog's back and then head toward Sister Jane's."

The kennels were at Sister Jane's farm, Roughneck Farm. Jane Arnold had been master of the Jefferson Hunt Club for over thirty years. Her late husband had also been a master.

"Vote." Felicity thought this would short-circuit Valentina's protest since Valentina hated agreeing readily with Tootie.

"You don't have to vote." Valentina turned toward Tootie, the mist rising a bit, swirling around the beautiful girl. "It's a good plan."

"I can't believe you said that," Tootie giggled. "F., we'd better remember this day."

They would, but for quite different reasons.

They backtracked fifty yards from the creek crossing.

"Why?" Felicity asked.

"Because the other horses will smell ours," Tootie sensibly replied. "Go on back a little more."

"Tootie, we'll lose them again." Valentina was more worried about Bunny and Mrs. Norton, the headmistress, than she cared to admit.

"No, we won't. Let me be in front this time."

Tootie rode tail during the entire hunt, which is one

of the reasons they got lost. Felicity, in front, didn't have the best sense of direction. When the whole field jumped a black coop in the fog, they landed into a woods, ground covered with pine needles. Those needles soaked up the sound of hoofbeats. By the time Tootie got over the fence, Felicity had turned left instead of right with the others. It was too late to catch them. For ten minutes they couldn't hear a thing, not the horses, not the hounds, not the horn. So Tootie led them south along Broad Creek since she could hear the water.

Neither Valentina nor Felicity argued, since both knew Tootie was a homing pigeon.

They quietly waited.

A splash sent the ears of all three horses forward. The humans heard it, too.

Comet reached their side of the bank, shook, then sauntered toward them.

"You three are as useless as tits on a boar hog," the male gray fox insulted them.

"Tally ho," Felicity whispered as though the other two couldn't see the fox sitting right in front of them.

Tootie glared at her. One should not speak when the fox was close or when hounds were close. The correct response would be to take off your cap, point in the direction in which the fox would be traveling, and point your horse's head in that direction also.

"Tally human." Comet flicked his tail, tilted his head. He could gauge the sound of the hounds far more accurately than the three girls before him. *"Well,*

21

chums, think I'll motor on. You look ridiculous sitting here in the middle of the covert, you know."

He vanished.

"He barked at us!" Valentina was thrilled.

"I've never been that close to a fox." Felicity was awed and a little scared to look the quarry square in the eye.

The beautiful music of hounds in full cry came closer. The girls stopped talking, almost holding their breath.

Moneybags, Valentina's big boy, started the chortle that leads to a whinny. She leaned over, pressing her fingers along his neck, which he liked.

"Money, shut up."

He did just as the head hound, a large tricolor, Dragon, vaulted off the far bank into the water. Trident, Diana, and Dreamboat followed closely behind the lead hound.

Within a minute, the girls heard the larger splashing sound of Showboat, the huntsman's horse, fording the creek, deep, thanks to recent steady, heavy rains.

Another four minutes elapsed before Keepsake, Sister Jane's hardy nine-year-old Thoroughbred/quarter horse cross, managed the waters. After that the cacophony of splashing hooves and grunts from riders, faces wet from the horses in front of them, filled the air.

"Come on," Tootie said as loudly as she dared.

The three crept forward just as the noise seemed finished. Crawford Howard suddenly crossed, though. He'd fallen behind. He was startled to see the three young women riding out of the mists, as was his horse, Czpaka, who shied, unseating Crawford right in the middle of Broad Creek.

"Oh, shit," Valentina said low.

"One dollar." Felicity truly was single-minded.

"Not now, F. We've got to get him up, apologize, and get with the field before we lose them again." Tootie hopped off Iota, her horse, handing the reins to Valentina.

"Mr. Howard, this is my fault. I am so sorry." She waded into the creek, cold water spilling over her boots down into her socks.

Swiftly, she grabbed Czpaka's reins, still over his head. Czpaka considered charging out and leaving Crawford. A warm-blood, big-bodied fellow, he wasn't overfond of his owner.

"Whoa," Tootie firmly said.

"Oh, bother. I hope he freezes his ass." The horse did stand still, though.

"Then he'll kick yours," called out Parson, Felicity's horse.

"I can dump him anytime I want," Czpaka bragged. *"The only reason I let him sit up there like a damned tick is I like following the hounds and being with all you guys."*

Tootie led Czpaka out. He stepped up on the bank. Crawford sloshed out. While he could be pompous on occasion he did see the humor of his situation. Besides, foxhunters had to expect the occasional opportunity to show off their breaststroke.

23

The mist rose slowly, the sun higher in the sky now on this brisk October day. But one could still only see fifty feet. Tootie looked for a place where Crawford could stand to mount his big horse. The huge knees of the gnarly tree wouldn't do. They'd be slippery, adding insult to injury.

"Val, you hold Czpaka while I give Mr. Howard a leg up."

Valentina, at six feet one inch, one inch taller than Sister Jane, was stronger than Tootie, who stood at five feet four inches. "You hold. I'll give him the leg up." She handed Iota to Felicity and Moneybags, too.

"Girls, I'll be fine," he demurred.

"Well, your boots are wet and the soles will be pretty slippery, sir. It's only cubbing. No reason to risk an injury before the season really starts." Tootie's judgment belied her years. She'd always been that way, even as a little thing.

"Good thinking." He reached up to grasp Czpaka's mane with his left hand, resting his right on the pommel of his Hermès saddle with knee roll. He bent his left leg as Val cupped her hands under it, lifting him as he pushed off with his right leg.

The tall blonde was grateful he pushed off. Some people, like sacks of potatoes, just stand there and you have to lift all of them up. Hernia time.

Tootie held the right stirrup iron to steady the saddle, releasing her hand and the reins once Crawford was secure.

Both young women gracefully mounted up, except

that water spilled from Tootie's right boot when she swung her leg high and over.

Hounds, screaming, were moving on at speed.

"Let's put the pedal to the metal." He clapped his leg on Czpaka, who shot off like a cannonball.

Moneybags, Iota, and Parson gleefully followed.

Within a few minutes they came up behind the field of twenty-five. As it was a Thursday hunt, the number of riders was smaller than on a Saturday. The mists kept lifting like a slippery veil.

Marty, Crawford's wife, turned to see her wet husband as they galloped along. She said nothing because hounds were speaking, but then, even if at a check, she would have remained silent.

In some ways, the checks separated the sheep from the goats for foxhunters. It was a far better test of one's foxhunting etiquette than taking a whopping big fence in style. Though one had to admit, the latter was far more exciting.

They thundered on. Water spritzed off Crawford's coat, his cap, and Czpaka's sleek coat.

They checked hard. Hounds bolted up toward a thick overgrown hillock. By now the riders could see, as the mists hung above their heads.

Sister waited for a moment. She didn't want to crowd hounds or her huntsman, Shaker Crown. As field master she kept the riders together, tried to keep hounds in sight yet stay out of the way.

Shaker hopped off Showboat as Dr. Walter Lungrun, the joint master, trotted up to hold the horse's reins.

Down low in the hayfield they'd just ridden across stood Betty Franklin, longtime honorary whipper-in. An old apple orchard was on the left by the deeply sunken farm road leading up to Hangman's Ridge.

Although she couldn't be seen, Sybil Bancroft, waiting in there, caught her breath after the hard run.

She, too, was an honorary whipper-in, which meant she wasn't paid for the tremendous time and effort she put into Jefferson Hunt.

Both paid and unpaid staff routinely perform heroic duties. Even if paid for it, no one enters hunt service without a grand passion for the game. You can't handle it otherwise. It's much too tough for modern people accustomed to the cocoon of physical comfort.

Comet had a den on the other side of Soldier Road, a two-lane paved ribbon, east-west, two and a half miles from this spot as the crow flies. As it was, St. Just, the king of the crows, was circling. He hated foxes and wanted to make sure he knew where Comet was.

Shaker took a few steps upward but couldn't get through the pricker bushes and old still-blooming pink tea roses. The remains of a stone foundation could be glimpsed through the overgrowth.

Comet dashed into an old den there that had been vacant for four years. The original tenant, a large red dog fox, had been shot and killed.

No foxhunter can abide anyone who kills a fox in such a manner.

Few American foxhunters want to kill a fox. Even if

they were vulpicides, they wouldn't murder too many. The land, the crops planted, and the ethos of American foxhunting mitigated against the kill.

Once in the old den, Comet immediately saw room for improvement and decided he'd abandon his den at Foxglove Farm for this one. He'd be hunting in his sister's territory, but he was sure he and Inky could accommodate each other.

Like all fox dens, this one was cleverly placed, drainage good, fresh water close by. The original tenants had created many entrances and exits, strategically placed.

"Dig him out!" Trident's paws flew in the soft earth.

Hearing the frenzy, Comet laughed. *"You can dig all the way to China, you nitwit. You'll never get me."*

"Did you hear that?" Little Diddy couldn't believe her ears.

"Blowhard." Dragon dug harder than Trident.

"Not as bad as Target. That's the most conceited fox that's ever lived." Diana mentioned a red dog fox who lived over at the Bancrofts.

"Good hounds, good hounds." Shaker blew "gone to ground," praised his hounds a bit more, then took the reins from Walter, lightly lifted himself into the saddle, and blew hounds away from the den. "Boss?" He looked to Sister Jane even though Walter had been joint master for a year now.

Walter took no offense because Sister was in charge of breeding the hounds, training them with Shaker. His responsibility revolved around taking territory duties off her shoulders. They both handled landowners, usually a pleasure.

Walter, however, studied bloodlines, preparing for that distant day when the weight of this would fall on him. He prayed the day would be very distant because she knew so much, and also because Jane Arnold was beloved by most, hated by few.

Walter believed you can judge a person by her enemies as well as her friends.

"Let's go in, Shaker. No point in getting the hounds footsore, and we've been going hard for most of two hours."

"All right, then." He blew a note evenly, then lifted it with a lilt so his hounds knew they were walking in, as did his two whippers-in, sweating although it was forty-nine degrees out.

The horses blew out of their large nostrils. Everyone was glad to be turning back toward the trailers and toward an impromptu tailgate.

Bunny, riding with Mrs. Norton, her boss and dear friend, pulled off to the side, then fell in with Crawford, Marty, and the three girls, whom she called "The Three Amuses."

"Where were you?" She stared accusingly at Tootie, wet from the knees down. Her eyes passed to a very silent Valentina and Felicity.

Crawford quickly answered. "I fell behind and the girls stayed with me and then I had the bad luck to slip in Broad Creek. If it weren't for Tootie, Czpaka would have run off. You've trained your girls well,

Bunny. I'm certainly grateful."

She beamed at the praise. Bunny's ego rested close to the surface. "I'm so glad they could be of service to you, Crawford."

"Yes, thank you, girls." Marty smiled broadly at the three kids, each pretty in her own way, although Tootie's green eyes just jumped out at one.

As Bunny turned to ride up to Charlotte Norton, Crawford winked.

"Mr. Howard, she would have torn us a new one," Valentina sighed. "Thank you."

"Yes, I owe you one, sir. It's our fault Czpaka spooked." Tootie truly was contrite.

"This is foxhunting," he said and winked again. "All for one and one for all."

Each Custis Hall student made note that she'd heard that earlier. They would find out soon enough how critical and testing that philosophy was: simple, true, and to the bone.

CHAPTER 2

After the tailgate, the rigs pulled out and Sister returned to the kennels. Her house dogs—Raleigh, a Doberman, and Rooster, a harrier—bounded along as the mercury climbed to the low sixties, the mists dissipated, and the dew sparkled on the still-green grass.

Golliwog, the calico, long-hair cat, sauntered

behind, not wishing to appear to be part of the group.

Sister opened the kennel door as Shaker was walking toward the office.

"Good day, really," he beamed.

"Indeed. The fog gets disorienting but—" Sister didn't finish her sentence as Betty, wearing her ancient Wellies, trooped toward her.

"New den."

"Old one, new fox." Sister smiled.

"Spooky out there for a little bit, wasn't it?" Betty, having lost twenty pounds, now back to her schoolgirl weight, burst with energy.

"Clammy damp." Shaker heard a yelp. He walked back down the wide aisle. "All right now."

"He started it," Dreamboat, a hound, tattled.

"I did not. All I did was step on his tail," Doughboy defended himself.

Shaker sternly peered into the young boys' run, as they called it. "You all did very well today. Don't spoil it."

The youngsters wagged their tails, eyes bright. They'd put their fox to ground, working right along with the "big kids."

Shaker returned to his master and whipper-in. "Sybil said her ears played tricks on her at the base of Hangman's Ridge. She thought she heard a truck motor up there."

"Sound bounced like a ball." Sister liked Sybil. Her mother, Tedi, was a friend of fifty years.

"Where is Sybil?"

"Had to hurry home. Board meeting in town. Marty Howard convinced her to serve on her literacy campaign group. Say, before I forget, Shaker, Halloween night, the boys from the Miller School will be doing something up on Hangman's Ridge. I said I didn't care as long as they cleaned up their mess. They're going to the big dance at Custis Hall and then Charlotte has allowed the girls to go to the ridge, chaperoned, of course, for an hour of fright after the dance. Guess it will be big beans."

Betty grimaced. "Too many hanged ghosts. Aren't there eighteen or something like that?"

"Think so." Shaker rubbed his chin. He'd missed a spot, fingered the stubble.

Sister thought of the souls wandering on the ridge as well as the souls of all those they harmed in life. "Well, the world's full of anguish. Let's keep it at bay."

"I'll go start on the tack." Betty wiped her hands on the coveralls she'd slipped over her britches. "That's my contribution to keeping anguish at bay."

"The Custis Hall girls already did it."

"They did?" Betty smiled.

"Their own idea. Neither Charlotte nor Bunny pushed them to it." Sister, a board member of Custis Hall, was pleased at the young women's thoughtfulness. "Good job, too."

"Bunny Taliaferro makes them break down the tack and clean it with toothbrushes," Betty laughed. "Not every day, of course."

"She's a hard nut, that one." Among these two friends, Shaker could freely express himself.

"Yes, she is. A good-looking woman, but stern," Sister agreed.

"Sure knows how to turn riders into horsemen. Got to give her that." Betty folded her arms over her chest, then noticed a cobweb up in the corner of the office that she had to attack immediately with the crop Shaker had placed on the desk. "Gotcha."

"Spider will haunt you," Sister laughed.

"I didn't kill her. I've only invited her to spin her web elsewhere."

"I sure miss Jennifer and Sari," Sister changed the subject. "Not just because they cleaned tack. Those two were a tonic."

Jennifer was Betty's youngest daughter. Her oldest, Cody, languished in jail, having fallen by the wayside thanks to drugs. Sari Rusmussen was Jennifer's best friend and the daughter of Shaker's girlfriend of one year.

"Well, she loves, loves, loves Colby College. I tell her, you keep loving it, honey, wait until that Maine winter settles in for eight months. She and Sari talk to each other every day via e-mail even though they're roommates."

"Why in the world do they do that?" Sister, although a fan of her iMac G5, still considered using it drudgery.

"They have one other roommate," Betty said and burst out laughing. "And they can't stand her, of course."

"What do you hear?" Sister asked Shaker.

32

"Thriving." He paused. "Lorraine's not. In the last month she's sent four care packages, one a week." He smiled a warm, engaging smile.

A knock on the door turned their heads in that direction.

"Come on in," Sister called out.

Marty opened it and stuck her head inside. "You didn't forget our meeting, did you?"

Betty and Sister looked at each other, because they had.

"Oh, Marty, I'm so sorry. I saw Sam drive away with Crawford in the passenger seat and I blanked out. Betty, come on."

"Let me get out of my coveralls and Wellies."

"You make a fashion statement," Marty teased her.

"The aroma of horse manure is a bonus. Be right up."

As Sister left with Marty, the two dogs fell in behind and Golly brought up the rear.

"Black bottom, you got 'em." Golly sang a few notes from the old 1926 song.

"She's referring to you." Rooster's pink tongue stuck out between his teeth.

"I'm not paying any attention to her." Raleigh lifted his noble head higher.

"How much is that doggy in the window?" Golly moved forward in time to Patti Page's 1953 hit song.

"Golly, what's the matter with you, going mental on us again?" Rooster loved to torment the cat. It was mutual.

"Death to all dogs!" she screamed, shot forward, jumped off the ground, and hit Rooster on the side with all four paws. She bounded off like a swimmer making a turn in a pool, then she scorched ahead of the dogs, blasted past the humans, and climbed up the old pawpaw tree, where she immediately struck a pose on a large branch.

"You're very impressive," Sister drily commented as she and Marty passed under the pawpaw tree.

"I am who I am! I am the mightiest cat in all Christendom. Dogs shudder at the mention of my name, Killer Kitty!"

"I'm going to throw up," Rooster coughed.

"Roundworms," Golly taunted.

Raleigh, on his hind legs, tried to reach the branch.

Betty, hurrying to catch up, called out to the sleek animal. "Your mother will give you such a smack."

Sister turned and beheld Raleigh, Rooster waiting at the bottom of the tree. "Boys, leave her alone."

"You're lucky she protects you or I'd be throwing up a big hairball: you," Rooster barked with mock menace.

Sister called over her shoulder, "Boys, she's not worth it."

"Ha!" Raleigh dropped to all fours and pranced toward the three women as Betty caught up.

Rooster followed.

"She doesn't protect me. I can blind you with a single blow. I can tear out your whiskers one by one. I can bite your tail in two."

"Ignore her," Sister said in a singsong voice.

"You're afraid of me. Admit it!" Golly ratcheted up the volume. She huffed, she thrashed her tail. No response. The two dogs didn't even turn to watch her. Disgruntled, she backed down the tree, grumbling loudly, so loudly that Cora, the head bitch, could hear it in the big girls' run.

"Golly, pipe down, I need my beauty rest," Cora said as she stretched out.

"Face it, girl, you need plastic surgery," Golly fired back again at high volume. She then dug her claws in the grass, wiggled her behind, and tore off, flying past the dogs and humans. She soared over the chrysanthemums filling richly glazed pots by the mudroom door. She then sat down to lick her front paws as the people approached.

"Golly certainly has a high opinion of herself," Betty laughed.

"Don't they all?" Sister laughed in turn.

CHAPTER 3

As Sister, Betty, and Marty walked toward the house, Comet was enlarging the den in the stone ruins. His den across Soldier Road on Cindy Chandler's farm appeared shabby to him compared to this. The other motivation for switching dens involved his housekeeping skills. He had none. His old den was filling up with bones, feathers, and fur. Some foxes are good organizers, others aren't.

He cheerfully lined the main section with grass, made note of good places for extra entrances and exits, and was particularly pleased that the creek gurgled one hundred yards below him. He was close to water but in no danger of flooding. To make the site even better, the pricker bushes and rambling old tea roses would keep out the nosy.

The hands that cut and placed the stone vanished from the earth in 1787. The small house was eventually abandoned as the next generation prospered to build the first section of Roughneck Farm, the simple but large, graceful house that Sister and her husband, Raymond, bought when young marrieds. It had a roof and walls but the staircases had collapsed. It was a ruin. Together they restored the place, doing much of the work themselves. In good time, Raymond began to make a lot of money. By the time they reached their mid-thirties they could pay for any repairs or improvements.

While Sister knew of this old, well-built foundation, she never cleared it. She recognized a splendid site for a den as well as Comet. She wanted Roughneck Farm to appeal to foxes the way Murray Hill appeals to a certain kind of Manhattan resident.

Comet carried in more sweetgrass and suddenly dropped to his belly, hearing a light flutter of mighty wings. These wings were silent until it was too late.

A pair of huge balled-up talons raked his back.

He snarled, then bolted for the main entrance. He

heard a large bird walking around the opening to his den and cursed that he hadn't time to dig out more exits.

"Oh, come on out, you big chicken," a deep voice chortled.

"Athena." He popped his head out as the two-foot great horned owl turned her head nearly upside down to stare at him.

"Scared you," she laughed again.

"Nah, I wanted to make you feel good," he lied.

She blinked, her large golden eyes both beautiful and hypnotizing. *"You are too clever by half. Take care, Comet, that you don't come to a bad end. You put me in mind of Dragon, that arrogant hound. He's another one who pays no heed to good sense."*

Comet emerged from his den. Arguing with Athena could bring reprisals. She wasn't just the queen of the night, she was the queen, period, but her authority irritated him. On the other hand, foxes and owls were allies and it was best not to disturb the equilibrium.

"Isn't death always a bad end?"

"No." She unruffled her feathers, the sunlight warming her.

"H-m-m. I don't want to go anytime soon."

"Who does unless they're suffering?" She paused, turned her head around almost backward to behold Bitsy, the screech owl, flying toward them. *"God, I hope she isn't going to sing to us."*

Bitsy lived in Sister's barn. A little thing, but her voice could wake the dead. She so wanted to be like the great horned owl whose voice, sonorous and low, filled the forests and meadows with melancholy beauty.

As hunting had been good for all the prey animals, they lingered in the soft early-morning light before retiring to their nests and dens. The foxes, on such a warming autumn day, would find flat rocks on which to sunbathe.

"Guess what?" Bitsy also lived for gossip.

"What?" Comet humored her.

"You scared the bejabbers out of those Custis Hall girls. I heard them talking at the tailgate."

"This pipsqueak scared them?" Athena asked, which thrilled the screech owl, who felt she had important information.

"They were separated from the others, wandering about in the mist. Comet popped out right in front of them, uttered a few unkind words, and took off. It's a pity humans have such poor senses. Those girls, when they first took the wrong turn, couldn't have been more than a hundred yards from the other humans, yet they couldn't smell horse or human. They rode left, everyone else rode right. It's a wonder humans have survived."

"Herd animals. They can't survive without one another," Comet astutely noted.

"That doesn't explain their inability to smell. What's the difference if there's one human or one thousand? They still don't know what's under their nose, literally." Bitsy puffed out her plump breast.

"Now, Bitsy, every creature on earth has figured out what it must do to live. Humans are day hunters, we're night hunters. Their eyes aren't too bad in the light. Nothing like ours, naturally, but they're perfectly serviceable. They can climb trees, build things. They are so successful now that most of them don't realize how weak they are. Ah, well, it will all come to a bad end," Athena said and sighed.

"That's what you said about me and that snot, Dragon."

"Really!" Bitsy's huge eyes grew even larger as she listened to Comet. She then turned to her heroine. *"Did you say that?"*

"I did. And now, of course, you want to know why." Athena raised her right eyebrow. *"Because both of them are too clever by half. Sooner or later, they'll reach too far."*

Comet smiled. *"Is that an observation or a prophecy?"*

"Both," Athena succinctly replied.

"Any other prophecies?" He unfurled his long pink tongue.

"Here's an observation before a prophecy. You're in Inky's territory. You'd better reach an accord."

Inky, a gray fox whose coat was so dark she shone glistening black, was a beloved friend of most of the other animals as well as Sister and the hounds. Everyone knew Inky. She visited the kennels nightly as she made her rounds. The only animal who didn't like Inky was Golly.

"There's so much game this season. I don't think Inky will mind." He considered Athena's advice, though. *"But you're right. No point getting on her bad side. And I can't take her for granted even though we are littermates."*

"Her cubs are leaving the den. They're making their way in the world. What if one of them wanted this den?" Bitsy kept tabs on the neighborhoods.

"I'll cross that bridge when I come to it." Comet had no intention of surrendering his new apartment. *"Athena, your prophecy?"*

"We're a week from All Hallow's Eve. Propitiate the dead."

"Some dead can't be satisfied." Bitsy believed in ghosts. She'd seen them.

Comet, like most animals, was sensitive to what humans especially couldn't explain. They often felt spirits around them, but the species was hag-ridden by logic. Few would admit to the experience. *"Not a good time to go to Hangman's Ridge."*

Athena's voice lowered. *"And it will be black as pitch on All Hallow's Eve, beware."*

CHAPTER 4

The bricks of Custis Hall's original four buildings around the quad had faded over the two centuries of their existence into a glowing paprika. Mt. Holyoke, founded on November 8, 1837, boasted being the first institution of higher learning for young ladies. But Custis Hall, a preparatory school, predated Mt. Holyoke by twenty-five years. It masqueraded as a finishing school. The girls learned management, mathematics, Latin, French, embroidery (a good hand was considered one of the gracious arts), a smattering of history, and a bit of literature, although the reading of modern novels was discouraged by the administration. Novels were considered racy. A copy of *Moll Flanders* or *Les Liaisons Dangereuses* could park a pretty bottom on a hard bench in front of the headmistress.

Charlotte Norton smiled to herself thinking about the history of Custis Hall as she eased off the accelerator, turned right onto the campus, passing through the monstrously large wrought-iron gates, the morning sun hitting the buildings so they shimmered. She never tired of seeing the restrained architecture. She loved her work and felt not one pang of jealousy when her former graduate school classmates moved ever closer to becoming presidents of universities, a few already presidents of smaller colleges. Her passion was secondary school.

She noticed, as she coasted into her parking space, a van with the local TV station's call letters and number on it. It was parked illegally alongside the main campus road and she had no idea where the campus police might be.

The only vehicles allowed beyond the parking lot were service vehicles. The door to her new Volvo

AWD VC70 station wagon closed with a comforting heavy thud. She heard chanting.

Her boot heels clicked as she hurried along the stone path, worn from use, toward the back of Old Main Hall. She'd intended to dash into her office, change clothes, and get on with her day. She'd left her cell phone to charge on her desk and now regretted that decision. Usually she called Teresa Bourbon, her assistant, at least once before reaching her office.

The chanting grew louder. She pulled open the back door to Old Main, the long polished wooden corridor before her.

"Plantation! Plantation! The Custis Hall Plantation."

"What the hell?" she muttered to herself, noticing, as she raced to her office, that no one was in theirs.

She skidded to her open door, Teresa commanding the anteroom.

"Mrs. Norton, we've got a situation." Teresa met her boss's gaze levelly as she used the old black expression.

"Jesus, what is going on?"

"There are fifty girls in the Main Hall, one TV reporter, and one print reporter. They have just discovered that Custis Hall was founded by a slave owner." Teresa, African American, held up her hand, her silver rings shining. "And they are deeply upset by the artifacts displayed in Main Hall."

A long stream of air blew out of Charlotte's delicately shaped nostrils, her nose slightly upturned. "I can't go out there in riding habit."

"Oh, why not?" Teresa wickedly smiled. "You'll confirm their idea that you're the Miss'us."

Charlotte loved Teresa. They'd worked cheek by jowl for nine years. The thirty-six-year-old woman knew exactly how to handle her. Charlotte flew into her paneled office, ran to the bathroom, shed her jacket, vest, and shirt, grunting as she pulled off her boots with the stand-up boot pull. She yanked a deep carmine cashmere turtleneck sweater over her head. This was followed by a pleated black skirt. She used her coveted staghandle boot pulls to pull up a pair of soft Italian leather boots. She took a very deep breath, then calmly walked out of her office as Teresa winked.

"Don't you want to witness this?"

"No. Gotta mind the store. If it gets really good, I'll lock the door and come fetch you home."

"Oh, Teresa," Charlotte smiled softly, "I think I'm about to be called a racist pig."

"Could be worse."

"I suppose it could." With that, Charlotte squared her shoulders, lifted her head, and strode to the great entry hall at the front of Old Main.

At the sight of her, students renewed their vigor and volume. Dwayne Rickman, fiftyish, a local celebrity as a TV reporter, moved toward her with the microphone.

She saw the two overwhelmed security fellows, men way past their prime but still wearing a uniform, swing toward him.

Knute Nilsson, treasurer, looked relieved as she took

over, as did Alfonso Perez, the director of alumnae affairs. They'd been holding the girls at bay, assisted by Amy Childers, the head of the science department, and her brother, a board member, Christopher Stoltenfuss. Knute, a natural leader, quick-thinking, told the other teachers to stay with their routine, don't leave the classroom. Amy happened to be coming in for an appointment with Charlotte and simply got caught in the middle. Her brother had come for a meeting with Knute so they felt like deer in headlights.

Al Perez had walked out of his office the minute he heard the chanting. He and Knute worked well together. They had things, more or less, under control. Everyone adored Al, a sunny personality in his early thirties, a new baby at home, career on the upswing. To date, he was the only Hispanic faculty member, and he adamantly pushed for hiring more Hispanic faculty.

"Mrs. Norton, what is Custis Hall doing to accommodate its African-American students?" Dwayne asked politely.

"Custis Hall's mission is to give each young woman a superior education, a grounding for life. Her race, her religion, her class background are irrelevant to that task but relevant to our knowledge of her. We have the highest number of scholarship students of any preparatory school on the East Coast." As she spoke her eyes swept over the fifty-odd girls. Perhaps one-third of them were students of color; the others, white, appeared even more impassioned than the African-American students. Her Hispanic and Asian students were conspicuous by their absence.

"Custis Hall is the plantation," Pamela Rene, the ringleader, began the chant.

The others took it up but quieted as Dwayne asked more questions. He signaled his cameraman to cut the lights.

"Mrs. Norton, thank you." He nodded to her.

Dwayne liked Charlotte Norton. She did a lot for the community. Her husband, Carter, head of neuro-surgery at the local hospital, was another tremendous asset. Dwayne had been around long enough to know a setup when he saw one. He'd do his best with the footage he shot to make sure Custis Hall and Charlotte came out ahead.

The print reporter evidenced no loyalty to Custis Hall or Charlotte. He was new to the area and this story held about as much appeal to him as covering brush fires in the county.

"Ladies," Charlotte addressed the assembled, who did give her the courtesy of silence, "I'd be untruthful if I didn't tell you I'm surprised. I had no idea you were uneasy about our founder, our beginnings, but as you can see, Mr. Nilsson, Mr. Perez, Mrs. Childers, and our board of directors member, Mr. Stoltenfuss, are in front of you. We'll listen, but we can't listen in this setting. A charged subject demands cool heads and a better place in which to discuss the issues."

Pamela spoke out, pointing to the locked glass cases

that contained artifacts of Miss Custis's life: George Washington's epaulettes; a dress worn by his wife, Martha; pots, iron skillets, plowshares, old bits. A marvelous carriage, impeccably equipped, sat on a dais in the center of Main Hall. All objects represented the life of Martha Washington's niece. "Slaves made these things but they get no credit! That's wrong."

Charlotte had to bite her tongue because the dress had been fashioned in Paris. This was clearly spelled out in the hand-painted cards identifying each item. However, Pamela was correct about the other artifacts. She neglected to mention that there was a brief gloss on slave labor. Didn't matter. It wasn't enough and it wasn't what Pamela wanted: attention.

"Ladies, I'm willing to meet with you one by one or in groups. But this calls for quiet thinking and a great deal of research."

Knute stepped in and spoke, for which Charlotte was grateful. "So much was destroyed between 1861 and 1865. We've lost a lot, including information about the Custis family. No one paid much attention to slaves or women. Their lives weren't well documented. Miss Custis merited attention because she was related to George and Martha Washington. We'll address your concerns as Mrs. Norton said. But let's take this one step at a time, calmly and deliberately." Knute felt no need to apologize for Custis Hall's founder. The past was the past. It certainly was open to reinterpretation, but he couldn't change a damned thing about it.

The situation cooled. The adults herded the girls out of the Main Hall. They promised to set up individual appointments. Also, this issue would be addressed at November's convocation, the first of the new school year. The all-school assembly was held the first Monday of each month.

Just as the girls moved out of Old Main, walking across the quad were Tootie, Valentina, and Felicity.

In a booming voice, Pamela shouted at Tootie, "Traitor!"

Tootie blanched but did not reply.

Valentina did. "Pamela, you aren't happy unless you're unhappy. Go sit on it."

Charlotte stepped forward. The three riders could now see her, as she'd been obscured by the crowd. "Ladies, that's quite enough for one day."

No one said a word, not even contentious Pamela, who stared daggers at Valentina.

When Charlotte reached the anteroom, Teresa looked up over Charlotte's head before she could open her mouth. Hard on Charlotte's well-shod heels tumbled Al, Knute, Christopher, and Amy.

Turning, Charlotte said in a sweet voice, "Come in. Let's sit down and have a cup of coffee."

"Coffee, hell, I want a drink," Knute good-naturedly said.

"I second the motion." Christopher wiped his brow with a Brooks Brothers linen handkerchief.

Knute, at forty-eight, maintained a boyish look and a trim body, his hair blond, lightly salted with gray.

Christopher, a few years older, carted around a pot-belly that even his expensive suits couldn't totally conceal. His complexion was florid, his manner brusque, which suited him as a prosecuting attorney aiming to run for governor. He bagged the high-pro-file cases and he won more often than not, even against the highly paid attorneys defendants hired. Christopher was a man to be reckoned with, to watch.

His sister evidenced the same incisive mind, although her field was the natural sciences. But like her brother, she had a combative nature. Being female, she tried to hide it, with mixed results.

Charlotte pointed the men to the bar, and Amy joined them. She stuck her head out of her office. "Teresa, call down to Dorothy and ask her to bring some sandwiches, more hot coffee, and hot tea; you know the drill."

Dorothy directed food services.

"Will do." Teresa, observant, keenly intelligent, and a touch shy, picked up the phone to buzz Dorothy.

Knute filled in Charlotte about the protest, for she'd missed only the first ten minutes. He said it appeared to be well organized.

"I'm open to all suggestions." Charlotte sat in a wing chair as the others, drinks in hand, settled themselves in leather chairs or the comfortable leather sofa.

Al waited for tea. He wasn't much of a drinker.

"Charlotte, the girls do have a point. We never gave much thought to what's in those cases except to dust the stuff."

"He's right." Amy gulped a gin and tonic, a bit of lime pulp catching in her teeth. She flicked it down with her tongue and bit into it—the tang of lime tasted wonderful. "Always looked like junk to me."

"Amy, if it isn't a mastodon's tooth, you aren't interested," her brother teased her.

Knute ignored them. He addressed Charlotte. "I'll help you call the board of directors if you like. We should schedule an emergency meeting."

"Good thinking, but I don't see how we can do that until Tuesday. It's hard to get people together quickly at the end of the month, and there are only four more days left in October, two of those being Saturday and Sunday. Also, I want to meet with some of these girls before I meet with the board."

"Good idea," Al agreed. "Want me to call our largest contributors?"

"No," Charlotte quickly said. "Not yet, Al. This may all blow over."

"M-m-m, let sleeping dogs lie." Knute held his shot of Johnnie Walker Blue under his nose for a moment.

Charlotte kept a well-stocked bar that she paid for herself. Knute would never open his wallet to buy such an expensive blended Scotch, but he was quite prepared to drink hers. Teresa locked the bar when she left each night if Charlotte didn't do it first.

"You've got to hand it to the kids who planned this. They didn't get destructive and had the forethought to call the media." Christopher wanted another drink but waited for the coffee and tea. It really was too early.

49

"How could all those kids keep their mouths shut?" Knute wondered out loud.

It crossed Charlotte's mind that Tootie may have known but refused to participate. Still, she, too, remained silent. Charlotte wanted to talk to Tootie, Valentina, and Felicity. Better to catch up with them after a hunt. As for the other girls, it was going to be a true sit-down.

"It's a strange time in life." Amy had now fished out the wedge of lime to suck on it. "They have good powers of thought, most of them, but they are emotionally retarded."

"I take issue with that," Al bristled. "Not every young person lacks experience. Nor is every girl blinded by her hormones."

"Al, you make excuses for them," Amy said, but not in an accusatory manner.

"I'm glad you care about them as you do." Charlotte hoped to defuse the ever-present tension between Al and Amy, oil and water.

"What do you think?" Christopher asked Charlotte.

"We can handle it. And we do need research. We need a new light on everything in those cases. That's an excellent task for all our history classes. The English classes can rewrite the descriptions. History classes can present the background of the time. Of course, this senior class will be out of here by the time all the evidence, if you will, is in. Still, it's a start and it ought to smooth things over."

"As in pacify them?" Al raised an eyebrow.

"Well, not exactly. Smooth things over is the wrong expression. Having the English and history departments involved means the girls really will be participating. Try to remember, Al, as headmistress I'd like this to be a harmonious place. As director of alumnae affairs I expect you'd like that as well."

"I do, I do, but I don't think we should trivialize their concerns."

"Oh, bull, Al, Pamela Rene has been a pain in the ass since her sophomore year. I'm surprised she hasn't thought of this before. She's furious because she wasn't elected class president. You will recall she accused Valentina of voter fraud. A bad apple," Knute said.

"She has a mother who was once the highest-paid model in New York and still wants the limelight, and a father who has built one of the largest trucking companies in America. There's not much time for Pamela." Amy knew the Rene family well. "As for those treasures in the cases, do we really want the kids handling them?"

"I hadn't thought of that." Al glanced quickly at Amy.

Dorothy and two assistants rolled in a table of sandwiches, cakes, freshly cut vegetables, dipping sauces, a large pot of coffee, and a large pot of tea.

"I didn't know how hungry I was," Knute said, waiting for Charlotte to stand.

"Please"—she indicated they should fill their plates. The two assistants poured coffee, helped with plates. Dorothy returned to her office over the dining hall, a room right out of Oxford, stained-glass windows shining bits of color on mahogany panels.

"Amy, Knute, Al, if there are any students you feel close to, talk to them. I'll ask our other faculty to also be on the alert for anyone who might need extra attention or guidance. Sometimes the girls need to vent." Charlotte couched her orders as thoughts while the others ate. "Christopher, I know you're overburdened, but perhaps you could put an assistant on researching any suits that have been pressed over similar issues."

"You know, that would be interesting," and he meant that, too.

"Knute, one more time," she smiled, "go over our budget and see if there's any fat that can be squeezed to send some of the girls on research trips, say to Poplar Forest or Mount Vernon."

"They can use the Internet," Amy replied before Knute could.

"They'll do that anyway," Charlotte answered. "If they go to places Miss Custis knew as a child, as a young woman their age, it will make it much more vivid." She turned to Knute. "Take a peek."

"All right." He settled in to a club sandwich.

They batted around more ideas. Charlotte discreetly kept her eye on the time.

"You know, we were lucky no one smashed a case," Al said. "How could we ever replace Washington's epaulettes? We were really lucky."

Knute replied, "That's exactly why I think the cases should stay locked, and I agree with Amy, the kids don't need their hands on those things."

"Do we have a value on that stuff?" Amy was curious.

"Well, we really don't." Charlotte wrinkled her brow for a second. "I guess we could hire an appraiser, but how would you value a page from George Washington's diary or his wife's hunting crop?"

"That's just it, Charlotte, someone has to, because those things are irreplaceable. National treasures." Christopher's pleasant voice filled the room. "Course, if the girls smash the cabinets, I'll have to get them on breaking and entering." He smiled.

"Would you like me to find an appraiser?" Al asked. "I'm sure many of our alumnae have valuable items and would be a source for recommendations."

"Al, with all due respect, I don't think we should go that route until the waters are becalmed." Knute sailed in his spare time and dotted his conversations with sailing terms.

"That's a thought." Charlotte leaned toward Knute. "If we discuss what we have in our care in terms of cold cash, at this moment, we may invite more reprisals. But I definitely think this is necessary for the near future and we must find someone whose credentials are impeccable."

"You know, if I'd known it was going to be this much trouble, I'd have picked the cotton myself," Amy commented and languidly sipped her coffee.

"That is so insensitive! Amy, you astonish me." Al's face reddened.

"For Christ's sake, get a sense of humor." She stared at him.

"But that's always it, isn't it?" He bore down on Amy. "The oppressed are supposed to laugh when the oppressor makes fun of them. How can you laugh at your own suffering? I mean, do you think it's funny if someone white wears blackface? Used to be a scream. Do you think it's funny if a man gets up in drag?"

"Watch it, Al, you'll kick off the transgender discussion." Christopher, unlike Amy, chose his words with some care.

"Oh, balls!" Al put down his coffee cup with force.

An assistant quickly took it away, replacing it with a filled one that hadn't spilled.

"Al, Amy is direct. Perhaps she is insensitive sometimes, but give her credit for being honest." Knute wearied of these two sparring.

"You can be honest and dead wrong," Al replied.

"I suppose you'd like to emphasize the dead." Amy did have a sense of humor.

"With all due respect, this has been a trying morning. I value each of you for your contributions, but I'm not up to being a referee for my faculty and staff at this exact moment." Charlotte's voice was firm. "Everyone here has appointments. If you haven't had enough to eat, take a sandwich, we can put a drink in a carry mug for you. But let's get back on course."

Charlotte cleared her office in ten minutes. She thanked the assistants, then she walked out to Teresa. "Can you believe those two?"

"I tune them out." Teresa glanced over a list of calls she'd taken while Charlotte met with the group. "Your husband called. He'll be home by six. He said he has a surprise." Teresa looked up and smiled. "Bunny called. Said call her back when you have a minute. Nothing urgent. Um, Sonny Shaeffer called, you'll receive an invitation for the bank's Christmas party but he wants you and Carter to put it on your calendar now, um-m, December sixteenth, Friday."

"Teresa, what do you think of all this?"

"I don't know."

"Are you saying that because I'm white?" Charlotte didn't hold back.

"After all we've been through? Now you're getting as sensitive as Al Perez." She waited a beat. "If I'd had reporters in my face and Pamela Rene, you know, I'd be a little touchy myself. I don't know what I think except—"

"Except what?"

"I have a strange feeling. I can't pin it on anything. I know you hate clichés but, Charlotte, I think this is the tip of the iceberg."

CHAPTER 5

"Lights, camera, action!" Marty Howard threw up her manicured hands, one magnificent marquise diamond catching the light. "Every year every hunt club puts on the standard, three-speed hunt ball. We're breaking out."

"As long as break out doesn't mean break bad," Sister slyly inserted into Marty's eruption of ideas.

"Oh, Sister, how bad can it be?"

At that, Betty roared, "You have no idea. Get a mess of foxhunters in their best duds liquored up, all that cleavage suddenly in view, and fistfights and running off with other people's spouses seems normal."

Marty exclaimed, "Nothing like that ever happened in Indiana."

"That's why you moved here, dear," Sister said in a silken voice.

Marty, while bright, missed the gradations of Virginia humor. She blinked. "Well, we came because Crawford wanted to retire at forty and get into the horse business, but I guess we got more than we bargained for. He's built the hunter barn, the steeplechase barn, and now he wants to breed Herefords, the kind with horns. He's either researching bloodlines on that computer he had built—to the tune of fifteen thousand dollars—or he's reading stock market quotes on it."

"Back to this hunt ball. Marty, I so appreciate you taking on this task. Getting Bill Wheatley and the theater students to help with decorating was a master stroke," Sister praised Marty. "And I know even if you don't make it public that you and Crawford have given a generous donation to Custis Hall for the theater department's services."

"We were happy to do it." Marty glowed, for she did like being useful, and after eleven years she was finally feeling like part of the group.

"Betty as vice chair—and I accentuate the *vice*—really does know where all the bodies are buried and she can take care of the table sittings." Sister smiled at Betty. "What else? Forgive me, by the way, for not being better organized. Over the years our social chairs have kept the Jefferson Hunt hopping and popping. I didn't have to do but so much. Also, I'm not too good at this kind of thing."

Betty was scribbling on a notebook Sister had given her. "Your job is to show sport. Our job is to show we're sports."

"What a good way to put it," Marty agreed. "Well, this will be the hunt ball to end all hunt balls."

"Key position: head of the silent auction. Hunt balls can't pay for themselves. The silent auction is your one hope to get in the black." Betty reminded them of the ever-present need for money. "How's Sorrel Buruss doing on getting items?"

"So far so good. She's gotten the usual stuff—framed prints, weekend getaway spots, and dinners.

What we're lacking are the big, flashy items," Marty answered.

They chatted awhile longer, drew up lists, again picked through the budget.

They experimented with different days over the years, throwing the ball the evening of Opening Hunt, or the evening of Closing Hunt. They found December to work the best. Everyone was in a holiday mood, people could get off work, and the bills had not rolled in to spoil everything. This year's ball was set for Saturday, December 17.

The venue, the Great Hall at Custis Hall, had been used by Jefferson Hunt for over one hundred years. The vaulted ceilings added a medieval air to the many celebrations, concerts, convocations that took place there.

Ten years ago the whole facility had been rewired, refurbished. A rock band could play without frying the electrical system.

The serving kitchen had also been updated.

The Great Hall supplied Custis Hall with bonus money, as groups would rent it to the tune of thirty-five hundred dollars before food, service, linens, tables.

Given the long relationship with Jefferson Hunt, the club need only pay for the food, service, and tableware.

Their century-plus relationship was the reason Jane Arnold sat on the board of directors. The senior master of the hunt club had served in this capacity since 1887.

As the ladies finished their coffee and biscuits, wrapping up details, Marty's cell rang.

"Hi, honey," she answered. "You're exactly right." She listened some more. "I'll be home shortly. At least you and Sam could hunt this morning before all this happened." More listening. "You know best." She made a big smooching sound. "Bye bye." She pressed the off button. "His computer blew up again. I use my Dell, got a good deal, and I have a real nice printer. Whole thing about nine-fifty." She laughed. "But Crawford hires some geek from New York, builds the whole deal, has to have an ASUS motherboard, this bell and that whistle. And now my dear, darling husband is on the phone once a day to this computer whiz because he can't figure out how to work the expensive piece of junk." She sighed dramatically. "Men."

"Boys and their toys," Betty laughed.

"I can't pick on them. I'm just as bad. If there's a gadget in the hardware store that promises bliss, I buy it." Sister's workshop bore testimony to this small passion.

"Before I forget. Are you going to make an appearance at Custis Hall's Halloween party?" Betty asked the master.

"No, are you?"

"We'll be there," Betty replied.

"Crawford and I will be going, too. That's our second stop that Saturday. Halloween is a major party night." Marty smiled. "Full moon on the seventeenth. There won't be enough light to cast an eerie glow."

Halloween fell on Monday this year, but all the parties would be on Saturday, naturally.

"Well, I know Charlotte will be glad you all are attending. I can't go. Delia might whelp that night. I don't want to leave her because I told Shaker he could go to the party with Lorraine at the firehouse. He was going to sit up with Delia. He hardly ever gets out. He is the most conscientious man. We're lucky to have him."

"Hear. Hear." Betty adored the huntsman.

"This thing with Lorraine might just work out," Sister winked.

The phone rang. Sister got up. Caller I.D. showed the number was Charlotte Norton's.

"Excuse me, girls." Sister picked up the phone. "Charlotte, hello." She listened. Then she listened intently. "I see." She was quiet again, then said, "Well, it can't be ignored, but perhaps it can be contained." More listening. "A special meeting Tuesday afternoon." She checked her wall calendar. "I'll be there. We'll be finished hunting. Actually, you might need the exercise to get your blood up for all this." She scribbled on the calendar with a 0.7 thickness of lead mechanical pencil. "I'll be there and let me know if there's anything I can do."

As she hung up, Betty's eyebrows raised, she pursed her lips. "What?"

"There's been a protest at Custis Hall. About fifty girls, black and white, called the school a plantation. They appear to be particularly upset over the displays."

"What, a bunch of dresses and hair ribbons?" Betty threw up her hands.

"The girls feel there has to be better recognition of slave contributions. That's what I've gotten out of this so far. Charlotte said she'll be meeting with the girls to dig underneath."

"The girls may have gone about it the wrong way, but we do need to recognize slaves' work. History, at least the way they taught it in Indiana when I was in school, was and probably still is about great men and wars." Marty, a liberal in most respects, instinctively sided with the protesters.

"Who will ever know the truth?" Sister shrugged as she sat back down. "Whoever wins writes history. The truth has nothing to do with it." She stopped herself. "Well, I doubt this protest will dampen the Halloween dance."

"Oh, it will all blow over," Betty predicted.

CHAPTER 6

The ivy climbing over the brick buildings of Custis Hall swayed gently in the light breeze.

This October 29 the twilight surrendered to darkness after a sunset of flame gold and violet.

The air already carried a bite to it. Revelers slipped through the various quads. The parking lot behind the Great Hall was filled with faculty cars, administration cars, and one white Miller School bus disgorging the boys in costumes. One fellow came dressed as Queen Christina of Sweden, an interesting twist since she often dressed as a man. The other young men wore clothes reflecting manly images: pirates, cowboys, spacemen, Batman, Spiderman, a robot, generals from all epochs, Richard Nixon, and a few desultory ghosts.

William Wheatley, head of the theater department, prided himself on the high level of teaching in his department.

Tonight, the girls specializing in set design made him proud. Bill was nearing retirement. This year would be his last hurrah.

Al Perez, one of the chaperones, dressed as Zorro, stood outside the massive front doors to greet the partyers. Valentina Smith, as senior class president, stood next to him. Charlotte Norton flanked her. The other uncostumed chaperones—Amy Childers, Knute Nilsson, Bunny Taliaferro, and Bill Wheatley— moved through the crowd, stopping to talk to students. From time to time, Knute would slip out back to check the parking lot. The kids were ingenious in sneaking weed and booze.

Green light bathed the outside doors. Inside, three-foot wall sconces flickered with fake flames, while the other sconces were held by dismembered hands à la Cocteau's *Beauty and the Beast*. The girls had done good work.

The light from both the permanent and the theater-built sconces infused the Great Hall with splashes of light in ponds of shadow.

A giant spiderweb hung overhead with a large black widow, her red eyes complementing the red hourglass on her body. She slid up and down the main strands of her web, causing shrieks from the costumed humans below. Smaller spiderwebs, dusted in various colors, blacklit, added to the scary decor. Witches flew about on brooms, the whir of motors distinguished as they passed over. The moan of a werewolf swelled into a howl and blended into the screams. A fake moon rose behind the stage constructed for the band.

Outside, the darkness contrasted with the false moon inside the Great Hall. Betty and Bobby as well as Crawford and Marty left at ten-thirty, bidding Zorro, who guarded the front doors, good-bye. The kids would dance until midnight, then load up on school buses, go to Hangman's Ridge, then back to the dorms after an hour there.

The Miller School boys were dazzled by the technical display.

At midnight, the sconces were extinguished. The spider's eyes glowed in the blackness. She slid down to the center of the web, and from her silkjets came a stream of little sparkly flashlights, which clattered to the floor. The girls who built all this picked them up first and turned them on. Tiny blue lights, red lights, white lights beamed. The other students, now down on their hands and knees, scooped up the lights. Dots of light danced as the spider moved back up to the corner, the witches flew about one last time, jack-o'-lanterns cackled, and the ghosts groaned.

Charlotte and her husband, Carter, stood by the doors to send the revelers off while Bunny Taliaferro and Bill Wheatley rounded them up. Al Perez and Amy Childers, squabbling at low volume, shepherded everyone out to the parking lot.

School buses painted in school colors awaited the kids. The Custis Hall bus was parked immediately behind the Miller School bus. Bill Wheatley was already on the Custis Hall bus.

"Honey, I should be home by one-thirty," Charlotte said as she kissed Carter on the cheek.

"Oh, what the heck, I'll go with you." He grabbed her hand, and they walked to the station wagon as Zorro waved and sprinted by to his car.

As Charlotte settled behind the driver's seat, she leaned over, kissing Carter on the check. "Thanks, honey."

She turned on the motor and slowly backed out. As they drove out the winding, tree-lined road they noticed Zorro walking in the opposite direction.

"Al must have forgotten something," Charlotte smiled. "If he ever lost his Palm Pilot he wouldn't know his own name. As it is, he usually forgets something. Makes me laugh. At least he can laugh about it, too."

They glided through the large stone gates, turning onto the state road. Within five minutes they'd turn onto Soldier Road.

Given the darkness of the night and the few cars in front of them it took twenty minutes to reach

Hangman's Ridge from the Soldier Road side. The dark, dank mists hung in the lowlands, covering the last wild roses of the year. Cumulus clouds, gathering in the west, were moving toward the ridge.

"Sister said she'd clean up the bushes on this old road off Soldier Road." Charlotte held the steering wheel firmly as they bounced in the ruts. "She's a good sport about this. We didn't want to come in from the other direction. We'd disturb the hounds."

"Bet the boys have the usual—spaghetti in pots masquerading as brains, grapes as eyeballs. The boys aren't as imaginative as the girls. Course, they might surprise me." Carter watched the clouds move in swiftly, black against black.

"Guts, gore, screams," Charlotte laughed.

Carter peered up at the sky. "You know, honey, I really do think the damned ridge is haunted."

"It will be tonight," she agreed.

Inky, on the far side of the ridge, heard the school buses laboring to climb up the twisting dirt road. Usually she avoided Hangman's Ridge, but the grinding of gears intrigued her. Who could be negotiating that road this time of night?

As the black fox picked her way through the underbrush, she felt a dip in temperature, a bit of breeze from the west. Hangman's Ridge ran southeast to northwest and winds would rake its long flat expanse.

The girls jostled behind the boys' bus.

"How did women wear these things?" Tootie kicked up her skirt. She was dressed as Madame du Barry and made a note never to do that again.

Valentina looked sleek in her Catwoman outfit and Felicity settled on being a witch.

Pamela, two rows back, as Little Bo Beep, touched Tootie on the shoulder with her shepherd's crook. "You'll answer to me, you little black sheep."

Her devotees giggled.

Bill, sitting behind the driver, was unaware of the exchange.

"You're so tiring," Tootie called back.

"You're so chicken," Pamela replied.

"Shove it." Valentina, next to Tootie, turned around, speaking over Felicity, immediately behind them.

The buses finally made it to the top, cars behind them. The boys poured out first, darting to the girls' bus.

"Close your eyes!" Terry Durkin, one of the leaders, told them. There was no need to close their eyes as they were plunged into unrelieved darkness. Charlotte and Carter parked behind the Custis Hall bus. Amy parked behind them. Knute pulled up behind Amy.

As the girls approached the tree they began to peek and turned on their little sparkly flashlights from the black widow.

Felicity screamed as she drew closer. All the girls opened their eyes and screamed at the sight of two corpses hanging from the tree. One was dressed as Lawrence Pollard, the first man hung, in 1702, because of a real estate swindle. The other corpse was dressed as Zorro, wearing the mask.

Only Tootie refused to scream. "Mannequins."

Valentina peered up. "Yeah."

Felicity remained frightened. "Zorro looks real."

"Oh, he does not," Valentina said. "You are so—"

"Who strung up the second victim?" Terry asked another boy, who shrugged.

Tootie walked under the corpses, followed by Valentina. They pressed their tiny lights upward. The Miller School chaperones assumed the boys had gilded the lily. The boys also assumed one of their number had done so.

Inky stuck her glossy head out from under the mountain laurel. She was fifty yards from the huge tree. The effluvia of a freshly hung human assailed her nostrils. Fresh death. The small muscles that go into rigor mortis first hadn't even tightened up.

Tootie, directly underneath, could smell him, too. She gazed up into bloodshot eyes bulging through the openings in the silk mask. This was no fake.

CHAPTER 7

Delia delivered seven healthy puppies. Sister had fallen asleep sitting on a low chair next to the brood box; a long heat lamp, overhead, glowing with dimmed light.

The dog hounds gave cry when the first screams were heard flying down from Hangman's Ridge like an arrow of fear.

Sister opened an eye, then closed it again, smiling. She imagined the girls spooked up on the ridge, the Miller School boys proud of their accomplishment. The next set of screams aroused the gyps sleeping out in the toasty large boxes on stilts in the large runs. The boxes had porches, the interiors filled with fresh straw. All the outdoor runs, dotted with spreading old trees, provided room to play or sleep. Younger hounds lived inside the main brick kennels. The arrangement gave each hound plenty of personal space so tempers didn't flare from overcrowding.

The continued screams awakened everyone.

Again Sister opened an eye, sighed, then opened both eyes. The sound of two sirens in the far distance presaged something terribly wrong. She patted Delia on the head, hurried to the small bathroom off the office, splashed water on her face, dashed outside, hopped into her pickup, and drove up Hangman's Ridge.

She reached the back side of the ridge just as the sheriff's squad car crested the Soldier Road side. The blue lights washed over the two hanging corpses. She knew immediately that one of the hanged men was real. Swaying slightly, his back to her, the angle of his neck gave it away. The young people, some crying, stood at their respective buses, the chaperones attempting to comfort the more obviously distressed. Tootie, Valentina, and Pamela also did what they could to help others. Felicity shook like a leaf but was in control of herself. Sister noted the remarkable poise of the three young women. Charlotte and Carter greeted Sheriff Ben Sidel as he stepped out of the car.

The rescue squad van pulled up behind the sheriff's car.

Sister waited until Ben, Charlotte, and Carter walked toward the tree, the rescue squad following at a discreet distance.

Ben spoke to Sister, "Hell of a Halloween."

She simply replied, "Yes, it is hellish."

Charlotte, the muscles in her face tight, met Sister's gaze as the older woman walked toward her.

Sister now faced the corpse, Zorro. She registered disbelief.

"Al Perez," Charlotte whispered to Sister.

Ben carefully checked the ground underneath, motioning for a deputy, Ty Banks, to come over. Deputy Banks, flashlight in hand, listened intently as Ben Sidel, in a quiet voice, gave him instructions.

Sister noted Inky still as a stone.

"What happened?" Ben asked Charlotte.

Briefly she explained the after-party plan by the Miller School boys, how at first they thought this was part of their night of fright, as they called it.

Ty examined the bark on the tree, and, like the sheriff, he inspected the ground underneath the corpse. Four imprints from a stepladder pressed into the earth. "Sheriff." He wordlessly pointed to the ladder footmarks, scanning to see if footprints were visible. The earth, fairly dry except for the light dew that would turn to frost, yielded no sign of footprints.

"Yes, I noticed that, too. Was he dead before he was hanged or was he killed by hanging?" Ben thought out loud.

"He couldn't have been dead longer than half an hour," Carter opined. "Warm, no rigor even in the small muscles."

When the students were walked back to the buses, Carter carefully touched Al's leg to feel for body temperature. He did not touch any other part of the hanged man's body for fear of damaging evidence.

"My husband wanted to make sure Al was, well, dead. If by any chance he wasn't, we would have cut him down and done our best to revive him. I mean, Carter would," Charlotte spoke.

"I understand," Ben said sympathetically.

"Will you need to question the students?" Charlotte thought first of her flock.

"Not now." Ben knew that some of the kids were aflutter from hysteria, despite the efforts of Knute, Bill, Amy, Bunny, and the other girls. "Did any of them see anything unusual?"

"No."

Charlie Thompson, chaperone for the Miller School, quietly approached. "Sheriff, three of my boys strung up the mannequin. They were alone. I guess you'd like to interrogate them."

"Well, that might be too strong a word. Mr. Thompson, take them back to school. I'll ring you first and then talk to the boys. Right now, these kids need your attention. You can all leave. I'll be in touch."

Charlotte looked to her husband, then back at Ben. "Should we tell his wife?"

"No, I'll do it. I hope no one has called her," Ben responded.

"No, I made that clear to all," Charlotte firmly replied.

"It's the worst part of this job," Ben flatly stated. "You all can go as well."

As the Custis Hall people and the Miller School people left, Ben asked Sister, "Hear anyone come up on your side of the ridge?"

"No, nothing. I was in the kennel whelping room. I would have heard a car or truck."

As the buses and cars dipped over the ridge onto the rutted road, Ben's eyes followed the receding red dots of light. "You have an opinion on Al Perez?"

"He was pleasant, competent, very upbeat. I knew him from serving on the board of directors."

"Enemies?"

"I don't know. Charlotte would know better than I. Custis Hall is her bailiwick." She hesitated a moment. "He didn't get along with Amy Childers—old romance—but we all have a few of those. We don't usually hang for it."

"One hopes."

Ben, not a country boy, learned to ride when he came to Jefferson County four years ago. He discovered that riding wasn't easy, but he enjoyed the challenge. He'd reached the point where he rode with the Hilltoppers. He was working toward riding up with

71

first flight, taking all those exciting jumps.

He had keen powers of observation, trained powers. He also had a sense of people's character, having heard every lie known to man, so he particularly valued an honest person. Sister Jane was rock-solid honest. Her powers of observation were also highly trained. She proved a shrewd judge of character, too, where humans were concerned.

Sister raised her eyes to Al's darkening face. "Hanging is a definite form of suicide. Anyone who hangs himself truly wants to die, but you've seen the stepladder prints, as did I. Al Perez didn't hang himself. Whoever killed him wants to tie the past to the present, to scare the hell out of all of us. This is the place of public execution."

Ty, twenty-nine, in thrall to his work, drank in every word. He'd not thought of that.

"A warning?" Ben thought out loud.

"Yes, but to whom? This is just a feeling, but the warning involves the school."

"Why do you say that?"

Sister paused. "If this person only wanted to warn and warn publicly, he could have hung Al somewhere else, or shot him, dumping him in a public place or a well-traveled spot. But it seems you've got a fevered imagination at work."

Ben felt the cold slice of breeze from the northwest. He reached in his pocket for a small round hard candy. He offered Sister one, then Ty. "In charge of alumnae affairs. Important post. Financially critical."

72

Sister folded her arms over her chest. "I doubt very much Al Perez is an innocent victim."

"M-m-m." Ben was thinking the same thing.

As Sister walked back to her truck, Inky shadowed her. Inky liked Sister. It was mutual.

Sister put her hand on the door handle, stopped to call back to Ben. "Shrouds have no pockets."

"What?"

"Shrouds have no pockets. I don't know why that popped into my mind, except that a lot of money flowed through his hands."

CHAPTER 8

Hounds ate at six-thirty this Sunday to the sound of the power washer cleaning the kennels. The jets of water hit the walls and floors with such force, every speck of debris and dirt was dislodged, swirling into a huge central drain, a big trap underneath it. Shaker cut off the washer.

Sister, who had slept fitfully, walked into the feeding room. Raleigh and Rooster remained in the kennel office. They got along with the hounds but it wasn't wise to allow them into the feeding room. They hated being separated from Sister, grumbling whenever they were left.

Shaker walked back into the feeding room just as Sister did. He took one look at her face. "What's wrong?"

"Al Perez was hanged last night at Hangman's Ridge." She gave him the details as she knew them.

"Jesus, there are sickos out there. Why didn't you call me?"

"You rarely get time to yourself. I figured after the firehouse party you spent the night out."

"Yep." He paused. "Gruesome end, gruesome. I liked Al. He was a nice guy."

"It wasn't clear whether he was hung to death or dead before he was hung. I studied the body as best I could under the circumstances. I didn't smell blood or powder burns. And my nose is pretty good." She then apologized to her hounds. "For a human my nose is good, but no one is as good as you all."

Trident, a lovely young hound, smiled at Sister before diving back into the feed trough.

"Why'd you go up there, or did Ben come for you?"

"Forgot to tell you that. I heard the screams. Woke me up. I didn't think too much of it since I knew the boys had planned their Halloween surprise. Then I heard the sirens."

"You would have heard someone drive through here."

She replied, "No one did." She switched gears. "How are the puppies?"

"Nursing. Delia's a good mother. Even if you'd been sound asleep next to her, she would have warned you if someone drove through the farm. You would have known. It's a crazy thing, isn't it?"

"It is."

"Sooner or later, they'll catch 'em."

"One hopes." She reached for a gallon of corn oil.

Shaker opened the door for the fed group of young hounds to return to their runs. He then washed out the troughs, refilling them with kibble. Sister poured a line of corn oil over the feed as Shaker opened another run door for older hounds to enter. They rushed up to Sister in greeting, then dove for the chow.

"It's supposed to rain Tuesday, temperature's supposed to drop, too." Shaker checked with the Weather Channel constantly.

"Yeah, I saw that, too. But I'm betting the rain will come in after we wrap it up at Mud Fence." She named that day's fixture, an old estate whose fences in the mid-eighteenth century were made of mud. The first settlers lacked the money for nails. They could fell trees and plane boards but nails were very expensive. Eventually they built snake fences once the work of clearing began in earnest. One didn't need nails for that. Some folks had to make do with a mud fence until they could clear more land, get more timber.

"Want to bet?"

"Five dollars."

"Bet." He held out his hand and she shook it. "Boss, ever consider murder?"

"You mean me killing someone or someone killing me?"

He laughed. "Ever consider what drives someone to it?"

"Sure."

"I expect any of us can kill. Just need the right or wrong circumstances."

"We might be mad enough to kill yet we don't. We don't step over the line." She listened to the hounds chewing their kibble, a comforting sound. "If one of these hounds kills another hound, why does it happen?"

"Sometimes they know a hound is weak, sickening. They take him out. Maybe that's canine mercy killing. Doesn't happen often." He thought a bit more. "If there's a fight, it's a challenge, a top-dog thing."

"Same with horses. They rarely kill but they can sure kick the powder out of one another if they take a notion."

"You're saying we murder, they don't." Shaker kept an eye on Dragon, growling. "That's enough, Dragon, shut up."

"Apart from war or self-defense, if we kill it's revenge, that's straightforward. Sex killing or serial killing is men against women. Sickness and anger, I reckon. Then there's money. Always that."

"And a challenge to authority. The top-dog deal." Shaker's auburn curls caught the light.

"Right. For the life of me I can't figure out how Al Perez, a mild fellow, fits any category. Can't see him as a sex criminal taken out by an enraged victim or father of same." She noted Shaker's expression. "Well, Custis Hall bursts with girls becoming women. That's a potent cocktail for a certain kind of man.

76

Money? He raised millions for the school. But he didn't work on a percentage basis. Yes, he received a big Christmas bonus. Being on the board, I'm privy to the financial life of the school, but I can't divulge details. He could have gotten resentful and figured he should get more given all that he raised for the school. It's possible."

"Yep."

"As to the challenge idea. I can't even imagine him challenging a dog."

"People can fool you." He whistled low to Asa, an older hound, who had finished his breakfast.

Asa walked over, put his head under Shaker's hand. *"Isn't it a good morning?"*

Sister smiled when Asa crooned. "You're a gentleman, Asa."

"Now, Boss, your curiosity getting up, is it?"

"Isn't yours?"

"Some."

"In a community as tight as ours, any death touches the rest of us eventually. I'm afraid of what we don't know."

CHAPTER 9

When the Good Lord jerks your chain, you're going." Sam Lorillard brushed Easy Able, one of Crawford Howard's steeplechase horses, a big rangy fellow who was winning the brush races.

Rory Ackerman scrubbed down the wash stall with disinfectant. Sam, in charge of the 'chaser stable, was fanatical about cleanliness, although this sense of organization was not reflected in his own house. "I don't know."

"Think about it," the wiry African American said. "You die when you are supposed to die. Now, we can all be horrified at Perez's murder, but if he didn't die that way, he would have gone to glory another way. It was his time and no one can change that."

"Then how do you explain that I was just about dead when you hauled me down to Fellowship Hall? You saved my life." Rory, an alcoholic like Sam, both recovering, thought fate no substitute for free will.

"You'd have stunk up heaven with Thunderbird. God prefers better fragrances." Sam laughed, for Rory used to reek of cheap liquor.

The square-built dark-haired man cut off the hose while he scrubbed the wash stall walls with a long-handled brush. "Whatever the reasons, I'm glad I'm still here and I'm glad Crawford hired me."

"He's a funny guy." Sam ran both hands down Easy's forelegs. "Doesn't know squat about horses. Likes to make a big noise, you know, be the man, but he's all right. He's fair. How many of our fine-born Virginians would have given you or me a chance? He did."

"That's the point. He didn't grow up with us." Rory laughed as he turned the water back on, squirting down the yellowish foam on the walls.

"Well—" Sam didn't finish as Crawford strode into the barn.

Inhaling the scent of cedar shavings, ground to a fine grade, Crawford rubbed his hands, for this Monday morning was overcast, quite cool. "Hell of a note."

"Perez?"

He nodded his head, yes. "Charlotte's called an emergency board meeting tonight. Ought to be interesting."

Rory, quiet, continued washing. Not a horseman, but he was strong, liked physical labor, happy to do whatever Sam told him. He watched Sam because he wanted to learn, not to ride, but to learn on the ground how to properly care for a horse.

"Who do you think did it, Mr. Howard?" Sam politely asked.

"Damned if I know. I can't see that Alfonso Perez was worth hanging. Milktoast. A man's got to have balls. This 'the meek shall inherit the kingdom of heaven' is exactly right because they won't inherit a damned thing on earth."

"Right." Sam stayed on the good side of Crawford by keeping most of his personal opinions to himself. He'd tell the boss what he thought about horses, tracks, running conditions, other trainers and horses but he kept his mouth shut otherwise, if possible.

"Unless this emergency meeting goes into the wee smalls," he meant late into the night, "I'm going to hunt tomorrow. Might not be a bad day to bring out a young horse."

"What time, sir?"

"We ought to pull out of here by six-thirty. Gives us time just in case."

Since the country roads, two lanes, bore all traffic, one could crawl behind a timber truck hauling logs to the sawmill or a school bus that stopped every fifty feet. You stopped with it when the lights flashed. The other early-morning hazard was the paper delivery lady, who flew along the roads like an amphetamine-crazed maniac.

"Mrs. Howard hunting tomorrow?"

"Yes."

"We'll be ready to roll," Sam said. "Six-thirty." Crawford reaffirmed the time and then left.

Fairy Partlow worked Crawford's hunters while Sam managed the whole equine operation at Beasley Hall. In a way, Fairy had been demoted since she worked for Crawford before Sam's arrival. If she minded, she didn't show it. Sam thought Fairy was happy not to have too much responsibility. All she wanted to do was make and ride the hunters. So far things were smooth as glass.

"Can't picture Al Perez," Rory said as he finished the scrubdown.

"You've seen him plenty of times." Sam rubbed a little Absorbine on Easy's back, gently massaging the long muscles by the spine. Easy groaned in pleasure.

"Those guys make the best crooks."

80

"What guys?"

"The ones you don't remember."

That evening, the board of directors convened in the large conference room on the second floor of Old Main. A huge painting of the first headmistress, the founder herself, hung behind the headmistress's chair. Paintings of subsequent headmistresses surrounded those seated at the oblong walnut table.

The faculty representatives—Amy Childers, William Wheatley, and Alpha Rawnsley, notebooks in front of them—sat on one side of the table, along with Christopher Stoltenfuss.

The administration was represented by Knute Nilsson and Jake Walford, in charge of maintenance, along with Charlotte, of course.

Apart from Christopher, the other community members were Sister Jane, Crawford Howard, Darla Coleridge, a stockbroker in her early forties and an alumna, and Samson "Sonny" Shaeffer, president of Farmers Trust Bank, married to an alumna, Liz, now in her early sixties.

With dignity, Charlotte opened the meeting. She assured the board that counselors were available for the students and that an assembly had taken place that morning to comfort them.

"—get to the bottom of this. I know you want this as devoutly as I do and I ask your help in solving this terrible crime, in restoring balance at Custis Hall."

Behind her, Teresa Bourbon took notes in shorthand, rarely raising her head.

Sonny spoke first. "Charlotte, board members, this is a profound shock to us all and I can't look at the empty seat without thinking of Al, who efficiently and with no fanfare accomplished all that was asked of him. It doesn't seem real, yet when I look at his seat, I know it is." He looked at Knute, the treasurer, then back to Charlotte. "We can expect some students to be withdrawn, I'm afraid."

"We're doing all we can to reassure the parents," Charlotte forthrightly added, "but until whoever committed this heinous act is brought to justice . . . what can I say to you," she looked at Alpha, Amy, then Bill, her faculty members, "to reassure parents and students. Also, at this point there is no motive," she paused, "and that's deeply disquieting."

Bill Wheatley, voice equal to the occasion, thanks to decades of training, said, "There are some things we can say that might help allay these justifiable fears. One is that this is not a crime against women. Obvious as that may seem, it may need to be expressly stated. This is a girls' preparatory school. They are becoming young women, and sexual predators are a sad fact of life. But this is not such a crime. The other thing we can do—and I know, Charlotte, that you and Knute have already taken measures—is we must hire additional security. It will greatly help all, even ourselves, to see a protective presence until this dreadful thing is behind us. Our campus police are too few in number." Diplomatically, he did not mention that the campus police were not up to the job.

Knute spoke up, "We've hired Abattis Security and Jack has oriented them, given them maps, whatever they need. They are already on the job."

"Strong beginning," Crawford said as he folded his hands. "Charlotte, I want to congratulate you on how you handled the television interviews. Being able to present yourself is an advantage. It's print reporters like Greg Baghout who ought to be horsewhipped. His article in the paper was inflammatory, irresponsible. He insinuated that Al's murder is connected to the issue of slavery in Custis Hall's heritage. He's a menace."

"Menace he may be, but until more facts are brought to light, menace he will continue to be." Alpha Rawnsley, wise, watchful, and now worried, carefully chose her words.

A silence followed. Charlotte asked almost plaintively, "Does anyone here have any idea how this could happen? What is going on?"

"I can tell you what is going on," Knute, face now red, said. "Someone hated Al."

"Or hates Custis Hall," Amy Childers replied. "Wants to make us look racist." When everyone stared at her, she added, "He was Latino, you know. We're in the middle of this, um, slave labor stuff."

Charlotte looked at the attractive science teacher and thought how nine years ago, when she became headmistress, Amy had been a fresh, enthusiastic woman eager for life. She was turning into an embittered woman, entering the lists of early middle age.

"For God's sake!" Knute threw up his hands. "That's far-fetched."

"We do represent the old WASP ways," Bill intoned.

"We have the best diversity program on the East Coast"—the color rose to Charlotte's cheeks—"second to none."

"But not in terms of faculty hiring," Amy bluntly stated.

Sister, her voice deep, soothing, finally spoke. "Stereotypes die hard: the money-grubbing Jew, the lazy black, the Mafia-connected Italian, the sex-crazed homosexual. Even though this institution has reached out to the community, done a wonderful job of attracting the best students of all races, the general perception is still that Custis Hall serves rich, spoiled white girls who will go on to Mt. Holyoke. Sorry, Alpha," she nodded to Alpha, a Mt. Holyoke graduate from the early 1970s, "Smith, Radcliffe, Wellesley, and marry a rich white boy from Harvard, Yale, Princeton, Dartmouth. Now, untrue as that stereotype may be, I doubt it is cause for murder. And I doubt the lack of Hispanics or a better proportion of African Americans on the faculty or administration is cause for murder."

"Well, what then?" Amy was upset, shaken, and frustrated.

"One kills out of passion, greed, or self-protection. Normal people kill. Abnormal people hear voices or whatever and they kill for quite different reasons, it seems to me. Hanging Al Perez from Hangman's Tree, if you think about it, was brilliant." Sister held up her hand to forestall comments. "It's hard to give credit to such a repulsive act when everyone is grieving, but here we are focusing on the repercussions of that act. A great deal of energy and money will be spent to calm students, parents, and the faculty. The killer has us all focused, worried. I have learned from my quarry, the fox, that things are not always what they seem. Al's killer has distracted us from his scent."

"What exactly do you mean?" Bill leaned forward, eyebrows quizzically raised, since he hunted when he could.

"I mean our fox has fouled his scent. The public nature of the act stunned all of us. He's scooted away for now."

"But he's close?" Charlotte understood the language.

"Charlotte, board members, forgive me for using foxhunting terminology," Sister gravely said. "He is close, he is part of this community, and he obviously has powerful reasons to kill. He's a fox in the henhouse."

Crawford bit his lips.

Knute blurted out, "Good God. But I still can't see why anyone would take out Al. We all worked with Al. He was so good-natured, so good with the alumnae. You had to like him. Everyone liked him."

Bill twiddled his pencil. "Maybe he was running drugs that came in through Mexico. Amy made a point about his background. Well, he'd be able to talk to people in a way we couldn't. It's not impossible, you know, that he may have been involved in something criminal."

"Oh, Bill, really." Alpha's eyelids fluttered.

"We have to think of everything no matter how absurd," Bill defended himself.

"He's right, Alpha. Much as we all liked Al, we can't neglect the possibility that there may have been unsavory aspects to Al's life." Knute slumped a bit in his seat, weary from the weight of the hours. "But I can't think of a one."

"Sister, you divided killers into normal and abnormal categories. Hanging a man from a tree at the place of former public executions the night of a Halloween party in front of children, that doesn't seem normal to me," Amy remarked.

Christopher answered his sister, "Maybe that's just what the killer wants us to think, that he's some nutcase."

"Sick as it is, I don't think our killer is a nutcase. What we do know," Sister's voice was hypnotic, "is that he or she is strong, strong enough to string up a grown man. Bold. The killer was on that ridge not fifteen minutes before the girls and boys arrived. He knew the territory, never forget that. He knows us, and he understands symbolism."

A long silence followed her assessment.

Charlotte pulled back her shoulders, saying, "Sister, there's a reason you're master of foxhounds, and I thank you for bringing us back on the line." Her eyes swept the room. "Allow me to amend something Sister Jane said. Yes, he thinks he knows us, but what he doesn't know is that nothing is going to destroy this school. Custis Hall survived the War of 1812, the War Between the States, two world wars, the Great Depression, Korea, and Vietnam. We will survive this, which is a different, personal threat, but we are more resourceful than this disgusting human being can know. He will be found, he will be brought to justice for what he's done to Al, and we will come through this stronger."

Knute Nilsson started to open his mouth but closed it. He was going to say, "We might be stronger, but we'll probably be poorer for years. It will affect alumnae pledges." Under the circumstances this very real concern seemed a little crass. He'd discuss this with Charlotte in private.

CHAPTER 10

At sixteen pounds, Target qualified as a major fox. In the fullness of maturity, his coat fluffed out deep red, but his mask betrayed a few gray hairs near his dainty nose. Indian summer returned to central Virginia so he blew off the fact that the Jefferson Hunt Club would be at Mud Fence. With the mercury happily showing in the mid-fifties, skies of robin's-egg blue, and, even better from his point of view, a stiff breeze from the west, scent would be awful.

So he dillied and dallied, rooting around the corn-fields bordered by rows of tall fir trees to break the wind. Corn tasted delicious. Why burn calories chasing rabbits, mice, moles, and small birds when all he had to do was nibble kernels off the ears lower on the plant, for this was left as a silage field and wouldn't be cut for months. He paid no attention to the mice chattering in their high voices when they got a whiff of him. He heard their tiny claws clatter over the husks fallen to the ground, stiff and brown now. He'd eaten so much he felt a little drowsy, but considered that it was a long way home and he ought to begin walking, as his den was on After All Farm, per-haps five miles as the crow flies. Target hated crows, which is not why he didn't always travel in a straight line. Given his high intelligence there were so many enticements. He noticed a nest of digger bees, so he watched them fly in and out of their underground nest. Bears liked bees, but he avoided eating them. His aunt Netty would sometimes pick up what bears had left after they ripped open a tree, the side of an old building filled with honey. She liked the bee taste. He hated eating bees, although he liked honey well enough.

Target craved sweets.

He left the cornfield. The digger bees made their nest in a row and he strolled across the farm road onto the field of mown orchard grass, rolled up and tied. Goldfinches hurled a few rude remarks, as did the purple finches, cardinals, and blue jays. He paid them no mind. He listened to the loud tapping of the pileated woodpecker. He was tempted to go into the woods to seek out the very tree and have a discussion about grubs and wood-boring insects, too, but decided the dew was thick and might hold scent for a brief time.

The sound of Shaker's horn pricked up his ears. Why didn't the damned man cast into the wind? He was casting crosswind and Target hadn't considered that. Well, he was far enough ahead. He decided not to linger even if he passed other foxes or the many bobcats who had taken over this part of Mud Fence Farm. This year crops flourished, as did game. There was enough for all and tensions among the hunters lessened. Usually the fights erupted over territory disputes. No one fought over water, as there was so much of it.

As Target walked northward, Shaker cast wide as he headed for the silage corn. If he was going to hit it today he had to hit it soon, for once the dew evaporated all scent would rise with it. Of course, being a man who loved his work, Shaker would draw along western banks where the sun hadn't warmed the earth or he'd look for cold wind currents, but scent would be spotty even then. With such warmth at nine-thirty, he figured they'd be cooked by ten-thirty. But there was always the chance of pushing out a fox sunbathing minus bikini and sunglasses and stretched in full glory like any bathing beauty on the sands of

Miami Beach. Foxes adored a good sunbath.

The field of thirty-nine riders was out for a few reasons. The real foxhunters on green horses figured it would be a slow day and therefore perfect for a green horse. The fair-weather hunters wanted to trot around in their lovely ratcatcher kits, so the sunshine appealed to them. The real foxhunters on made horses who loved hound work especially enjoyed watching hounds go to it on the difficult days. Any pack looks good on a good day; the great packs are the ones who do all they can on the hard days. Truth be told, one sees more good hound work on a "bad" day than on a good day.

Then again, as the red foxes always bragged, it doesn't matter how great a pack of hounds may be, it's foxes that make foxhunting.

Target was about to prove this, however unwillingly, because Cora, the strike hound, edged a little forward, springing into the cornfield. Shaker didn't call her back as he trusted her. She wouldn't shoot off. Her phenomenal drive salvaged many a so-so day.

The grackles in the corn flew up like pepper, black dots against a blue sky. Their irritation was evidenced by the curses called down to the pack, now all in the cornfield. They circled since they knew the hounds wouldn't be in there long. The mice simply scurried out of the way of the hounds, diving into little bundles of corn husks if necessary.

"It's Target!" Cora triumphantly inhaled a remnant of his scent.

The other hounds flew to her. Cora made very few mistakes.

Young Doughboy, in his second year out, yelped with excitement.

"Lower your voice, you twit," Dragon growled. *"You'll sound like you're on deer."*

"Sorry," the chastened youngster replied.

"Dragon, you can be such an ass." His brother and littermate, Dasher, picked up a lovely stream of fading scent. *"Heading north."*

The hounds opened, honoring Cora's initial voice. Shaker blew three quick notes in succession, waited a second, blew the call again.

Hounds were away.

Sister, on Rickyroo, a seven-year-old Thoroughbred, grinned. What could be better?

Behind her a few riders slipped their hands down to check their girths. Crawford had dropped his reins during the cast and when Czpaka bolted forward he fished frantically for them. Riders hadn't figured on such a quick hit, but that's the beauty of foxhunting: expect the unexpected.

Bunny brought six students today. Charlotte agreed when Bunny asked to go. They both thought keeping everyone in their routine, rewarding those who were making good grades and improving as riders, would be for the best; anything to dissipate the claustrophobia of nervousness.

The Custis Hall girls might be nervous, but it was not over Al Perez at this moment.

Before they knew it they flanked the cornfield, rumbled across the farm road, and blasted into the orchard grass field distinguished by the fir trees on one side to break the wind and southern hawthorns on the eastern perimeter, a gift from visiting birds. The owner of Mud Fence three generations back so admired the southern hawthorn, also called green hawthorn, with its bright red berries now in evidence, that he imported enough to line this forty-acre hayfield. In spring the trees delighted with showy white flowers.

"Bother," Target grumbled to himself. He picked up an easy lope heading straight for home.

Three coops in a row marked off another farm road and a small pasture off that. Hit them right and they were a piece of cake, hit them wrong and you'd lurch over or worse, get stuck between them, the rest of the field balled up behind you trying not to cuss you out.

Sister cleared them all, noting that the footing, thanks to the dew still on the northern slope, proved slippery. Pine needles and leaves would be slippery, too, if they were still dewy.

Not much time to think about that because Target picked up the pace, now making a beeline for After All Farm. Within fifteen minutes they'd covered two miles of uneven terrain, jump after jump, and were now fording the lower branch of Broad Creek. Silt built up on the far bank and Rickyroo struggled to get through it.

Sister stopped. She called back to Tedi, in front.

"Tedi, find another crossing. By the fourth horse this one will be impassable."

"I'll head up toward Tattenhall Station." She mentioned an abandoned tiny white clapboard train station a half mile away. It once served a spur line for Norfolk and Southern. The railroad had built a serviceable bridge across the creek so employees could get to work. The railroad track ran parallel to the creek at that point.

"I'll stay with the hounds," Sister called back as Tedi touched her cap with her crop. They'd have a hell of a gallop to catch up but what a way to spend the morning.

As the sound of hoofbeats disappeared, Sister squeezed Rickyroo. Shaker, in sight, was flying flat out across a millet field, another coop, and into second-growth woods.

With his Thoroughbred speed and great heart, the young horse was soon within fifty yards of the huntsman.

The winding trail through the woods opened onto another hayfield, unfenced. They thundered across the green expanse, the hounds before them, then crossed a thin ribbon of a creek, over a log jump and into a peach orchard.

Sister assumed she'd not see the field again, but by the time they reached the old metal windmill put up in the 1930s, still turning, she could see Tedi, riding hard toward the sound of the horn and the hounds.

"She's good," Sister thought to herself and then

laughed, since Tedi, at seventy-one, like Sister, could have ridden most anyone into the ground.

Target, wishing he hadn't stuffed himself full of corn, hit top speed, twenty-five miles an hour. He knew this pack and somehow they'd managed to stick to his scent despite conditions. Five more minutes and his odor would have risen over their heads. He knew how fast the American hound can be. Still, he stayed straight as an arrow until he turned to see Dragon and Cora perhaps one hundred yards behind. He turned hard right in midair, ducked down low, and shot for the state road. The asphalt would help him since the tar smell would kill his scent. It was an old two-lane highway and he reached it—no cars as it was in the back of the beyond, so he tiptoed across it—then blasted into the pine plantation.

Dragon and Cora were flying so fast they overshot the line. Diana, a bit more deliberate, turned hard right.

Before she could open her mouth, Trinity, a third-year hound, a brilliant child, bellowed, *"To the right."*

Dragon whirled almost as gracefully as Target to rejoin the pack. Cora breathed on his heels. Cora hated any hound getting in front of her. She was jealous of her position to the degree that Dragon was arrogant and wanted it for himself. The two would never get along.

The Custis Hall girls hung tight. Tootie had never been on a run this fast. The thrill of it diminished the hazards. Valentina, too, proved tight in the tack.

Felicity, even though Parson was good as gold, experienced butterflies at some of the stouter jumps. Pamela Rene, not to be outshone by Tootie or Valentina, didn't bat an eye. She rode right up, for the girls had begun to pass some of the field members whose horses were slowing in the heat.

The etiquette was that the girls should ride in the rear, but once a run unfolded the rule became whoever could keep up should. So if a younger member passed an older member or if a person without their colors passed someone with their colors (even though this was cubbing, everyone knew who had colors and who did not), it was acceptable. Yes, it irritated, sometimes, those who were passed, but at this level, with this distance being covered at warp speed, whoever had the best horses moved to the front. The Custis Hall girls, thanks to the wealth of their families, rode top-flight horses. Nothing instills confidence like a great horse. Nothing shakes one's nerves like a second-rate one.

Sister felt the sweat roll between her breasts. The back of her shirt stuck to her. Her mouth felt parched. Thank God, she'd clipped her horses. She pitied any animal today with the beginning of its winter coat. Surely its rider would have brains enough to pull up and spare the horse.

The hounds, too, felt the heat, but their drive was so great, later on they'd fling themselves into a creek or even a water bucket—but only after they'd accounted for Target.

The heat affected the big red, too. He began to sink

with one mile to go. He zigged, he zagged. Finally he noticed a large tree that had been uprooted in a windstorm. He nimbly leapt up, ran all the way up, then dropped fifteen feet below.

The hounds threw up, or lost the scent, for a moment at the huge old sycamore. Sycamores grow in moisture, often by creeks or river branches. This one had been uprooted thirty yards from Broad Creek so Target plunged straight down into the creek, swimming up toward After All Farm. The water felt good.

Gingerly, Ardent, an older hound, tried and true, sniffed the tree trunk. *"He went up the trunk."*

Most of the Jefferson hounds, fast but sixty to seventy pounds, were too big to attempt to follow the line. Little Diddy, the runt of the whole pack, only in her second year, surprised everyone by hopping onto the trunk, pieces of bark flaking off, exposing the lighter color underneath. Carefully she picked her way up, the angle at thirty degrees.

"He made it to here," she called down, the branches obscuring her, for she'd gone up quite far.

"Thanks." Diana and Trudy walked under the end of the tree, jumped in the creek, swimming to the other side. The others followed, noses to the ground, once on land.

"Here!" Trudy called, the other hounds flocking to her.

They spoke at once, then came up against a bend in the creek. Trinity jumped in and swam straight across but he found no scent there.

96

"Work both sides of the bank," Diana ordered. *"He's heading back to his den so he went north."* She figured he crisscrossed the creek again at the bend to throw them off.

It took four minutes of intense searching but finally Doughboy came up with the line, very good work for a second-year hound.

They opened. Shaker blew them on.

Target reached the spot where Snake Creek feeds into the larger, fast-moving Broad Creek, he turned left, staying on the left side of Snake Creek; He was now on After All Farm.

He reached the covered bridge, ran across it, then made a loop, coming back to Snake Creek, where he recrossed it. It was an obvious ploy but it would buy him just enough time. He could hear the hounds closing and he prayed they were as hot and tired as he was. If only he hadn't been such a damned pig.

He traveled right over Nola Bancroft's grave, Tedi and Edward's daughter, who died in 1981 at twenty-four. She was buried with Peppermint, her favorite horse. He outlived her, making it to thirty-four. A beautiful stone fence enclosed the plot.

The hounds tore across the bridge. The field clattered over it, hooves reverberating inside, the noise deafening.

"Reverse!" Sister quickly turned when she saw the hounds jump back into Snake Creek.

Shaker knew he'd get balled up in the bridge because someone wouldn't be able to turn their horse around. He jumped down the steep bank, into the water, grabbed mane, stood up, and leaned forward on HoJo. A young horse who didn't make it on the steeplechase circuit struggled to find purchase.

Tootie, thinking ahead, turned her horse's head and slid by everyone else as soon as Sister called "Reverse."

The Custis Hall girls and Bunny followed.

Marty Howard stuck a minute, but she finally got herself around. Her horse spooked at some goblin seen only by himself.

Sister knew better than to try to pass them all, so she waited, tried not to bitch and moan, then hurried through as Tedi finally managed to get them out of the way. "Good job, girl."

Tedi smiled and quickly fell in behind her old friend. The hounds leapt over the stone wall, ran over Nola and Peppermint's grave.

Far from aggrieving Tedi, the sight of hounds running over her firstborn made her happy. For a fox or hound to cross a foxhunter's grave is a sign from heaven. It's to be wished for, not avoided.

With a maniacal burst of energy, Target skidded through fallen leaves, hoisted himself over a larger stone wall, this one separating fields closer to the main house. The outer fields had three-board fencing.

His den in sight, he soared into it like a basketball that doesn't touch the rim. *"Thank God!"*

Dragon, Cora, and Doughboy reached the den first. Little Diddy had had a bit of a time getting off the tree and had needed Walter's help. They brought up the rear as everyone tried to pile into the opening.

The remnants of a nice pattypan squash as well as a pumpkin littered Target's den. He'd meant to clean it out but the morning, fresh with hope, lured him outside.

"Come on out!" Dragon dug.

Target kicked pumpkin seeds at him.

Betty rode up, as she'd come in from the left, took HoJo's reins. She knew they were all on, no point in staying out there. Wouldn't be a second cast in this heat.

Shaker blew and praised his hounds. As he withdrew them from the den, he watched pumpkin and squash seeds spew out like a tiny white and orange Vesuvius.

Sister saw it, as did those closest to her.

He paused. More seeds were tossed into the morning light.

"He thinks he's so cute." Ardent smiled.

Shaker laughed until the tears rolled down his cheeks. Betty, too.

They thought they'd seen it all but this reminded them, foxes do have imagination.

Shaker didn't mount up but walked over to Snake Creek. HoJo was too hot at that moment to drink but he called all the hounds into the creek. They gratefully plunged in, cooling off and drinking.

"I have never seen anything like that in my life." Sister rode up, laughing.

"I bet if we opened up dens we'd find missing

99

watches and old love letters." He laughed along with her.

"None of mine, I hope," Sister giggled. "I can't write a line."

"Ha." Betty rolled her eyes heavenward as Magellan, her second horse and a Thoroughbred, drank. "You probably have a stack of envelopes tied up with powder blue ribbons."

"Sure." Sister wiped her brow with the embroidered handkerchief she'd stuck in her pocket. "You know, we're so close to the farm, let's hack over. I'll see if someone can go back to Mud Fence and bring the rig and my truck. I need two warm bodies."

"Only two?" Shaker finally remounted.

"What did you have in mind?" she asked.

"Actually, after this run, a long drink of anything cold."

"Oh, I wish you hadn't said that." Betty was parched and she didn't want to drink from anyone's flask as it would only make her thirstier.

Sister turned Rickyroo toward the field, sweat running down their faces and in some cases mascara as well. "Folks, let's hack back to Roughneck Farm. It doesn't make any sense to ride all the way back to Mud Fence. Some of your horses are spent." She noticed that Sam Lorillard's horse was in splendid condition. The man could train and ride. "If anyone wants to let their horse drink in the creek, go ahead. Use your judgment. Back at the farm you can untack them, we'll put them on a tie line if they can get along, you can wash them down or whatever, and then we'll figure out a way to get everyone back to their trailers."

This process took two hours but it went off without a hitch. Sister brought down drinks for everyone as they washed their horses. Tootie took care of Rickyroo while Valentina washed HoJo. Then the two girls washed their own horses.

Using the old farm truck as well as Sister's new truck, they piled everyone in the beds. This took three trips, but all went well.

Tootie and Valentina squeezed into the cab with Sister on the last run out since she invited them, too.

"Well, ladies, what'd you think?"

"I've never had so much fun in my life," Valentina effused.

"Me, too," Tootie concurred.

"For the record, if you need someone to talk to, I can listen. I know things are crazy right now. And if your parents will allow it and Mrs. Norton, if you want to stay here some night before hunting, I'd love to have you. Now, I can't take everyone in the riding program so we'll have to discuss numbers."

"I'm not telling. I don't want to share," Valentina honestly blurted out.

"Sister, we don't all get along. I mean, we can't stand Pamela Rene."

"Ah."

"She's a good rider and all, but she's, uh—" Valentina paused.

"Off the chain," Tootie said.

"I see. Well, let's just keep it between us, and when you're ready, let me know. I'll talk to Mrs. Norton. It's a nice way to know the hounds better."

"It's a nice way to know you better," Tootie said and meant it, and it pleased Sister.

"We don't want to sound negative, I mean, about Pamela. She's real competitive and she's always trying to buck us off, you know," Valentina whispered. "She said to Tootie that Tootie thinks she's better than her, Pamela, I mean. She said Tootie thinks she's part of the Niggerati."

"She didn't say that!" Sister was surprised.

"When I called her on it she told me to shut up because I'm white." Valentina's voice returned to normal.

"Well, Tootie, what do you think?" Sister wisely asked the beautiful young woman.

"I think that word in any form ought to be banished from the English language," Tootie replied without rancor. "She's mad at me because I wouldn't be part of the protest. You know, Sister, I do think Custis Hall ought to pay more attention to its history. Those buildings were built, the early ones, by slaves. But I don't think confrontation is the way to do it. I mean, that is so sixties."

As they neared the entrance to Mud Fence, Sister slowed even more since the bed was jammed with people. "Anything weird at school? Anything that makes you kind of take notice, apart from what just happened?"

"Like sex perverts?" Valentina put her arm around Tootie's shoulder.

"Val."

"I'm not the pervert. I'm in the middle, Tootie, and I'm squishing up next to you on the turn."

"Oh, sure, Val, I bet you say that to all the girls."

They made Sister laugh. She felt like a schoolgirl in their presence. She couldn't say they made her feel young again because she didn't feel old despite what the calendar said. She had no idea where those seventy-odd years went and she had to remind herself that she had had a birthday in August. Seventy-two! She kept thinking she was seventy-one, as if it much mattered.

"Well, you know," Tootie said as the remaining trailers came into view, "Mr. Wheatley always finds an excuse when we're trying on costumes."

"The old devil!" Sister blurted that out.

"He likes big boobs." Valentina added that juicy tidbit. "That's why he likes all those plays from the eighteenth century. He can put everyone in low-cut dresses. I swear it's the truth."

"Do you think he touches anyone?" Sister was more than curious, she was slightly worried.

"If he did, we'd know. Really. I mean, we know who's sleeping with whom," Valentina bragged.

"I can hardly wait for our slumber party." Sister laughed but she was beginning to feel that Custis Hall sheltered many secrets. Why had she not thought of it before?

CHAPTER 11

Had circumstances been otherwise, Sister would not have contacted Charlotte Norton. She met her at seven that evening, the campus paths illuminated by the ornate, graceful cast-iron lights installed in 1877.

Teresa had gone home. They sat in Charlotte's office eating a shepherd's pie that Sister had made, knowing Charlotte probably hadn't eaten much that day.

"—three."

"Well, if that's all, you'll weather this storm." Sister reassured her as three students had immediately been withdrawn from Custis Hall.

"Then Knute came in wringing his hands about the potential for lost alumnae funds and what were we going to do about the position of director of alumnae affairs? I told him we could at least wait a few weeks, then appoint a temporary person. This is no time for a search committee."

"Wise choice. I'm surprised Knute would be insensitive."

"Doesn't mean to be. He's worried because hiring a security firm put a big dent in his carefully wrought budget and we need so many things above and beyond simple maintenance. Well, I don't have to tell you. Think of all that goes into running the Jefferson Hunt. It's the same meat," she smiled, dark circles under her eyes from exhaustion, "different gravy."

"I like the decisions. I like the problems even. Not sure I'd like your current problem, but anything, even something as bizarre as Al's death, does give one a chance to ferret out weakness in the organization."

"That's one way to look at it. How we will replace him I don't know. He had the right personality for the job. And he was so much fun to be around. I miss him more each day as it sinks in that he's really gone." Charlotte poured Sister another cup of steaming Constant Comment tea, then one for herself. "Did you want something stronger? Forgive me for not asking sooner."

"No, thank you. Charlotte, you have so much on you. If there's anything I can do to help, call me."

"Well, what I heard today was a barn burner. If I'd been out, that would have restored my spirits." Charlotte placed the silver teapot on the intricate brass Custis Hall cypher.

The cyphers, placed beneath hot pots, were made at Virginia Metalcrafters in Waynesboro. Beautiful cyphers for William and Mary, or Washington's initials, or Jefferson's made one realize how aesthetically advanced that superb generation was, far more advanced than current generations.

"Try to make Opening Hunt this Saturday even though it's usually a big parade."

"I'll try. We've organized a special parents' meeting beginning Saturday afternoon. There's no point in ignoring this. We've got to take the bull by the horns.

Knute opposed. So did Amy. They think it keeps the problem in front of everyone. Alpha's for it. The other board members are for it and I hope you are, too."

"You have to meet the issue head on. What people need more than anything is contact with you, the administration, and faculty. They need to be heard and of course they need reassurance. You'll be exhausted. Can Carter help, at all?"

"He's canceled his appointments, even his beloved Sunday golf game. Bless him."

"Good for you, good for the parents. Carter has that wonderful bedside manner. How are the girls taking it?"

"The assembly helped. The students have all met with their faculty advisers. They can come see me, too."

"Anyone taken you up on it?"

"Pamela Rene."

"Of course." Sister smiled. "She's an angry child."

"I suppose if I had a mother who told me how to walk, talk, dress, and that I'd never be the woman she was, it would wear me down, but," she paused, "her situation isn't unique. So many children of wealth are psychologically abused. Let me amend that, many children are abused, period. The odd thing about Americans is that we seem to think that money cures all things. There's sympathy for the middle-class child, outpouring of concern for the poor one, but for the rich, well, people have little. You know, Sister, I don't care how much money a person inherits, you can't buy yourself a loving mother or a loving father."

"No, you can't. That's one reason why I try to include the girls who can ride into hunting. We can't make up for what is lacking at home, if it is—obviously not all rich kids are ignored or bedeviled—but we can make them feel valued. Many a young person has flirted with trouble, and thanks to hunting, pulled themselves out of it."

"Horses help. I truly believe horses are healers." She smiled a true smile. "And the club members are very warm." Charlotte continued on a sterner note. "It's horses or drugs. Whenever I hear a parent complain about the cost of buying and keeping horses I say to myself, 'You'll pay it in wrecked cars, plunging grades, and drug rehabilitation.' I've seen too much of it."

"In a way, that brings me to why I came in tonight. After today's hunt we had to shuttle people back to Mud Fence."

"I heard. The girls loved it! Another adventure."

"On the last trip I had Tootie and Valentina in the cab of the truck with me. They told me that Bill Wheatley comes in during custom fittings and he, well, I don't know how to put this. He's not grabbing them, but according to the girls, he likes to catch them in states of undress and he is particularly fond of girls with big racks." Sister leaned toward Charlotte and touched her hand. "I hope I haven't added to your troubles, and this is hearsay. Given what has happened, anything and everything may be important."

Charlotte's face registered the news. "Damn. Damn him if it's true, the old fool."

"Both girls said he never touched them and they've never heard of him touching anyone else."

"That's cold comfort."

"I know," Sister sighed. "Charlotte, what was Al's relationship with Bill?"

Charlotte blinked. "They weren't close. Al showed off the theater department to alumnae, but who wouldn't? Our theater department and our riding program are sensational. The theater is easy to show. It's much more difficult to highlight your English department unless an alumna or a parent will sit through one of Alpha's remarkable lectures."

"She is remarkable." Sister admired Alpha for her knowledge and for her demeanor. "It's just the two of us—the walls don't have ears—what about Amy? Was it over?"

"For him, not for her. When Al married Rachel, Amy broke bad. Soured. She never bounced back. Of course, they kept their affair quiet while it was going on. And I don't know how you feel about this, but I don't disapprove of relationships between staff or administration. Neither was married. And as I said, they kept it off campus. I don't know why it ended, only that she was heartbroken and then angry."

"Angry enough to kill?"

"No. She might have wished him dead, but no."

"Dead end?"

"So far." Charlotte passed a tray of lemon curd tarts.

"Doesn't quite go with shepherd's pie, but it's all I could scare up from the dining room."

"I like lemon curd tarts," Sister said, picking one off the plate. "Are there other affairs of which you know?"

"No," Charlotte wavered. "Well, none that I'm certain about."

"Such as."

"Knute. I think Knute may be sleeping with Bunny. I asked her. We're friends. She denied it, but she also knows the consequences. He's married. Something like that could cause harm to the school if it came out."

"Speaking of coming out—the girls. I assume some of them are sleeping with one another."

"They are."

"In the old days they'd have been expelled."

"Their faculty advisers talk to them. On the one hand, we don't berate them, on the other hand, we don't encourage them. But you know, that's been going on at same-sex schools since the earth was cooling. I pride myself that we're honest about it. We offer counseling if they ask for it. It's an age of experimentation. I think, not that I'd say it publicly, that if they don't at least get crushes on one another, they aren't developing. It's part of growing up."

"Yes, it is. Do you think that might have something to do with Pamela's behavior?"

"I've thought about it. She doesn't seem to feel affection for anybody."

"A bad sign."

"I know."

"Is it possible Al Perez could have crossed the line with any student?"

"No," Charlotte forcibly replied. "No. Why he was killed, I don't know. I can't come up with a thing. But he didn't sleep with students. If he had, he'd have been out of here so fast, no one would have seen his dust."

"I am sorry to come with troublesome news. You're going through a terrible time. I wish I could do something for you."

"Being here helps. Knowing I can tell you anything."

"Tootie did mention something else of interest. She said Pamela was mad at her because she wouldn't take part in the protest, but she thought Custis Hall should do more, should look into its history. She's level-headed, that Tootie."

"I love that kid. She's one of those special ones. Valentina is, too, in a completely different way. One is thoughtful, highly intelligent, and reserved. The other one is charismatic, bright, and high-spirited."

"They are beguiling, as is Felicity, quiet and steady."

"So you know, I appointed Tootie and Pamela as well as Valentina to search for a person who can evaluate the artifacts. They also have to find someone who can counsel us on the period in which Custis Hall was built, and lastly, they need to come up with research and writing projects for students. I've put them to work and I'm hoping by making them work together some of their hostilities will abate. Each of them is capable, it's the emotional component, but then it always is, isn't it, regardless of age?"

"In theory we get better at working with people who go about a task differently than we do."

"In theory."

"Still, it's hard to work with people we plain don't like."

CHAPTER 1 2

Tradition binds us to the dead for good or for ill. Hunting defines human cooperation. It was probably the first large-scale enterprise we undertook as a species. Language and technology started with the chase. Architecture developed later, agriculture is even more recent in the lurching progress of *Homo sapiens,* agriculture being perhaps fourteen thousand years old.

Drawings on Egyptian tombs show hounds walking out on long couple straps prior to being released to chase, by sight, their quarry. Homer mentions hunting with hounds in *The Odyssey.* Asian and European civilizations hunted, but it took the English to raise hunting to an art.

Then as now, the money flowed to those who could handle hounds, horses. Blacksmiths, saddlers, bootmakers, tailors, purveyors of foodstuffs for humans, horses, hounds, real estate agents all benefited from hunting. Herdsmen did, too, as hunts removed their fallen stock, saving the farmer or shepherd a great deal of effort.

Originally hunting foxes fell into the lower class of venery. Stag hunting, boar hunting had pride of place. By the end of the seventeenth century, at the dawn of the great eighteenth century, foxhunting took over. The venue for those seeking to make a place for themselves in politics, in society, now rested with a cunning foe, the fox.

The Enclosure Laws ensured that the fields of England, for the most part, were divided into lovely squares bound by hedges, fences, or double ditches. The rest of Europe kept to the old village-and-commons system, which is apparent if one flies low over France. But England went her separate way just as she went her separate way over religion during the reign of Henry VIII. Both divergences ensured a nation of freethinkers or, as a foxhunter would say, people who take their own line.

Chasing that red devil meant one would soar over wooden fences, oxers—a type of double jump— bullfinch (nasty) hedges, the odd gate, stone walls, deep ditches, and whatever else the farmer had constructed to keep his stock where it belonged.

The English also believed in giving the quarry a sporting chance. Americans refined this even further, in part because their lands were and remain much wilder. Also, cattle not sheep are the dominant animal in American pastures. The fox isn't a pest in America unless you keep poultry. There is no need to kill foxes. The English farmer is within his rights to kill them as they destroy his newborn lambs just as a Wyoming sheep farmer is within his rights to shoot a coyote.

The traditions for the United Kingdom, the United States, Canada, Australia, in fact, wherever English is the language, remain unchanged. If a fox is viewed, hounds not yet on the line, the huntsman, ideally, should count to twenty before swinging hounds that way. Give the fox a fair chance to get moving. No hole, drain, or culvert can be stopped. The fox has every opportunity to pop down whatever underground chamber appeals to him. This has been the case in America but has only recently been put into practice in England.

The other tradition is that hounds have the right-of-way. There is no exception to this. A horse who kicks a hound must leave the field.

In counties where hunting is prevalent, those driving a car automatically slow. People should anyway as a matter of course, but those who don't, if recognized, soon find themselves verbally accosted or in the social deep freeze. Hounds always have the right-of-way.

Never speak to a hound. Even if you were present at its birth, even if you walk out the pack daily, never speak to a hound. Only the huntsman and whippers-in may speak to the animal. Too many voices can confuse the hound and, worse, your big flannel mouth may cause the animal to lift its head.

The sound of "Hike to him," "Hark," or "Leave it" from a member of the field has caused huntsmen to just go off, a torrent of abuse following. Other, more diplomatic huntsmen, if hearing the sin, call the hound to them as quickly as possible. But the tradition is as it was in the time of the pharaohs: Never speak to a hound when hunting.

The animal wants to chase a fox, has been bred, trained, and loved so that it will do its job. There are more less-than-perfect-weather days than perfect, which means the hound is trying very hard to get a line, a thin enticing ribbon of scent. It never fails: the slow days are the days when sooner or later, the field starts talking. If ever hounds needed quiet, it's on the difficult days. On great scenting days, even if some damned fool is blowing her mouth off, hounds won't be distracted. The problem is, for true foxhunters, that most of the field hunt to ride instead of riding to hunt. If they aren't tearing across the countryside, lurching over jumps, they're bored. Good hound work means nothing to them. In fact, they don't know it when they see it. And not one member out of a hundred will know the signs of a dishonest huntsman or master, ones who "arrange" for foxes or scent to appear. Honest masters and staff tolerate the rider types because they pay their subscription fees, which keep the whole show in business. It would be a barefaced liar of a huntsman or master who would say they didn't love the days best when the field was small, weather bitter or iffy. The people in the field then are the true blues, the ones who love hounds, love the game.

By tradition, not only should one not speak to hounds, but one should not speak to the other hunters, especially at a check, when they sit and wait for hounds to recast themselves and find scent. Rarely is this observed, and even the best field master, if the field is huge, can't enforce silence without sending an offender home. No one likes being draconian, but sometimes someone must be sent home because of bad manners. It certainly wakes everyone else up.

Sister Jane thought of these things as she prepared her kit for Opening Hunt. Always a gala occasion, she wanted to ensure that she presented a good example. Like most masters, she knew the real hunting would begin on the other side of the festive day.

In England, foxhunting begins November 1, the formal season. Americans usually determine Opening Hunt according to their latitude. Someone in upstate New York might start formal hunting in early October. By December the northern hunts, Canadian hunts, often shut down.

In Virginia, Opening Hunt will generally fall on the last Saturday of October or the first Saturday of November.

The Jefferson Hunt held to the first Saturday in November, in part because it's close to November 3, St. Hubert's Day, the patron saint of hunting. This particular Opening Hunt Saturday fell on November 5, the feast day of Zachary and Elizabeth, parents of

John the Baptist. Still, it was close enough to St. Hubert's Day.

The legend is that St. Hubert, a dissolute youth, was hunting on Good Friday when an enormous stag appeared, the cross shining between his mighty antlers. Thus was St. Hubert converted. He continued to hunt and breed hounds named for him, even when bishop of Maastricht and Liege. He died in A.D. 727, revered to this day. Churches are named after him, his blessings invoked by those in search of their quarry. Dedicated hunters, regardless of quarry, often have a St. Hubert's medal tucked somewhere on their person or even a ring, the stag with the cross between its antlers.

Sister wore a St. Hubert's ring on her wedding ring finger. Raymond bought it for her at a lovely jewelry store in Vienna, right across from the Spanish school. She wore it with her wedding ring. Adorned with oak leaves and acorns on the sides, it had worn down over the last forty years. Her wedding ring finally broke in two, ten years after Ray's death, which was in 1991. What remained was St. Hubert's ring, which seemed fitting.

On her right hand, the third finger, she wore a red-gold signet ring, a fox mask beautifully engraved. Her son gave it to her when he was thirteen. He paid for it himself, no help from his father, out of money he had earned repairing tack. RayRay liked working with his hands. Sister, not given to gusts of emotion, cried when she opened the green Keller & George box, to behold the simple, beautiful ring. She never took that ring off her finger. Ray Jr. was dead by the next Christmas.

Like most people, she harbored superstitions. She wore her grandfather's pocket watch when hunting. Many's the time as a child when, out hunting, she'd see her grandfather pull out his watch, flick open the case, and check the time.

So often her mind would go back to her husband and her son, two handsome men, in her estimation, anyway, and she'd remember them riding together, flying their fences, big smiles on their faces. She had hoped RayRay would inherit the mantle of master of foxhounds as well as his great-grandfather's pocket watch.

Life has a funny way of working things out. Last year, after decades alone at the helm, she finally took on a joint master, Dr. Walter Lungrun, her husband's natural son. It seemed that everyone knew but her. Even Walter's father, while he lived, knew. When she found out she thought "The Lord moves in mysterious ways His wonders to perform." As for Big Ray engaging in affairs, she didn't hold it against him because she was having affairs of her own. However, she didn't become pregnant. Now she rather wished she had.

Every marriage creates its own world, and while Sister's marriage wasn't conventional it was solid. They did love and support each other.

But that was all so long ago, and Opening Hunt was tomorrow. She refocused her attention on her attire.

Her top hat, her black shadbelly, her canary breeches hung in the closet. Her fourfold stock tie, pressed, was folded over a hanger. Her shirt, the banded collar fitting her neck with a half inch to spare, also hung there. Her canary gloves, buttersoft, rested on her Dehner boots, the patent-leather tops gleaming. Her hammerhead spurs sparkled. Her hat cord was already attached to the top hat so she wouldn't fumble for it in the morning. All she would need to do was hook it on the inside back loop of her shadbelly collar.

She'd been foxhunting since she was six years old. Before that her mother and grandfather would take her out on a leadline. Even so, at seventy-two, she kept a list of everything she needed taped to her bureau. Sister had a horror of being incorrect in any fashion. Her only cheat was the thin garter strap that slipped through the tab at the back of her hunting boots. Before Velcro, a row of small flat buttons closed the breeches on your calf. The buttons ran all the way up to the knee. The garter strap slipped between the upper buttons. There were those who said it should go between the second and third button and those who argued for the first and second button. Centuries ago, the garter strap kept the boots in place. A few people argued that the garter strap kept the breeches in place. She finally gave it up because the leather rubbed her leg. She'd come back from the High Holy Days, Opening Hunt, Thanksgiving Hunt, Christmas Hunt, and New Year's Hunt, with bloody legs. So far, no one commented on her slight rebellion. Then again, few knew the difference.

"Golly, that's it. I can't do any more." She flopped into bed glad the fire in the fireplace warmed the room, which faced the northwest. "Don't bring me any mice tonight. I need my sleep."

"How about a juicy spider?" Golly teased.

"Even I won't eat a spider," Rooster mumbled as he rolled over on the rug beside the bed.

"You eat everything else." Raleigh put his big paw on the harrier's back leg.

"Is this going to be a chatty night? I need to sleep." The phone rang.

Golly put her paw on the receiver. *"Hollywood calling."*

"Hello."

"Honey, I'm at the airport. Sam's coming to pick me up. I just couldn't let Opening Hunt go without being there." Gray Lorillard's voice lifted her.

"I can't believe you! You've come all the way back from San Francisco for Opening Hunt? I'm so happy!"

"I'll see you in the morning. Did I ever tell you how good you look in a shadbelly?" He laughed. "I know you need your sleep so bye."

"Bye." She hung up the phone. "Gray's home! I can't believe it. Thank God I had my hair and nails done yesterday."

"Why do women do their nails? They don't have real nails." Rooster thought it odd.

119

"Color," Golly spoke authoritatively. *"Humans don't have much color. Their eyes, their hair but other than that they're one color, white, black, brown, you get the idea. See, if a lady paints her nails it perks up the rather drab affair."*

"Oh, that makes sense," Rooster replied.

"They wear clothes. That's colorful," Raleigh said and lifted his paw off Rooster's hind leg.

"Sure, but when they're naked, no color." Golly kept to her idea.

"What about men? Why don't they do their nails?" Rooster was fascinated.

"Well, they do, I mean the ones who are very successful in business, but they don't paint them. They buff them. Men can't be colorful like women."

"What about the pictures in some of the books Sister reads? Feathers and ruffles and stuff like that?" Raleigh noticed everything.

"That was when men were peacocks. All gone now." Golly warmed to her subject. *"Now the most powerful thing a man can wear is black and white, or gray with stripes for a morning suit, or white tie at night. White tie is even more powerful than black tie. All black and white."*

"You'd think they'd imitate us. We have varied coats." Rooster was proud of his rich tricolor coat.

"Black and white." Golly swayed a little.

"Not tomorrow. The men wear scarlet and the women are in black." Raleigh liked getting one up on Golly, who was every bit as smart as he was and

therefore a challenge.

"They get to be peacocks?" Rooster's voice rose.

"A peacock that sits on its tail feathers is just another turkey." Golly, irritated that Raleigh had found the exception that proves the rule, turned her back on the dogs on the floor to curl up by Sister's side.

The phone rang again.

"Goddammit!" Sister picked it up and said in a modulated voice, "Hello."

"Sister, this is Marty Howard and I'd like to bring a guest tomorrow."

"That's fine, Marty."

"Well, it's a last-minute thing and she only has black field boots. Might you overlook it?"

"If you can't call around and find a pair of boots to fit her, of course."

"Thank you. Good night."

"Good night." She hung up the phone. "Now I'm wide awake." She grabbed the book next to the table, *The Life of Frank Freeman, Huntsman* by Guy Pagent, published in 1948 by Alfred Tacey, Limited, Leicester, England.

The phone rang again.

"I am going to rip this infernal thing out of the wall! Why are people calling me this late?" She picked it up. "Hello."

A deep voice said, "If I reveal myself I'll be killed. Al Perez had his hand in the till. He's not alone."

"What?"

121

Click.

She sat there for a moment, phone in hand, then put it back in the cradle. The odd tinty sound of the caller's voice was unnerving.

"Close to home," she said aloud as she dialed Ben Sidel.

CHAPTER 13

Today, the summation of fall, was flooded with soft sunshine. As fall lingered long this year many trees still dazzled red, orange, yellow, and true scarlet. The sky, an intense blue, was cloudless. The mercury at ten A.M. sat on the sixty-six-degree line but would surely climb. This was a perfect day for everything but foxhunting.

As the Reverend Judy Parrish from Trinity Episcopal Church blessed the hounds on the beginning of the one hundred and eighteenth season, the crowd of two hundred people smiled. The hounds gathered around the divine as she stood on a mounting block so people could see her and so the dog hounds wouldn't take a notion to offer their own blessing.

Diana observed the Reverend Parrish's vestments flowing slightly in the light breeze. People's clothing fascinated her and she thought it must be a bother to have to decide what to wear and be confined in it. Paying for it was the final insult. She had only to wash her sleek coat and go about her day.

Diana wondered why the Reverend Parrish's robe was white with a multicolored surplice whereas the Reverend Daniel Wheeler's robe was black, his surplice representing the ecclesiastical season. The Reverend Wheeler gave a blessing on Thanksgiving as that was the Children's Hunt and the youngsters adored the Reverend Wheeler.

Diana considered asking Cora, who was older and wiser, but knew if she so much as opened her mouth a dirty look would shoot her way from the huntsman.

As they disembarked from the party wagon, their special van, he told them sternly, "No loose tongues. Be respectful."

Sister, on Lafayette, stood to the left of the hounds; Shaker, on Gunpowder, was on the right. Betty and Sybil discreetly stood farther back just in case.

Tedi and Edward opened their house for this special day. Hospitality, second nature to them, made everyone feel part of the ceremony even if they'd not so much as fed a carrot to a horse in their life.

As the hounds, the horses, the foxes, and lastly the humans were blessed, Sister lifted her eyes to take in the large field, all one hundred and thirty of them. This number, unwieldy for a field master, was dwarfed by the four hundred or so who would take to the field on Boxing Day in England. Entire villages poured out along the road to cheer them on. For an American hunt, one hundred and thirty people in the field and another two hundred on the ground constituted a sizable number. She knew her people could ride. About the visitors, well, they'd either hang on or dot the landscape in their best clothes.

The best riders of Custis Hall came. Charlotte and Bunny sat beside each other. Bill Wheatley, in a weazlebelly with a robin's egg blue silk stock tie, not incorrect if one studies the mid-eighteenth-century prints, was also there. Bill's theatrical nature would leach out somehow. He had to be noticed.

Sister was glad Charlotte kept the girls on their schedule. Charlotte's judgment impressed Sister. Over the last nine years she had ample opportunity to observe what to her was a young woman. At seventy-two, someone forty-three is young.

Her eyes lingered on Gray Lorillard next to his brother, Sam, and Crawford and Marty. They hadn't a minute to catch up, although he did sprint to her truck when she pulled in to give her a big hug and a kiss. He made her feel like the most special woman in the world. And he was handsome. His hair was salt and pepper, his military mustache set off his straight white teeth, and his deep voice had a melodic, hypnotic quality. The other thing she noticed about Gray when they'd begun dating last year was his hands, slender but strong.

Bunny Taliaferro also had lovely hands.

She really didn't know why she looked at hands. Maybe it was because a horseman needs good hands, but not necessarily pretty ones. She valued both.

A moment of silence, then Shaker coughed.

She smiled gratefully at Shaker, for he brought her back to the task at hand. "Hounds, please."

He clapped his cap on his auburn curls, the cap tails dangling. They walked at a stately pace down the long winding drive; at the covered bridge he put his horn to his lips, pointed Gunpowder to the right, and blew for the hounds to get to work. "Lieu in there."

"Finally!" An exasperated Dragon bolted along Snake Creek.

For all his eagerness and everyone else's the day was a blank. No master wants a blank day even if Jesus Christ himself couldn't get a fox up on a day with a high-pressure system overhead, dry, bright, and now seventy-two degrees. Still, everyone enjoyed a gorgeous ride and came back to the trailers in two hours. Even at the leisurely pace at which they moved along some people managed to part company with their horses.

As the hounds drank water back at the party wagon, Crawford walked over and said to Shaker, "That bitch has drive."

He had pointed to Dragon.

"Dog hound," Shaker simply replied.

"Ah, well, you ought to breed him." Then Crawford walked toward his wife, who had just emerged from their dressing room in the horse trailer.

Shaker seethed.

Sister shrugged. "He has to be the authority."

"No authority on manners and doesn't know squat about hounds." Shaker stroked Diddy's head.

"You're right about that."

A hunt member should never presume to tell staff or the master what to do or how to do it. Crawford had told the huntsman what hound to breed, thereby committing two sins. First, he had breached etiquette. Second, he had revealed a dangerous ignorance should he ever get the opportunity to breed a pack. Beware being seduced by a brilliant individual. Always study the families, study the bloodlines.

The breakfast exceeded even the last Opening Hunt breakfast. This time Tedi and Edward brought down an oysterman from the Chesapeake Bay who shucked oysters right out of an ice-crammed barrel. There were clams, too. Half a pig turned on the outdoor spit over open coals, as did half a lamb on a second spit, the roasting pit glowing orange. Twelve people had been employed to serve the guests; blue-and-white-striped tents set up outside provided shade since it proved so hot.

Two bars, four bartenders, worked feverishly. Foxhunters have hollow legs, but in the heat even the abstentious developed a powerful thirst.

The muffin hounds, like Knute Nilsson, who didn't ride but came for the party, to see friends off, were in line for breakfast, which started at noon. The riders needed to sponge down their horses, water them. Tedi and Edward, having hosted many a breakfast, knew to keep the food coming. No rider should go home hungry.

Each long table had a low fall display, sheaves of

wheat, with a miniature French hunting horn in the middle.

Tedi thought of everything. Sister, Walter, Tedi, and Edward moved from table to table making sure everyone had what they needed.

The girls from Custis Hall, thrilled to be part of the big day, and equally thrilled not to be eating Custis Hall food even though it was pretty good, sang, and then prompted others to join in.

Bill stood up, held up his hands like a conductor, and they belted out "Do ye ke'en John Peel."

At the last chorus everyone joined in. Many guests now felt no pain.

Charlotte, who managed to attend Opening Hunt after all, touched Sister's sleeve as she passed the table. "Thank you, Master. Another wonderful Opening Hunt."

"Given the temperature, we could have gone fishing instead." Sister laughed.

Charlotte pulled her down and whispered in her ear, "I'll talk with Bill on Monday. I wanted to do some investigating of my own first and I thank you, too, for alerting me to something so sensitive."

Sister squeezed Charlotte's shoulder and moved on.

Ben Sidel, elbow to elbow with Henry Xavier, nick-named X, a boyhood friend of RayRay's and therefore dear to Sister, was extolling the virtues of his horse, Nonni.

Sister chatted with the men, then moved along.

As Ben's eyes followed her, X remarked, "I'll bet

she's pissed about Al Perez being hanged on her property."

Ronnie Haslip, another childhood friend of RayRay's, said, "Who wouldn't be?"

"Yes, but the difference is she'll figure it out. No offense to you, Ben," X declared, his vest unbuttoned since he really was becoming rotund.

"No offense taken," the genial Ben replied.

"Any ideas?" Ronnie liked being close to the action and gossip, and he liked the sheriff.

"Ideas are one thing, hard facts are another. The only thing I can tell you is he was hanged to death. He wasn't killed somewhere else, then strung up."

Ronnie shuddered. "Hope it was fast."

"It wasn't. He didn't drop far, so his neck didn't snap. He strangled to death."

Ronnie and X looked at each other, then at Ben.

X dabbed his mouth with a napkin. He may have been fat, but he was dainty. "Doesn't make sense."

"It will. Once all the pieces are in place there's something inevitable about the puzzle." Ben knew talking business was part of his job, just as being a doctor meant you heard everyone's symptoms. He noticed Walter Lungrun getting an earful from neighbor Alice Ramy.

As Sister swept by one of the end tables she noticed a small bespectacled figure walking toward the tents. A woman, perhaps in her early fifties, her hair pulled back in a severe bun, eyes searching, came toward Sister as Sister extended her hand.

"Hello, I'm Jane Arnold, welcome."

In a faltering voice, the lady held out her small hand. "I'm Professor Frances Kennedy from Brown University. Is Mrs. Norton here?"

"She is. Let me take you to her, but please make sure you get something to eat. Can I get you a drink?" Sister also noticed that she wore beautifully made monkey's fist gold earrings and one simple old ring, oval, with a black onyx stone, a crest engraved thereon.

"No, thank you," Professor Kennedy respectfully declined.

Sister noted, making her way through the people, that Professor Kennedy was frail, not just thin. She wore a pleated skirt in the Kennedy tartan, a crisp white blouse, a Celtic brooch on her left shoulder. Her features were Caucasian, although she was African American, which made Sister wonder if her people weren't originally Ethiopian, as they so often have sharp features.

People's ancestry fascinated Sister, but that could be said of most Virginians, who, try as they might to avoid it, find that chickens come home to roost in middle age. By that time you look like your people. Blood tells.

"Charlotte, this is Professor Frances Kennedy. Professor Kennedy, this is Mrs. Charlotte Norton, headmistress of Custis Hall."

The look on Charlotte's face, welcoming but questioning, left Sister to wonder just what was going on.

Then she noticed that Pamela Rene beat a hasty retreat to the smorgasbord.

Charlotte made the student next to her give her seat to Professor Kennedy and she sent Valentina for a plate of food and Tootie for a drink once she extracted what libation the quiet-spoken lady preferred.

"I'm here to examine your artifacts." Professor Kennedy smiled shyly as she gratefully sipped iced tea, a sprig of mint floating on top.

CHAPTER 14

Face flushed even to the roots of his wavy silver hair, Bill Wheatley sputtered, "I demand to know who is spreading filth and calumnies about me!"

"Bill," Charlotte's voice remained calm, "I can understand your being upset, but no one is spreading filth. This came as an observation from students and I took the precaution of calling former students. No one has accused you of improper conduct or sexual harassment."

"Well, they're calling me a Peeping Tom!"

"Now, Bill, what the girls have said is that you often walk in and out of their costume fittings and changes. Peeping Tom hasn't escaped anyone's lips. Just try to remain calm and explain this, uh, habit to me."

"I'm head of the theater department for Christ's sake, Charlotte. I oversee all the plays, every aspect of production. And you know, costume design was where

I made my name before marriage and three children forced me to think about job security."

"I appreciate that. You need to fit and refit costumes. And I repeat, no one has implied that you have touched them or said anything inappropriate. It's just that you seem to pop in when they are in, shall we say, states of undress."

"I don't care. I don't even notice!" He lied a little.

"Now, Bill, you don't expect me to believe that, do you? I'm a woman. Even I'd notice."

He stopped, stared hard at her, then looked up at the ceiling. "Well, if one of the girls is, well, you know," he motioned with both hands rolling outward over his chest, "how can I not see them? Not that the girls are topless. Just, well, Charlotte, what do you want me to say?"

"Nothing. I want to clarify the issue and let you know that some of the girls feel uncomfortable."

"They're at that age, terribly self-conscious." He nodded. "Growing pains and all that. I'm getting close to retirement age, adolescence in reverse. That's how I think of it. My legs buckle and my belt doesn't."

She smiled. "Just don't go in the dressing room anymore. Everyone's on pins and needles. I'd hate to see this get blown out of proportion."

His gray eyebrows shot upward. "A suit? You mean someone would bring a lawsuit against me?"

"No." She shook her head. "I don't think anything would go that far."

"Oh, Charlotte, all a judge has to do is see a young

woman cry in the dock and whoever is accused, even if he's as innocent as John the Baptist, his head will roll." He inhaled deeply. "I have loved teaching here. This is my home. But I'm glad retirement is near. Things have changed, Charlotte, not for the better. If you hug a student, it could be sexual harassment. If you say anything, even in explaining our past, that could be construed as sexist, racist, or demeaning to some group. You're put in the stocks and rotten eggs are thrown at you. And then you resign. It's crazy. It's out of control."

"I agree, Bill, it's gone too far, but I also know that for centuries, those with power thought nothing of mocking those without. I can sympathize with over-sensitivity."

"Oversensitivity is one thing, using it to harm others or climb up over their backs is quite another. That Pamela Rene is a little shit, I'm telling you. She's stirred up a hornet's nest over those artifacts. Do you know what she did last week? We're rehearsing *A Raisin in the Sun*, one of my favorite plays. Talk about a slice of history. Well, she didn't know her lines. I reprimanded her and she said why not use cue cards? She's a spoiled brat and she hates Valentina and Tootie."

"Why do you say that?"

"They're more popular. She tries to bulldoze people. Valentina, in particular, has already mastered the art of consensus. If she can hold it together, that kid will be our first female governor or senator."

"I agree. But back to the subject at hand. Do you agree not to go into the dressing rooms?"

"How am I going to check costumes?"

"Why can't a girl come to you?"

"All right." He folded his hands in his lap. "I see your point but I go on record as saying this is a bit silly."

"Silly or not, Bill, we have a major problem facing us and this school doesn't need any more jolts."

His face reddened again but he agreed. "All right." He paused. "Who is that tiny little black lady in Main Hall?"

"Ah, yes, Teresa and I need to alert all the faculty. Administration knows but I haven't gotten to faculty yet. She's an expert on slave life and labor from 1800 to 1840. She's a kind of social archaeologist."

"From where?"

"Brown University."

"Ah, then she is big beans."

"Seems to be."

"That was fast. I thought the search would take longer."

"Let's just say that Pamela has stolen a march on us." She held up her hand. "But she really has found the right person to assess our treasures."

"Have you checked her credentials?"

"I called the president of Brown this morning and, I'm happy to say, she called right back. Professor Kennedy teaches two classes a week, Wednesday and Friday, and we will pay her way back and forth until this is finished."

"My God, how long will she be here? Knute Nilsson will have a cow!"

"So far he's given birth to a small calf," Charlotte remarked. "Professor Kennedy thinks she can complete a thorough physical examination in two weeks' time, so that's two trips to Rhode Island and back. She'll take photographs and can work from those. It could be worse from a financial standpoint."

"Yes, but you'd think there would be someone from UVA or William and Mary."

"Bill, of course there are. Professor Kennedy comes from a school north of the Mason-Dixon line and, under the circumstances, that's to our benefit."

"Because anyone from a Virginia school is tainted by being southern? Even if they're African American?"

"M-m-m, I wouldn't put it in those words. The woman is at the top of her field. That's our insurance policy. That she hails from Brown just ups the premium, if you will."

He sighed. "I never was any good at politics. You are, and we're better off for it." He unfolded his hands. "Like I said, I'm glad retirement is near."

"Custis Hall won't be rejoicing." She reached over and touched his hand.

"Thank you."

"I had one other matter."

"What?" He was wary.

"Did you design the Zorro costume that Al Perez wore?"

"Yes. Remember when we did *The Mark of Zorro*? Well, it's quite simple. I can't take too much credit for it."

"And Al asked to borrow the costume?"

"Yes. That's not unusual."

"No, not at all. Although I hope you encourage them to make small donations."

He laughed. "I don't. See, I'm just not political and I guess I'm not much good at business either."

"Did you make sure the costume fit?"

"No. He tried it on and said it was fine. Al wasn't tall or stout. I thought he looked good in it."

"Do you know who took him back into the costume storage area?"

"Uh, let me think. Pamela. She didn't stay with him of course. He picked it up the day before the party."

"I know you're overburdened, but would you write this as a report? Write it, have Pamela read it and sign it also, and turn it in to me. I doubt it will have bearing on the case but I think it would be prudent if you were proactive."

He frowned. "I guess it would be And no one has any idea?"

"No."

"What a horrible sight that was."

"None of us will ever forget it." She noticed Teresa was buzzing her with the light on the intercom as directed.

Charlotte would give her the time frame for each

meeting and when the time was up, she'd buzz or set off the flasher.

Bill knew the drill. He stood up, then sat down because Charlotte hadn't stood up. "Sorry."

"Wait a minute." She rose, walked over to her desk, and hit the intercom. "Teresa, thank you." Then she returned to Bill. "How many Zorro costumes did the department make?"

"Two. One would be cleaned while one was being worn. The cape was a light wool, so it would hang properly. I showed the students how to sew chains, thin bracelet-sized chains, into the hem of the cape. Chains kept the cape down but the actor could still flip the cape up and out. If I hadn't put in the chains every time Zorro, it was Randi Walsh, remember?" He paused.

"Yes, she was quite athletic." Charlotte nodded.

"Well, every time she passed an air duct the cape would have fluttered up. Hence using light wool with the chains."

"How smart."

"Coco Chanel beat me to it." He smiled broadly. "Only she sewed hers, little gold chains, on the inside of the jackets, allowing them to show. I buried mine inside the lining." He waited a moment. "Which reminds me. When will Al be buried?"

"Rachel is sending his body to his family in San Antonio. They'll have the service there."

"What about here?" His eyes misted. "I miss him. I especially liked eating lunch at the faculty table because Al could be funny." He paused. "We visited

Rachel right after Al's death but, really, I don't know what to do. Should my wife and I go over more often or leave Rachel alone?"

"Rachel advised me that she would prefer something after Christmas vacation." Charlotte felt so sorry for the young widow and mother. "She's exhausted at having to go through this and plan the family funeral. Of course, she wants it to be special when we have a service. And she doesn't want it before the holidays. As for stopping by regularly, Rachel, like anyone who has suffered a shock, needs support."

"You're right." He changed the subject. "So the coroner is finished with the autopsy?"

"Yes, but I didn't ask for details, obviously."

Charlotte rose and this time Bill rose with her.

He held out his hand. "I apologize for losing my temper."

"Apology accepted. As for losing your temper, I think I would, too."

"No, you wouldn't. You're cool under pressure. I admire that. We all do," he finished as she clasped his hand. "I'm glad you told me the scuttlebutt. It would have been far worse to hear it from someone else. And I will not walk into the dressing room." He released her hand. "God only knows what else will come up. This tragedy has let the genie out of the bottle."

"Emotional upheavals bring all kinds of debris to the surface, but we'll get through it."

That afternoon the temperature began to drop. Indian

summer crept away in the fading sunlight. Sister and Shaker rode up to Hangman's Ridge as they were working Keepsake and HoJo. It was their last set of horses who hadn't hunted Saturday. They'd ridden Lafayette, Aztec, and Showboat earlier.

Neither one especially liked Hangman's Ridge, but it was high so the sunlight lingered longer there, the meadowlands below already nestled in darkening shadows.

After twenty minutes of cantering and trotting along the wide expanse they turned for home, traveling the farm road, which was the way they had ridden up.

"Boss."

"What?"

"Mind if we walk down the narrow trail? There's enough light. I didn't clean it up before hunt season like I should have. I made a halfhearted pass at it in August. If we go down that way I'll see how much there is to do."

"Get Walter to organize a work party. Or I will. We've got a lot of territory to clean up and panel at Little Dalby." She cited a new fixture, a beauty of two thousand acres that backed up on Beveridge Hundred, an old fixture.

"Who convinced the new people, the Widemans, that they needed us?" He smiled.

"Marty Howard."

"She did?"

"She designed their gardens as well as giving them some ideas about creating allées of sugar maples, an unusual choice, but I'm interested to see how it turns out. She also mentioned the living brush fences at Montpelier, and I guess that set them off. Marty let it be known that if a hunt crosses your land your property values rise, and think of the statement it would make if the fences were brush. She selected English boxwoods. Can you imagine the cost?"

"Good girl, our Marty."

"She is, isn't she? Crawford's been bugging me to come along when I feed the foxes. Says he wants to learn more about the quarry."

"Can't stand him." Shaker said this with little emotion as it was an old topic. "I know he's important to the hunt, I know he's underwriting the hunt ball, but I just think he's an ass. And I don't like the way he looks at Lorraine. He even said to me that Lorraine was hot. I wanted to smash his face. I don't like that kind of talk."

"She's a beautiful woman. All men look at Lorraine."

"Not the way he does." Shaker closed his lips tight.

"He has strayed off the reservation. I can understand how you feel, but I don't think Crawford would be stupid enough to cross you or Marty. He's learned his lesson."

The trail wasn't as bad as they thought it might be.

"Wonder if that old den is in use again."

"The one just above the wildflower meadow? I don't know. Let's see." She was always eager to keep tabs on her foxes, with whom she felt a spiritual affinity.

"The young ones left their home dens around the beginning of November. We might have a new tenant."

"We used to have a wonderful running fox that lived there six years back."

He started to say that with the deer season upon them and coyote mating season firing up, the leaves brittle on the ground, releasing a pleasing but pungent odor, the next few weeks would be difficult for hunting, but she knew that. Shaker and Sister felt every nuance of their environment.

They slowed; the old den was on their right. With some of the underbrush now leafless, the den could be clearly seen. A clever location, it afforded good privacy, had many entrances and exits, and was less than two hundred yards from a clear, fast-moving feeder stream to Broad Creek. The wildflower field to the west was nice enough from a fox's point of view, but the hayfields to the east, the hay rolled and stacked alongside the edge of the fertile field, provided field mice, rabbits, and voles lovely places to make their homes. It was a convenience store for foxes.

Shaker noticed the clump first. "What the hell?" He quickly dismounted as Sister held HoJo's reins.

"I can't really see in there. What is it?"

He picked up a piece of cloak. "Zorro."

CHAPTER 15

The front moving through kicked up gusts of twenty knots, not enough to knock one down but enough to cut through a thin jacket. The cold was settling in along with the night.

Athena and Bitsy sat in the branches of a scrubby pine. Their luminous eyes observed everything. Both birds kept their backs to the wind.

Young Georgia, Inky's half-grown vixen daughter, huddled in the back reaches of her many-chambered den. She listened to the commotion at the wide entrance. This particular den, like an old pre–Revolutionary War home, had undergone many improvements over time. Hearing Sister's voice reassured Georgia that she had a friend out there among the other humans, but she loathed the fuss at her main entrance.

Given the grade of the topography, Ben Sidel couldn't set up tripod lights. Ty held a powerful beam, as did Gray Lorillard. Shaker was also pressed into service. Ben wanted foxhunters with him on this task. The only person he brought out from the department was Ty Banks, who had a real feel for police work.

Sister, on her hands and knees with Ben, pointed out the scraps of material.

Ben, wearing plastic gloves, carefully teased out long pieces of light wool, although most of the cloak, which Shaker first pulled out, was intact.

Shaker shone his flashlight right onto the spot.

"The cub has been working at it," Sister replied.

"It looks like the fox was pulling it in."

"She was. See." She pointed to triangular holes at the edge of the cloak, the lining torn, the chain just showing. "This will make wonderful bedding."

"Then why are other parts of the cloak outside the den?" Ben, like most foxhunters, knew precious little about their quarry.

In Ben's defense, he was new to the sport, but the majority of foxhunters do not study foxes. They listen to hearsay or read an article here and there. The only way to learn about foxes is to observe them, to live by them, although reading about them doesn't hurt.

"She took what she needed. The cloak isn't torn much," Sister replied.

"M-m-m." He started to reach down into the hole.

"Ben, don't do that."

"Why?"

"Because the cub is in there. The reason Shaker and I came this way was to check the path and to see if the den had a new occupant. She or he will bite you, and believe me, it hurts."

"Sheriff, you need prophylactic rabies shots," Gray suggested.

"Too late now," Ben grunted. "Ty, give me that flashlight."

Ty handed him the heavy flashlight run on a nine-volt battery. Ben tilted it to illuminate the deeper recess of the entranceway.

"Nothing," Sister remarked.

"How do I know this fox doesn't have more in the den?"

"You don't."

"Then I've got to dig the critter out."

"Shaker and I will do that. We can trap the cub without harming the animal or ourselves. We'll move her—I think it's a vixen—to another den. Shaker, how about that one in the apple orchard?"

"Yeah, that's empty."

"Why won't she come back here?" Ben was curious.

"We do a soft release. We'll put her in a big hound crate, with food and water. We'll put the crate in front of the new den. Every day we'll check on her. The third day, we'll put fresh straw by the den, a little sweet-smelling hay, and a five-pound feed bin with a lid on it, a small hole drilled in the bottom. We'll tie that to the closest tree. Come nightfall, we'll open the gate. She might run off for a few hundred yards, but it's too good a location. She'll be back."

"Why hasn't some other fox used it?" Ben handed the flashlight back to Ty.

"Oh, it was Uncle Yancy's and he's fickle that way. He moves around. If he were human he's the kind that would redecorate every year. You know the type."

Ben laughed. "You know the foxes as well as you know your hounds."

"Some. We'll pick up a fox on a new fixture or during breeding season, courting foxes. That's exciting because we're trying to figure them out. They've got us figured out."

"How long do you need to get the fox out of here?"

"If you and Ty will go down to the house and wait for me, Shaker and I should be able to do this pretty quickly. The reason I ask you to go to the house is that she can smell you, hear you. The more people there are, the more frightening for her. She might fight harder." She stood up. "Gray, will you go down with them and bring back the caller, the little trapping cage, and the heavy gloves? They're in the kennel storage room. Oh, bring a shovel, too. We'll have to stop up the other getaways."

"Georgia isn't going to like this," Bitsy chirped.

"Sister's right, though, the orchard den is much better than this one." Athena heard mice scuttling to their homes as the wind was stronger now.

"Little apples are tasty to foxes."

Athena, full of the devil, egged Bitsy on. *"While all the humans are here, why don't you give them a song?"*

The small screech owl puffed out, warbling what she thought was a little ditty she'd heard on the barn radio. *"Since my baby left me—"*

"Jesus!" Ty jumped out of his skin.

Even Shaker and Gray froze for a moment, then laughed.

"What the hell is that?"

"Son, that's Bitsy, the screech owl." Sister had to

144

laugh at him. "She lives in the barn."

"Well, what's she doing up here?" He regained his composure.

"Bitsy's the social sort. She likes to know what's going on." Sister enjoyed the little owl with her big eyes. "Sometimes she hangs out with the great horned owl. Bitsy's song might scare you, but Ty, if Athena ever flies over your head, that really will put the fear of God in you. She's huge and you don't know she's there until she's right on top of you. If she balls up her claws they are as big as your fists. Shaker and I call her 'The Queen of the Night.'"

"Hoo ho, hoo hoo." Athena let out her deep, soothing call.

"That's her," Shaker said.

"These animals are like people to you, aren't they?" Ty, a suburban boy, found it all strange.

"No, they are what they are, but we live with them and respect them. They have powers beyond what we can imagine. This earth belongs to all of us."

"Chiggers, too," Gray called over his shoulder as he started down the steep path.

Once the three men were out of sight, Sister and Shaker turned off their flashlights.

Wind at their backs, they squatted by the den, the dark aroma of fox filling the air.

Neither one spoke for a long time.

Bitsy flew closer, landing on a branch of a young fiddle oak. *"Did you like my song?"*

"Ha ha," Athena chortled, then joined Bitsy.

Sister and Shaker could see the outline of the two birds.

"She really is nosy." Shaker had grown accustomed to Bitsy.

She'd emerge from the rafters at twilight. If he was still in the kennels, she'd perch on a branch or even the weather vane to watch him.

"She reminds me of my aunt, who lived in great fear that she'd miss something. If she were alive today I expect she'd be the first person to buy a wrist TV." Sister grinned remembering Aunt Sian.

"Some people are like that."

"Did you all like my song?" Bitsy then broke into the chorus.

"Bitsy, for God's sake, have mercy." Sister grimaced.

"Ha ha," Athena laughed louder now.

"I remembered the words," Bitsy said and prepared for another go.

"Save your voice, dear. The night is young." Athena appealed to the little owl's ego.

"You're so right. I hadn't thought of that." Bitsy ruffled her light-colored chest feathers. *"Winter's here."*

"Yes." Athena watched the two humans sitting quietly. *"They have owl-like qualities, those two. They silently watch. Neither one is quick to move until sure of the game."*

"Still think it's a pity about their eyes." Bitsy made a crackling sound with her sharp beak.

"We don't need them mucking about in the dark.

146

They'd just get in the way. There's enough trouble with the coyote coming in and hunting at night. Imagine if the humans were out there with them. Between the two of them, they'd flush our game."

When Gray arrived with the required items, it didn't take Sister and Shaker longer than twenty minutes to get the pretty young gray fox into the cage. One of the reasons, apart from their skill, was that Athena called down to Georgia, telling her she'd be better off cooperating and a much better home awaited her.

Upon seeing her, Sister remarked, "She's dark gray but not black like her mother. Bet she has her mother's intelligence."

While Shaker settled Georgia into the big traveling crate, Sister met with Ben and Ty waiting in her kitchen.

Gray offered the men a drink, which they declined, but they eagerly downed Sister's fresh coffee. It might be a long night for them.

"I hope you can lift a print." Gray sat across from Ben at the old kitchen table.

"Not much chance, but we can always hope. A better shot is a strand of human hair, anything like that, a spot of blood."

Sister commented, "Whoever it is knows where the dens are. Has to be someone who has hunted with us for years."

"Could be a deer hunter." Ben had to consider every angle.

"Yes, it could. Donnie Swiegart knows where the

dens are. Not that he'd kill Al Perez." Swiegart was a local man who was as passionate about deer hunting as she was about foxhunting, the difference being that he ate what he brought down whereas she never brought anything down.

Shaker opened the door to the mudroom. They heard him stamp his feet. He hung up his worn buffalo plaid coat, then opened the door into the kitchen.

"Coffee?"

"How about green tea?"

"Green tea?" Ben's eyebrows raised.

"Lorraine got me hooked on drinking green tea at night." He smiled. "You know, I really feel better. I feel clean from the inside out, sort of."

"Better try it, Chief," Ty said, suppressing a smile.

"What's wrong with you?" Sister directed this at Ben.

"Nothing. I have a little insomnia, that's all."

"Green tea will help." Shaker flicked the round black knob on the big gas stove.

"So will milk. Ben, you have too much on you and this county just doesn't give you and your department enough money. No wonder you can't sleep. You can only do but so much. If you don't take care of yourself we're all up a creek without a paddle." Sister was sympathetic.

"Right." Ty smiled shyly at the master, then glanced at his mentor and superior.

The fire cracked in the huge walk-in fireplace, topped by a wooden mantel, the ax lines cut in 1788

148

still visible. The kitchen was the oldest part of the house. The rest had been built when the federal style was prevalent.

Gray leaned forward. "Two Zorros."

"Yes, it seems that way," Ben replied. "Charlotte and Carter passed a Zorro on the way to their car that night, then passed Zorro again going in the opposite direction. They assumed Al had forgotten something in his office."

"It's baffling. Al was in full costume when he was found, and now this." Sister rose as the teapot boiled.

"Boss, I'll get that." Shaker got up, too.

"I want one myself."

"Go sit down. I'll do it."

She returned to her seat.

"Bill Wheatley said there had only been one, the one Al checked out when I questioned him the day after the murder. He'd gone straight to the costume storage area to make certain the costume Al wore really was from Custis Hall. It was." Ben tapped his forefinger on the table.

"Two Zorros," Sister echoed Gray. "It occurs to me that while people thought they were seeing Al, they were seeing the second Zorro."

"Possible." Ben turned toward Ty. "Check out costume rentals in Virginia tomorrow. Might get lucky."

"I wonder if Al knew there was a second Zorro?" Gray found this all disquieting.

"You'd think he wouldn't willingly go off with another Zorro, now wouldn't you?" Shaker was baffled.

"You'd think." Ben dropped his eyes. "Like I told you last week, Sister, Al did not die by a clean snap of the neck. He strangled up there. Whoever killed him didn't or couldn't do it fast. And there wasn't a mark on him. No sign of a struggle."

Sister's eyes widened. "An ugly way to die."

Gray considered the situation. "Well, honey, if Al had been cleanly killed before he was hanged, that would be one thing. Actually, it would make this easier to understand. You'd think he'd fight like hell even with hands bound not to climb that ladder. Did he willingly put his neck in the noose or was he tricked into it?"

"He couldn't be that dumb," Shaker exploded.

"Dumb? Or trusting?" Sister evenly replied.

CHAPTER 16

C areful." Professor Kennedy's voice sharpened. "Sorry." Pamela, wearing thin plastic surgical gloves as did the others, placed an iron snaffle bit on white cloth.

As she arranged it, Felicity, using a digital camera, snapped photos.

Pamela started to pick it up.

"Pamela, where is your mind today?" The good professor was becoming irritated. "Tootie has to measure it."

"I forgot. I think my blood sugar is low." Pamela did

not sound convinced by her own excuse. Then she laughed. "My father's sister says, 'Got the suga', suga' runs in the family.'"

"Does. It's more prevalent among us than whites." Professor Kennedy leaned over with her magnifying glass. Finding nothing too interesting in the bit, which had been made in a mold, then sanded for smoothness, she indicated that it should be replaced.

Tootie thought the smoothness of the metal impressive. She tapped the small measuring tape, bright yellow, against her thigh.

Professor Kennedy brought out a pair of epaulettes. "H-m-m, color much better than I would have anticipated. Military uniforms were big business throughout Europe, Russia, the whole New World. When uniforms began to simplify, thousands of people were out of work. It's the little things like that that make history real."

Pamela gingerly took the epaulettes, the hanging gold tendrils of metallic thread springing slightly. Professor Kennedy took them back from her and peered intently through her magnifying glass. She said nothing but placed them herself on the white cloth.

"Shoot?" Felicity asked.

"Yes. And then shoot upside down, *carefully*. I need both sides."

Valentina, books under her arm, walked by as the bell rang. "Hey, I got out two minutes early. Hello, Professor Kennedy. I'm here to help."

"Good. You can—" She didn't finish, as Knute

Nilsson walked up from the wide hall leading to the administrative offices.

"Professor Kennedy, I'm surprised your eyes aren't red from mold and dust," he joked.

"Visine," she briskly replied, then added, "The cases and the objects are cleaner than I expected."

"Good. Good." He smiled broadly. "Mrs. Norton can't stand one gum wrapper on the floor. She runs a tight ship. Have you found anything that surprises you?"

Canny, she lied, "No. Not yet anyway. As you know, there's a wide range of articles here and authenticating some of them will take time. The dresses made in Paris, still lovely, aren't they?" He nodded yes and she continued, "Those of course are much easier because the French dressmakers to the aristocrats kept excellent records, measurements, types of materials. Many even made drawings, colored, too, to remind them of what their patronesses had ordered. Then, as now, no two ladies wish to appear at the same ball wearing the same gown."

"Easier for us men, isn't it?"

"Today, yes. But can you imagine the layers for your full-dress military uniform? Gentlemen had batmen, dressers, because no man could do it himself."

"How could they dance in boots?"

"They didn't. They wore their dress uniform but with silk stockings, expensive breeches, and equally expensive pumps. Society required money and lots of it." She warmed to her subject.

"Still does," Pamela said sourly. "My mother spends enough on clothes to pay for Argentina's army."

"I'm sure she's quite beautiful," Professor Kennedy replied.

"She is. Pamela's mother was Thaddea Bolendar, the famous model back in the late seventies. She made the cover of *Vogue*." Knute, like most men, went weak at the knees at the sight of Pamela's mother.

Professor Kennedy, a woman and therefore far more sensitive to the mother-daughter dynamic, instantly appreciated the source of some of Pamela's unhappiness, for Pamela, a little overweight, resembled her father more than her mother. In short, she would never be a beauty, but if she worked at it, she could be attractive. Her sharp eyes took in six-foot-one-inch Valentina's unforced, athletic beauty, all that gorgeous blonde hair, those blue eyes. Then there was petite Tootie, standing right next to Pamela. Poor Pamela suffered by comparison, for Tootie in her way was every bit as stunning as Pamela's famous and spoiled mother. As for Felicity, she was simply pretty. One had to study Felicity before realizing how pretty she was.

Professor Kennedy smiled brightly at Knute. "My experience is that the children of highly successful parents, once they learn not to compare themselves to their parents, go on to become successful themselves."

"That's an interesting observation." Knute clearly didn't get it.

Pamela did and she brightened. "Really?"

"Well, yes, because success, regardless of career, can be broken into discrete bits of practice, if you will, traits, behaviors. Even though you need special skills for different tasks, jobs, there are certain things that cut across all careers. For instance, something as simple as determination. No one gets anywhere without it."

"We've got that." Valentina beamed and then in one of those moments of insight, underrated in the young even though they have them, she grasped Pamela's discomfort. "I think Pamela is more determined than any of us."

Pamela didn't trust the compliment coming from her archrival, but she was glad of it.

Tootie, per usual, kept her thoughts to herself.

Bill Wheatley breezed in. Seeing the cases open, Knute standing there, he skidded to a halt. "Knute, I had no idea you were interested in our heritage."

Knute teased Bill back, "Now, Bill, just because I don't go into a rapture over a ribbon doesn't mean I don't care."

Bill chuckled, speaking to Professor Kennedy, "To tell the truth, Professor, I'm afraid few of us have paid much attention to the treasures in our display cases here much less to their manufacture. We're all so busy with our duties we forget to stop and smell the roses, if you will."

"You've studied the clothes," Knute contradicted him.

"Yes. It's been so helpful for costumes for plays set

in the beginning of the nineteenth century. Don't know beans about the rest of it." His eyes fell on the snaffle bit. "Valentina, Tootie, girls, this is right up your alley. And if you don't know, Sister Jane will."

"The master?" Professor Kennedy appreciated the social grace and skill with which Sister had made her feel welcome at the Opening Hunt breakfast.

"She has ancient pieces of tack, bits, boot pulls, you wouldn't believe the junk she has in the barn or up at the house. She's got one old curb chain from the time of Charles I! When an argument broke out about the introduction of the curb chain, damned if she didn't bring it out."

"A curb chain?" Professor Kennedy knew little about horses or their accoutrements.

"A chain under the horse's chin," Pamela replied. "Sometimes they have a larger link smack in the middle."

"You use them with a Pelham bit," Tootie added, pointing to the snaffle. "Wouldn't use it with this."

"Ah, well, as you can gather, the development of equipage is not my forte. I suppose I should learn the basics." She paused. "Until Henry Ford made cars affordable, we needed horses."

"Still do." Valentina loved her gelding, Moneybags.

"Luncheon with Sonny," Knute said as he checked his watch. "Professor, if you ever need help on sailing history, call me. In fact, I just bought a three-masted schooner, in need of T.L.C., but a beauty all the same. She'll be seaworthy by spring."

As Knute left, Bill filled in Professor Kennedy. "He really does know a lot about sailing. It's his grand passion."

"You certainly have a diverse administration."

"One of the strengths of Custis Hall." Bill checked his own watch, returning his gaze to the tiny lady. "Charlotte mentioned that your expertise is construction. We don't have much of that, I mean a few pegs and nails here and there."

"That's where I started because that's what I could see, more material, if you will. But I have tried to expand my knowledge into the living arts, kitchenware, even clothing, although I would never pass myself off as an expert in attire. I can grasp the fundamentals and it's my good fortune to have many colleagues I can turn to for advice."

"Interesting work?"

"I love it."

"As you can see, we have a hodgepodge."

"Yes, but there are items here of great cultural value."

"And no one cares. No one cares who made that bit or how they lived." Pamela's face flushed as she said this.

"People are beginning to care, Pamela. The past is always with us even when we aren't aware of it. Not knowing one's past is like being blind in one eye. You think you can see but you're hampered, deceived even," Professor Kennedy replied.

At the word "deceived" Bill perked up. "Yes, yes, of

course, I never thought of that." He checked his watch again. "Well, I have so enjoyed chatting with you, Professor, and I'm always glad to see my four favorite students. Her Most High has summoned me and I must repair." He bowed with a flourish, then disappeared down the administration hall.

Pamela's steely gaze followed him. She blurted out, "When I first came here I thought he was gay. He's not."

"He's a fop." Tootie giggled.

"Oh, let's just say he's theatrical," Valentina said as she wondered how she'd look in the low-cut ballgown that had pride of place in the adjoining case.

"Ladies, there have been times in history when men enjoyed a greater latitude of expression in dress and behavior than they do now. Nothing at all to do with gender issues. Think of the drawings and paintings of courtiers during the time of Elizabeth I. Think of the drawings of African kings from the nineteenth century." She paused. "But you see in those days the highest goal was glory, personal glory, hopefully in the service of one's king, queen, country. The goals have changed, and one doesn't hear the word 'glory' anymore. We have become dull, efficient, dry—men more so than women."

A moment passed while the four young ladies absorbed this, then Tootie piped up, "Not in the hunt field."

Bill Wheatley walked into Charlotte's office, Teresa

opening the door. The sight of Ben Sidel, in uniform, surprised him.

"Bill, sit down." Charlotte pointed to a leather chair. "I'll get right to the point. The sheriff has found a second Zorro costume. He's brought it for you to examine and perhaps identify." She paused. "Tell us why you told Ben you'd only made one Zorro costume. You told me two."

Bill stuttered, "An oversight. Of course, I had two made." He turned to Ben. "But you questioned me the very next day, the next day after that hideous sight. I don't remember one thing I said. Please forgive me."

Ben, not a trace of his inner thoughts showing, said, "Were there two costumes when Al Perez went in to try one on? Did you personally see both costumes?"

"I think so."

"When is the last time you saw both costumes?"

"The day Al tried on his costume. Before he came in, I'd gone back into the storage room for a bolt of gingham. I distinctly recall passing that rack, the outer rack. I'm sure I saw them."

It escaped neither Charlotte nor Ben that Bill was sweating.

"Will you look at what we've found?"

"Of course."

Ben stood up, picked a cardboard box off the long side table, and placed it before Bill. Charlotte handed over a pair of thin plastic gloves.

"Put those on, Bill," she directed him.

As he slipped on the surgical gloves he said, "Just

like what Professor Kennedy and the girls are using. Tight, aren't they?"

Ben indicated that he should pick articles out of the box. He held them as though they were soiled baby diapers.

"Do you recognize this?" Ben asked.

"Oh, yes, yes, my, yes. This is the costume." He pointed to the chain, touching it with his right forefinger. "Charlotte, there's the chain in the lining."

"Yes, so it is."

"Sheriff, where did you find this?"

Ben hesitated a moment. "Near the hanging tree."

"I thought you and your men combed that area."

"We did but the animals combed it more thoroughly than we did." Ben left it at that.

"I guess you're lucky the costume is in as good a shape as it is." Bill peeled off the gloves, folding them in half. "I know Al's car was in the parking lot here the next day. We all noticed it. I guess you all went over it with a fine-tooth comb."

"We did."

Bill didn't ask if the sheriff had found anything important to the case. He added, "Al willingly got in someone else's car, don't you think?"

"Yes, I do," Ben answered.

"Someone he knew." Bill sounded sad, fatigued.

"It does seem like that. There were no signs of struggle on Al's body. No bump on the head." Ben inclined his head to the side. "Is there anything you'd like to tell me? Anything else that has occurred to you?"

"No. I just thought about his car." Bill paused. "Sheriff, why would there be two Zorro costumes? Who else is involved?"

Ben said, "I don't know, but I will find out."

After both men had left, Charlotte sat at her desk, staring blankly at the silver tea service on the sideboard. A gift from the class of 1952, she loved the curving lines of the teapot, the burnish of the silver.

Teresa opened the door, peeking in. She started to close it.

Charlotte called her in, "Come on, T."

Teresa closed the door behind her. "Charlotte, you're worried."

Charlotte looked up at her. "I am. I am more worried now than I think I ever have been in my entire life. More worried than when I saw Al hanging from the tree. That was a shock. This is worry."

Teresa, warmhearted, nodded, "Well, I figure if the sheriff calls it can't be good."

Charlotte got up and walked around her desk; she took Teresa by the hand, walking her to the sofa. They sat down side by side.

"Teresa, I think Bill Wheatley is lying to me."

Teresa's face did not register surprise. "I know exactly what you mean."

"What tipped you off?"

"He's always been a little too cheery for me. Cheery is the only word I can think of, but lately, he's cheery underlined three times except when Al Perez's name comes up, and then he's grief underlined. It's all too . . ."

160

"Theatrical."

"That is his department," Teresa said drily. "Do you think this has anything to do with the dressing room discussion?"

Charlotte trusted Teresa completely. This trust was returned in full. She had asked her right-hand woman if she, too, had heard any rumors about Bill swooping into the dressing rooms. Teresa had heard the odd comment over the years but not enough to set off her radar.

"I wish I knew. I just know . . . he's different. Then again, we have a murder on our hands, and I could be reading into everyone's behavior. I find myself fighting down suspicions."

"That's natural."

"And disquieting." She sighed, leaning her head back on the sofa. She didn't have an Adam's apple but she had a tiny bulge there, Eve's orange. "I have this terrible premonition."

"What?"

She turned her head toward Teresa. "Not an event. I'm not seeing into the future. It's, well, it's that I think this is the beginning. Like you, I'm getting the creeps. And Teresa, I have no idea, not one, why or what."

A long, long silence followed. "Like I said last week, the old cliché, this is the tip of the iceberg."

CHAPTER 17

The cold front blew the last of the leaves off the trees except for those on a steep southward slope. A few pin oaks glowed rich red. Other oaks with orange or deep russet leaves rustled with the light winds. Eventually the color would fade to a dull brown; the leaves might stay put until spring, when the new buds pushed them off.

Nature fascinated Sister, whether plant or animal. Little Dalby's two thousand acres contained gorgeous ancient oaks, towering pines, and old hollies down in the bog that reached up a story and a half. The soil varied greatly from the eastern part of the old land-grant estate to the western, becoming more rocky, with boulders jutting up from pastures as one moved west.

Sister held a topo map for one quadrant of the farm. She turned, her back to the breeze, which was intensifying.

Betty held the left side of the map. "I thought the front moved through the other night."

"Did. This is just plain old wind." Sister pointed to a small cross on the map. "St. John's of the Cross. Remember the wonderful Christmas Eve services the Viaults used to have here? You were newly married when I met you and Bobby Christmas Eve."

"Bet the old vines and Virginia creeper are holding

it up. Holding us up, too." Betty thought back to old times.

Sister smiled. "That's true. If it weren't for honeysuckle some of my old fencing on the back acres would be down."

"We've marked half this farm." Betty reached into her pocket for a roll of hot pink surveyor's tape. "I bet we can knock it all out and the boys can get over here tomorrow. I heard Crawford bought two new Honda ATVs, so he can ride one and Marty can ride the other. He's going to use his to feed foxes on his farm when you show him how and give him a schedule. He'll need the ATV."

Sister inhaled deeply. "Deer."

"Make your eyes water. Where is he?"

"Moving along the edge of the woods. The wind carried the scent straight to us. Tell you what, sure makes me appreciate the hound work on a windy day."

"That's the truth. I can remember days when we'd see the fox when the wind blew the scent thirty yards off. Shaker knows how to swing them into it, though, in case they're struggling."

"He's a good huntsman. He's a good man."

"M-m-m," Betty murmured in agreement. "Well, want to see what's left of St. John's of the Cross?"

Sister hopped onto her ATV, a 2001 Kawasaki. Used daily but well maintained, she didn't think she could run the farm without it. She envied Crawford blowing into Wayne's Cycle and writing a check for two brand-new Hondas. Knowing him, he bought the 750cc monsters.

They rode up to the edge of the old pasture, broomsages coming up, waving thin golden wands in the wind.

Sister slowed at the edge of the woods. Calling over her shoulder, she shouted above the motor, "Fence not bad. Let's see if we can find an old farm road. We can mark a jump near the gate if there still is one."

The two cruised along the woods until coming to the farm road. The gate, handmade from wood, was rotting out, hanging crooked on big rusted hinges.

Sister cut the motor and they both climbed off.

Betty reached the three-board fence and deftly looped the surveyor's tape around the top board, leaving a tail to flutter. The jump site was twenty yards from the gate.

"St. John's will be maybe a half mile down the farm road. Looks different, doesn't it? Course, things change in eight years."

"Things can change in eight minutes." Sister laughed as she wiggled the old gate open. "Don't see many hand-built gates anymore. Too bad."

Betty fished in her pocket, holding up the sharp clippers. "Ready."

They climbed on the Kawasaki and followed the farm road as it crossed another deeply rutted road, the ruts made by wagon wheels, not tires.

Sister called over her shoulder, "Once upon a time

this was the old road to the gap. Guess it fell out of use around the turn of the last century."

"Later. When the state built the new road—the 1930s." Betty liked history. "Part of all the work F.D.R. cooked up."

"Old man Viault kept things clean right up until the day he died. He and Peter were in the army together." Her eyes twinkled. "Seems so long ago yet like yesterday. Those were men, weren't they? Hate to see this place so run-down."

"Marty says the Widemans are dedicated to restoring Little Dalby to its former glory." Betty noticed a woodcock fly up out of the brush. "How about that. I hope they make a comeback."

"Not much chance, Betty, not as long as all the raptors are federally protected. They're killing the ground nesters at a frightening rate."

"The runoff from pesticides is killing the ground nesters, too. I hate it." Betty hugged Sister's waist when they hit a bump.

A shift of hazy light, gold-filled with specks of dust, shone through the trees right onto the cross of St. John's.

Betty's hand flew to her heart. Then she hugged Sister and they both smiled as the tall woman cut the motor.

The roof, slate, held; the stone, covered in Virginia creeper leaves a bright fall red as Betty predicted, was in great shape. Some of the leaded-glass windows were broken, but not too many.

A big twisted wrought-iron handle on the blue wooden door worked fine. Sister pressed the thumb piece, the lock clicked. She swung the door open.

Covered in dust, the altar and the pews stood. All had been hand-carved.

Even the wooden cross, for the worshippers couldn't afford gold or even brass, stood on the ornate wooden altar.

A soft flutter of wings snapped their heads upward and a great horned owl, male, swept overhead, out the front door.

"Athena's boyfriend." Sister laughed—he came down so quickly, so silently, he startled them both.

"Nest in the steeple?"

"I don't know, but he knows how to get in and out. Well, it keeps the mice population in check."

"Think he's Athena's boyfriend?"

"I expect she has a fella closer to home. I also expect she gives the orders."

"Ever tell you about the time I saw a snowy owl? Big as Athena."

"You did? Lucky you. They come down from the north. Pickin's are good here." She coughed. "Dust."

"When do you think's the last time anyone was in here?"

"Eight years, at the least. Old man Viault didn't get around much at the end." She coughed again.

Betty thought a moment. "This was the slave church, wasn't it?"

"Was."

"You'd think the master wouldn't want a church in the woods."

"I don't think it was back then. Might have been on the edge, but if you look around at the trees out there, they aren't but one hundred years old, maybe one hundred and twenty. That one cigar tree is pretty old, a good one hundred years."

Cigar trees like moist spots.

"Maybe we should tell Professor Kennedy. I enjoyed meeting her the other night when you had her and Charlotte, Carter, Bobby, and me over for dinner. I like small gatherings best. She's a fascinating woman and from Portland, Maine, of all places."

"A real Yankee. Course I can get along with a true New Englander much easier than someone from the middle states most times. None of us can help where we were born." She smiled slyly.

"Hell, none of us can help being born." Betty laughed.

"That's a fact. What I can't figure is why some people are so unhappy with life." She pointed to the altar, a blade of light falling on the cross, the streaky windows behind washed many times over by rainstorms. "Make a joyful noise unto the Lord."

They walked outside, Sister closing the door behind her.

"We've let so much go. So much that has to do with slavery," Betty mused.

"Yes, but remember that we let a lot of everything go. There wasn't a penny after the war. Virginia didn't begin to feel good times until the 1920s, and that was nipped in the bud by the Depression. And think about it, who ran the show? White men." She held up her hand. "I'm not saying one thing against our forefathers, but it seems to me that people will preserve first what relates directly to them. So once a little money flowed south of the Potomac, the buildings that were shored up had to do with their history. It's only been in the last two decades that a recognition of preservation for black folks has taken root."

"And there's not a damned thing to preserve for women."

"Women's work perished in the using," Sister said with a shrug. "So it was. And in many ways so it is. I can't be bothered getting angry or feeling shoved aside. I remember the protests in the seventies. I wasn't against them but it was alien to me. I figure you make hell with what you have. I may be on the shorter end of the stick than the white man, but I've still got some say-so, some ability to relish this life."

"You're a different generation, Sister. Even myself, and what am I, twenty-five years younger than you? Of course, when I'm around you I usually feel twenty-five years older since I can't keep up." Betty laughed.

"Flatterer."

"No, it's true, you have some kind of primal energy."

"Because I'm living my true life and I'm my true self."

"It's also in the blood."

"Yeah, my mother and father both had energy. But anyway, here we are in the middle of the woods, the branches are waving, clouds are scattered, the fragrance of the earth and the leaves rises up to meet you. It's perfect and I'll bet you that some of the folks who worshipped here despite the hardship, the injustice of their lives, found moments of sheer beauty. They had to because you can't live without it."

"We can ask Professor Kennedy."

"A deep knowledge." Sister put her arm around Betty's shoulders.

They walked around the back of the church checking the foundation, fitted stone.

"Couple of gaps here big enough for a fox." Sister inhaled, a faint whiff of Reynard tingling in her nostrils.

"Here's a sizable one." Betty had stopped right at the back. "Almost big enough to crawl in."

"You and I could. Some of our members would get stuck."

Betty hunkered down. "Wouldn't take the Widemans much to repair the foundation. Really. It's in darned good shape."

"That, a few windows, and a thorough cleaning, St. John's of the Cross will be as good as new."

They walked back, getting on the ATV.

Once home that afternoon, Sister did call the Widemans. The lady of the house, Anselma, seemed very grateful for the news and said she was so looking forward to the hunt on Tuesday, November 29.

Sister hung up. Thanksgiving Hunt loomed before her. The two weeks since Opening Hunt flashed by in part because time always seemed to move faster after Opening Hunt, and partly because of the activity around Custis Hall, unpleasant as it was. She'd been working overtime, but hadn't thought much about the second High Holy Day. Here it was about to splat on her head. Well, chances were it wouldn't be blank.

She dialed Charlotte, informed her of the slave church, and thought she might want to tell Professor Kennedy. If the little lady wanted to see it she'd buzz her over, but she'd let Charlotte decide.

Then she reaffirmed that Valentina, Tootie, and Felicity could spend Thanksgiving with her, off campus for the holiday weekend. All three elected to stay back over Thanksgiving vacation. They wanted to foxhunt. Charlotte thought it a wonderful idea that they stay with the master.

Word got around, so other club members took in girls who wanted to stay and hunt.

Pamela Rene had promised her parents she'd be home for Thanksgiving. She already regretted it.

After finishing up her calls—she averaged twenty to thirty a day, most of them having to do with hunt activities—Sister threw on her sweater, her ancient Filson tin coat, the tan faded to wheat in spots.

Raleigh and Rooster followed along. Golly, hating wind, stayed inside, and the minute the dogs were out the door she ate some crunchies from their bowl. She liked her food better but getting away with something appealed to her.

Shaker sat in the kennel office, head bent over the small red books published by the Master of Fox-hounds Association of America. These were the stud books, a treasure for any breeder.

"Shaker, I thought you used the computer for that."

"Down."

"Again?" He nodded and she asked, "How old is that computer?"

He tapped the dark screen. "Five."

"Is it really? I quite forgot. Guess I need to buy one for Christmas, don't I?"

"I like the one you bought yourself." He grinned impishly.

"Well, then I know just what to get. You know, five years, can't complain. These things change so fast. I guess this Gateway is now a dinosaur."

"Computers turn over too fast. Think of the old truck Peter Wheeler willed to us. Runs like a top. Stuff should be like that."

"The 454 engine will go on when we're all dead. It's the brakes, the clutch, the alternator, the radiator that fritz out. Patch, patch, patch." She folded her arms across her chest. "Bought you the topos. Marked. Lots of jumps to build but not too much in the way of clearing. Between you and Walter's work crew, two days. Maybe one if enough people come out."

"November 29 is around the corner."

"So is Thanksgiving. We'll be over at Foxglove. Should be a little scent anyway."

"Never know. November is tough."

"Hey, how's the little girl doing?"

He knew she meant the fox they'd relocated. "She's fine. I'm pretty sure she's Inky's. I saw them together last night at twilight, up by the round hay bales. Sitting on top of them surveying their domain."

"Good."

"Anything more?"

" 'Bout what?"

"The Zorro stuff." He realized, close as they were, she couldn't read his mind.

"Nothing new."

"Stalled out?"

"I don't know. Legwork. Ben has to find and put together tiny pieces of tile until he gets the crime mosaic, if you will. He said that most times who the killer is is obvious but in something like this, not at all."

"His riding is getting better."

"So it is."

Shaker pondered a moment. "You know, Boss, I think Lorraine is just about perfect. If only she fox-hunted. That's my one complaint. Not that I say much. But I look at Ben. If he can do it, she can, too. Course, you have to want to do it."

Sister knew Lorraine was taking lessons from Sam Lorillard in secret. She wanted to surprise Shaker for Christmas Hunt. "Well, maybe one day she'll take a notion," she nonchalantly replied as she sat on the edge of the desk, picked up a stud book from 1971, flipping it to Green Spring Valley. She read absent-mindedly, then glanced at Shaker. "Funny thing."

"What? Their entry?"

"No, chemistry. You and Lorraine have good chemistry." She closed the small red book. "I keep coming back to this thing with Al Perez. Everyone liked him. Good chemistry. He was an agreeable man. Not charismatic but nice, and he extended himself to others. People miss him. They grieve over his death. And they miss his skills at Custis Hall. He was good at extracting money from the alumnae. So I ask myself, again, why? Circumstances?"

"Amy Childers could have hung him in a fit of jealousy." He said this without conviction.

"No. If she were going to do him bodily harm she would have done it when their relationship ended. I suppose Ben had to ask her uncomfortable questions but Amy didn't kill him."

"Circumstances or he crossed someone. You're on the scent, girl." He smiled; his teeth were straight. He knew her well.

CHAPTER 18

Tuesday, November 22, was the last day of classes until Monday, November 28. The brevity of Thanksgiving vacation ensured that many Custis Hall students stayed put.

A few left the previous Friday, having turned in their

papers, taken tests early. Pamela Rene was one of those. Her father sent the company jet for her, which impressed some students, infuriated others. Pamela took it as a birthright but she really didn't want to go home.

Professor Kennedy came to say good-bye to Charlotte before her own departure.

The two women sipped sherry. A misting rain coated the windows, small panes, original to the building.

"We've grown accustomed to you, Frances." Charlotte used Professor Kennedy's first name once the older woman had given her permission to do so.

"I've met some interesting people and I can't thank you enough for setting up the meeting with Sister Jane and the Widemans."

"I look forward to seeing St. John's of the Cross myself, but I expect it will be from the back of my horse, first time, anyway."

Professor Kennedy placed her sherry glass on the silver tray. She smoothed down her skirt. "Charlotte, I will have this report to you by the first of the year. It's painstaking. I want to do the best job for you that I can because this will be the template that future generations refer to and utilize."

"I know we'll be excited to read it."

She touched her tight bun for a second. "Refresh my memory, who has keys to the cases?"

"I do. Knute, as treasurer, has a backup key. Teresa knows where I keep my key. Jake Walford, in charge of buildings and grounds, has his own key."

"No one else?"

"No, why?"

She paused; a pained expression crossed her well-formed features. "I hesitate to discuss this. Part of me thinks I should wait until my report, wait for the fallout, but . . ."

"Yes?" Charlotte's heart beat faster.

"The man who is dead. Did he have a key?"

"No."

Professor Kennedy's faced seemed inscrutable. "Those cases would be easy to pry open. You'd know, though."

"Professor Kennedy, what's the problem?"

Speaking quickly and low, Professor Kennedy plunged right in. "There are irregularities among your artifacts."

"In what way?"

"I believe some of the items are not authentic."

Charlotte took this in. "I see. Do you think they were not from the Custis family when they were donated to the school?"

"No. I believe some of these items have been tampered with much more recently. But before I risk my reputation on this, I want to carefully go over the photographs and my descriptions with my colleagues."

"Yes, of course. I can appreciate your position."

"And I can appreciate yours," Professor Kennedy said sympathetically.

"Have you told anyone else?"

"No."

"Do you think anyone suspects? Do you have suspicions?" Charlotte leaned forward. She noticed Frances checking her watch. "I can take you to the airport."

"I have to drop off the rental car. I'm packed and ready to go." She sat up straight. "I'll have my report to you after the New Year." She paused. "I don't know the people here well enough to have suspicions. I hope I'm wrong, Charlotte, I truly do, but," she inhaled deeply, "I know I'm not. My report is going to hit Custis Hall like a bombshell."

CHAPTER 19

W *hy do I have to do it?"* Grace moaned.
"Because you live at Foxglove," Aunt Netty answered.

The two reds, one young, the other getting on in years but famous for her blazing speed, trotted by the steady, hypnotic flow of water from the upper pond to the lower pond at Foxglove Farm.

Athena called in the distance, *"Hoo hoo hoodoo hoodoo."*

A light frost coated the meadows silver.

The sun, an hour from rising, seemed on the other side of the world, for this time is the coldest time.

The two vixens reached Cindy Chandler's pretty stable. Cindy put out hard candies for them, which they demolished in short order. Then Aunt Netty, on her hind legs, stood as tall as she could to push up the latch into the sweet-feed bin in the feed room.

The effort it took both girls to flip up the lid was considerable. Once they caught their breath they hoisted themselves up, dropping into the sweet feed, the tiny bits of grain between their toes, the aroma intoxicating.

"I'd rather eat and sleep today."

"All right then, why don't we compromise?" Aunt Netty flicked a moist oat off her whiskers. *"You go by the ponds. Oh, make a big figure eight so they'll think they're running a gray. The humans, I mean. The hounds will know it's you. Then just pop into your den. That's easy enough. I'll take it from there and run to the old schoolhouse. I think my errant husband is under there. He left his old den. Lazy ass."* She sniffed. *"He used to keep a clean den but this last year, he hasn't. He was forever fickle about his living quarters, but really, he's gotten slovenly. All he wants to do is sit on the old window seat at Shaker's and watch the TV through the window. He's getting mental."*

Grace prudently did not mention what Uncle Yancy said about Netty, namely that she had turned into a harridan. *"He takes a notion,"* she said noncommittally, stuffing more sweet feed into her powerful, slender jaws.

So busy were the two vixens that they didn't hear Cindy Chandler come into the stable to braid her horse. Startled, when they heard the thump of the tack room door they leapt up, but the motion brought down the lid.

"Shit!" Aunt Netty allowed herself a profanity. *"What do we do?"*

"Nothing until she comes for a scoop of sweet feed. We'll scare the wits out of her when we jump out."

Cindy, however, wasn't going to laden her good mare, Caneel, with sweet feed. She put all the hay the mare wanted in her stall, tying the net up so she'd reach with her neck, not her usual practice. But as Caneel merrily tore at her feed net, Cindy knocked off the dust. She had washed the mare the previous night with Show Sheen, so her coat glistened.

Then she brought out a bucket of warm water, a small footstool, took off her gloves, wet a piece of mane, and began braiding.

Most people in the middle years hire kids to braid, but Cindy, having spent time on the show circuit at the highest levels plus training steeplechasers, put in a perfect, tight braid. Kindly and warm, she proved a perfectionist about braiding and turnout. She used a black braid for the mare's black mane. Every now and then she'd honor a holiday, braid with orange and black for Halloween, red and green for Christmas. Her delightful sense of humor was infectious.

The two foxes waited and waited.

"She's starving that mare," Grace whined.

"I don't know what she's doing." Aunt Netty felt drowsy. Too much sweet feed and sour ball hard candies.

There they sat.

At ten the eighty-nine riders resplendent for the

second of the High Holy Days gathered in front of the charming frame house at Foxglove Farm, hugged by English boxwoods. Cindy Chandler had a gift for landscaping and gardening. Wherever one looked there was something to involve the eye.

A prayer of Thanksgiving was given by the Reverend Daniel Wheeler. The hounds gave the good man with his musical voice their attention.

Then off they rode.

Sister and Shaker always discussed the day's cast the night before. They decided that since they'd had such good luck by the ponds last year they'd start there. The farm afforded many opportunities for a brisk ride since Cindy had paneled every fence, indulging in a few special jumps like a new tiger trap behind the stable that led into the pasture holding Clytemnestra, the giant Holstein cow, and her son, growing as large as his mother. The tiger trap at three feet six inches looked like teeth since each log stood up, forming a steeple. Quite impressive except that Cly would step over it and rub her belly. And if she felt bored she'd smash right through it. She evidenced a slight antisocial streak. Orestes, her son, mostly followed momma. He didn't have too many ideas of his own.

The Custis Hall girls as well as Charlotte, Bill, and Bunny rode in the middle of first flight.

When the whole pack of hounds charged into the stable the field watched with uncomprehending fascination.

Shaker called, "Come to me."

"The fox is here!" Cora shouted, knowing Shaker couldn't understand but he knew she was honest as the day is long.

Darby shot straight into the feed room. *"It's Grace and Aunt Netty."*

The whole pack in a frenzy squeezed into the feed room.

Shaker dismounted, handing his reins to Sister, who had ridden up.

"Betty, dismount and get in here with me," Shaker called through the stake.

Betty, on the other side of the stable by Clytemnestra's pasture, flung her right leg over the pommel of her saddle, kicked her left leg out of the stirrup, and hit the ground with both feet. Outlaw didn't need to be held. He stood there, ears forward since he could smell the foxes.

"Oh, this is going to be ripe," Outlaw said to himself.

The word spread from horse to horse, which made the hotter ones prance about. Humans not tight in the tack began to fret.

Cindy wondered what could be going on. She'd been in the stable before dawn and she didn't see any fox. Granted she picked up a whiff of eau de vulpus, but that was normal given the hard candy treats.

Shaker paused in the doorway to the feed room. The hounds stood on their hind legs. Tinsel, nimble, jumped onto the feed bin lid, slanted, and balanced there, giving tongue.

The din was deafening.

"Betty, call out to Sister. Tell her to try to hold hounds if they go out her end of the stable. I hope Sybil's where she's supposed to be. If the hounds get through Sister and the field she can keep up."

Betty ran to the opened large doors, called out to Sister, then hurried back to the other end of the stable. No point in telling Shaker when she mounted up. He'd never hear her with that racket.

"Leave it. Leave it," he ordered his hounds calmly, voice low.

"We'd better do what he says. Trust him." Diana did trust him but it took great willpower to vacate the feed room.

The last hound out, Dragon, grumbled.

"You leave it!" Shaker narrowed his eyes and Dragon knew he meant business. Shaker walked into the feed room.

He stood back, lifting one end of the bin top with the staghandle of his crop. Sure was useful, that staghandle.

"Go right. I'll go left!" Netty blasted out of there as if she'd been on a launch pad at Cape Canaveral.

"Split the pack!" Grace let Aunt Netty know she understood the wise old vixen's intent.

The two vixens shot out of the feed bin with such force that Shaker staggered back, gasping.

"Hold! Hold!" He had the presence of mind to keep his voice steady.

The hounds were levitating with the thrill of two

foxes brushing right through them.

Shaker, raised a good Irish Catholic, knew that November 24 is the feast day of St. Colman of Cloyne, who spread the good word in Limerick and Cork during the sixth century A.D. However, he didn't think the dear fellow could help him in his current predicament.

He called upon the saint of impossible causes, "St. Rita, keep my pack together," as he walked deliberately to Showboat, agog with excitement.

St. Rita must have been otherwise occupied at that moment because Dragon did not hold. He careened after Aunt Netty, who was running through the horses' legs. Crawford lurched forward as Czpaka snorted and whirled, but he hung on.

Walter, surprised by Rocketman getting light in front, slipped off as did a few others.

One could hear, even with the din, "Ommph," "Aargh," "Dammit."

As Netty caused maximum pandemonium, Shaker struggled to mount Showboat, who was backing up, taking Sister, holding tight on to the reins, with him.

"Hold still!" Keepsake snorted at the high-strung Showboat.

"Hounds are away!" Showboat knew his job was to be right up there with them. He was neglecting the fact that Shaker was supposed to be on his back.

"Do you want a Come-to-Jesus meeting?" Keepsake uttered the dreaded phrase that meant major discipline.

That reached the Thoroughbred. Finally Shaker swung his leg over.

While he was doing that, Grace dashed in front of Betty without so much as a "How do you do."

She slunk under Cly's fence, headed straight for the giant, making certain to step in every cow patty she could find. Cly's patties resembled small islands. Grace slipped through them and boy, could they foil scent.

"Tally ho!" Betty marked the fox just as half the pack blew right by her. She counted heads as quickly as she could but it was more than apparent that half the gang was going in the other direction. Her ears told her that.

Pretty soon the ninnies in the field were bellowing "Tally ho."

There was no need for this chorus, obviously, since everyone and God could see the redoubtable Aunt Netty. A field should always be silent.

The three masters of Deep Run, along with two ex-masters, Mary Robertson and Coleman Perrin, had come to enjoy the day. They were getting more than they bargained for, and Sister quietly cursed to herself that if your pack was going to piss off they'd wait until another master was present. It's the same principle as your well-behaved six-year-old blurting out some embarrassing personal information when company came calling. So much for saving face!

Shaker knew there was little point in blowing the pack back to him. He noted that Cora, Diana, Ardent,

183

Darby, and Diddy waited for him to tell them to go. He never loved hounds as much as he loved those five hounds at that moment.

"Hark to 'em." He smiled.

"Yippee!" Off they flew toward Aunt Netty's trail.

He then blew three short notes, blew them again, and doubled them, hoping the rest of the pack would swing to him even though they were on their own fresh fox.

Betty could read Shaker's mind. She jumped over the tiger trap the second the hounds streaked by her and she was straining to get ahead of them to turn them. No easy task in the best of circumstances. But now Cly took offense at what she saw as a triple disturbing of her repose. First came Grace, then the hounds, and now this two-legged twit borrowing the speed of a four-legged one.

She roared, *"Outta my pasture!"*

Orestes mooed, *"Ditto. You'd better do what mom says."*

With that, both bovines charged Betty and Outlaw.

Outlaw, tough as he was, wasn't going to play bumper cars with those humongous creatures. He shifted to the side. Betty, tight as a tick up there, rode it out with ease. Her goal was to get ahead of the split group. Outlaw's goal was to avoid this enraged and terribly stupid cow. As for Orestes, he wasn't even stupid. He was a blistering idiot.

Betty steered for the coop, rider up, on the other end of the pasture. Four feet sure enough but there wasn't a second to lift that rider off.

"Outlaw, let's boogie, baby boy."

"Piece of cake." He picked up speed since he was a compact 15.3 hands. He wasn't going to soar over with a few cantering strides like Showboat. But he took off a wee bit early, clearing it with ease.

Betty started laughing on the other side. My God, this was living.

Gaining on the hounds, she knew far better than to start blathering and cracking her whip. That would only send them on. She had to get in front of those suckers to turn them.

More pastures beckoned. She was now lapping the tail hounds.

"Son, I am deeply offended," and with that Cly lowered her head and crashed through the coop with the rider, pieces of black-painted board heaving into the air.

Orestes cantered after her, leaving perfect cloven imprints in the perfect footing.

"That bitch is coming after us!" Outlaw whinnied.

Hearing the cowbell, Betty turned. "Great day!" she whistled, using the old southern expression for disbelief. "Baby boy, we've still got to turn these hounds."

She urged him on and they finally reached Trident, up front. She cracked her whip and it reverberated like a rifle shot.

"Leave it!"

Trident hesitated. Betty cracked the whip again. "Leave it!"

The group reluctantly did as they were told because the next reprimand would be ratshot in the ass. They saw the .22 come out of the holster and those little birdy bits could sting.

They stopped. They could all hear the other part of the pack since sound carried beautifully on this overcast day.

"Hark to 'em! Hark to 'em." Betty's voice shook with excitement, for she could also hear Cly coming, ground shaking.

Bellowing *"Death to the human!"* Cly lumbered toward them like a large black-and-white freight train.

Behind her, parroting mom, was the son.

"Let's get out of Dodge!" Doughboy sprinted toward the sound of hounds moving fast in the opposite direction.

Betty, on the outside of them, shrewdly put the hounds between her and that damned cow.

Cly tossed her head to and fro and just thought she was the most fearsome beast in the land, a modern Minotaur. She may have been fat and ridiculous but she could hurt you.

Hounds, Outlaw, and Betty slipped by the two Holsteins. This didn't please them, so Cly decided to keep after them. She wasn't fast but she was determined, and she could still run faster than a human.

This became apparent when the company of creatures passed the other side of the stable, where a few humans were still on foot, trying to catch their horses or their breath.

Cly headed straight for them.

"Jesus Christ!" Bill Wheatley shouted as Cly zeroed in on him.

"Jesus can't help you now! Climb, man, climb!" Sam Lorillard shouted, as he'd stayed back to help.

Bill ran for all he was worth and in that instant vowed he would go to the gym and dump the excess weight. The old walnut by the stables had low branches, drooping with advanced age. Bill grabbed one and swung himself forward, trying to get his legs up over the branch. He managed but his lardass hung there, most tempting. Cly hooked his butt, tearing off a wide swatch of expensive corded material, but fortunately she didn't break the skin.

Sam, quick-witted and quick, had taken off his jacket, waving it in front of Cly. She charged; he sidestepped her while barely escaping a bone-crushing butt by Orestes, faster than mom.

By now, everyone on the ground found refuge in a tree or had made it into the barn, slamming a stall gate behind them.

"Let's blow this joint!" Cly snorted as she headed in the direction of the hounds.

Betty pushed up the hounds to the rest of the pack, and when those hounds passed Shaker he looked straight up to the sky and smiled.

Aunt Netty ran so fast one expected to see white jet trails behind her. Famous for her speed and cunning, she had no time to play with hounds today. She'd eaten too much and they were too close behind despite the efforts of Shaker to hold them.

No huntsman wants to chop a fox. If one is bolted close by, the rule is count to twenty. Well, he didn't get to count to two.

So Netty ran for her life on this Thanksgiving Day. She didn't bother to foil scent, swim small creeks, she ran flat out, belly to the ground.

With the schoolhouse in sight, she put on the after-burners and just made it to the hole in the foundation as Dragon's jaws snapped at her sparse brush. He got a few little hairs in his teeth for a reward.

By the time Sister and the field—what was left of it, given the speed and the jumps along the way—reached the schoolhouse, Shaker was blowing "gone to ground" and Netty, plopped on her side, was sending up a prayer of thanks to the Great Fox in the Sky.

This moment would have lasted longer except for the low tang of a cowbell coming ever closer.

Felicity, who had fallen back and rode at the rear, looked around. "It's a mad cow!"

Cindy Chandler turned. The sight of her pet and Cly's son on the rampage turned her face chalk white. "Oh, dear, she's uncontrollable when she gets like this."

Sister called to Shaker, "We've got to get out of here. Go over the in and out!"

Shaker did not question his master. He gracefully mounted, saw Sybil already on the other side of the wide dirt road. He squeezed Showboat over the first coop. Showboat knew better but he was still jangled from all the uproar, so he sucked back when his front hooves hit the dirt. Sometimes a horse will get a little tentative if the surface changes.

Shaker squeezed, touched him with the spurs, and whacked him proper on the hindquarters with his crop. If Showboat balked, then Keepsake might, doubtful, but he might. And other horses in the field would, too, so he had to get over.

With a surge, the Thoroughbred left a half stride early. Shaker leaned back a bit in the saddle but he was ready for it.

On the other side, hounds with him, he trotted down to the woods at the edge of the meadow and cast hounds. Soon enough the field got over.

Cly thundered up to the coop. She considered crashing it but she was tired. Her full figure didn't get much exercise and she'd been running and bellowing for half an hour.

"That ought to teach them a lesson!"

"What's the lesson, Mom?"

"That this is my farm and they'd better do as I say." She belched, the sickly sweet odor of cud emanating from her mouth and nostrils.

Turning to walk at a leisurely pace back to the stable where she hoped feed lay about, she noticed seven riders coming toward her, including Bill Wheatley, a piece of his britches flapping every time he stood up to post.

"Oh, let's have some fun." She lowered her head and rolled right for them.

189

Scattering them like ninepins, Cly shook her head, reveling in her power.

"You're hamburger, you old monster!" A rider angrily pointed his finger at her.

She turned, pawed the ground, lowered her head as did Orestes, and scared him so bad he burnt the wind getting out of there.

"What's hamburger?"

"Nothing to concern yourself about, son." It was occurring to the huge old girl that she may have crossed the line. She decided not to rummage the stable. *"Let's go back to the pasture and have a nap."*

Shaker and the pack, all together, got up another fox, and had a good fifteen-minute burst. But people were ragged out from the adventure. So he swung hounds low and back toward the house. It took forty-five minutes to get there and they did get two more short runs in the bargain.

Sam Lorillard, on hearing the horn, turned back toward the stables. He had a pretty good idea that Shaker was drawing back and he'd just seen the devil cow go back that way.

He walked behind her at a respectful distance. When she walked into the pasture and dropped to her knees, asleep almost instantly, he put his horse in a stall.

Sam kept tools in his truck and trailer, as did most smart foxhunters. He pulled out his toolbox, got a hammer and some nails, and walked around to the side where Cly had smashed up the coop. Unsalvageable.

He walked back to his truck, fired it up, and drove around to the shed where Cindy kept her supplies. He loaded up boards, drove around the outside of the pasture, and nailed them up.

That would at least keep Cly from aimlessly wandering out until the men of the club could get back here and rebuild the jump.

He knew Cly well enough to know she only smashed through fences and jumps when playful or angry. Her usual modus operandi was to eat and sleep and then eat some more.

By the time the field got back, all was secure.

Crawford handsomely tipped him for it and Sam gratefully accepted. Then Crawford, expansive, since he'd managed to ride out this wild hunt, offered a beautiful bronze sculpture for the hunt ball silent auction. Sorrel Buruss, chair of the silent action, waxed ecstatic, rode over to him, and kissed him from horseback.

When Bill dismounted, Charlotte laughed at him. "Well, Bill, I now know you're a boxer man and not a briefs man."

"I'm just glad to be in one piece."

"Your pants look like Zorro slashed them into a 'Z,'" Valentina giggled, then apologized, "Sorry. I forgot."

Bill smiled up at her, "It's all right, Val. Life goes on."

Shaker hopped off Showboat to open the party wagon door. Hounds walked in happy with this exciting day.

Sister, Keepsake at the trailer, walked over, "Never, never in my life have I hunted a day like today. How you and Betty got those hounds all on was a miracle."

"May the saints preserve us." He beamed.

Showboat, standing by the party wagon, laughed. *"I preserved you, not the saints."* All the other horses in earshot laughed.

CHAPTER 20

The heavenly aroma of turkey filled the house, along with the sweet scent of sweet potatoes, corn bread, cranberry sauce, special fried grits cakes, all manner of sauces, spices, vegetables, and salads.

Golly stayed at her window post behind the sink. She knew if she behaved many tidbits would be tossed her way as Sister and Lorraine put on the finishing touches to the meal.

Tootie, Valentina, and Felicity set the tables while Gray made everyone drinks. The house overflowed with people. Sam came and of course Sister invited Rory, Crawford's farmhand, as he had no people left who would have him. Shaker, still beaming, regaled the girls with hunt tales as he folded linen napkins. He liked to be useful and never thought of chores as women's work or men's work.

Tedi and Edward came. Sybil, too, and she brought her two sons. Edward III, called Neddie by everyone, even though still in grade school showed every sign of growing to be taller than his grandfather.

Walter came and brought as his date Sorrel Buruss. That would set tongues wagging, mostly because it happened under everyone's nose. Ah, what an offense to those who had to know everything about everybody because their own lives were such a bloody bore.

Mandy, Gray's daughter, drove down from Washington. She looked more like her mother than her father, but she had her father's quiet sense of command as well as his wonderful way with color. Over the last year Sister and Mandy learned to value each other.

Marty and Crawford Howard came, and Sister told Shaker, who strongly disliked them, that he had to abide Crawford. The Howards would always be invited to the big parties or functions where Crawford's checkbook was hotly desired. But no one invited them to the family dinners, the true gatherings of the clan. Once Sister discovered this she thought she'd set it to rights. Crawford wasn't so bad. He needed to stop bragging about himself, a sign of weakness, but Sister wanted to give him a chance.

The dogs barked as another car pulled up.

Betty and her husband, Bobby, came in through the back door.

"Sorry we're late." Bobby hung up his coat on the peg by the door.

"That Magellan jumped out of the paddock so everyone else had to follow. And of course, we were all dressed up. Don't you think the mud stains on my skirt add to my fashion statement?" Betty, too, was in fine spirits.

Gray, Bobby, and Crawford located extra chairs to accommodate all the guests since the dining room chairs only numbered twelve. They'd set up extra tables in the huge dining room. When the "new" part of Roughneck Farm was built in 1824, this room doubled as a small ballroom, so each end boasted a beautiful fireplace. The small orchestras used back then would play on a raised dais against the outside wall. If the weather was warm all the French doors would be thrown open and dancing would be outside as well as in.

When Big Ray lived he threw fabulous parties, this room overflowing. Once he died, Sister rarely used it. But today it seemed perfect.

Between the food, the stories, having all the young people around, it was one of the best Thanksgivings Sister could remember.

After the last dish was carried out and the table cleared, they all repaired to the living room, where Sorrel opened the grand piano and played song after song. The schoolgirls knew the words to Cole Porter's songs because Custis Hall put on *Anything Goes*. They all got hooked on his witty lyrics and melodies.

By midnight, the last of the guests had left. They'd thrilled to a hard day's riding, the joy of one another's company. Lorraine protested that she should stay to clean up, as did Betty, but Sister pushed them out the door, saying she'd abuse the Custis Hall students.

With Golly, Raleigh, and Rooster cleaning plates the only thing to do was to load the dishwasher. Up to her elbows in soapy water, washing the crystal, Sister handed glasses to the girls, standing in a row. Gray filled up the fireplaces, then returned to the kitchen.

"What can I do?"

"Sit by the fire and look handsome."

More tired than he cared to admit, he dropped into the old cane rocking chair, propped his feet up by the huge walk-in fireplace.

"What a day." He smiled.

"Aunt Netty is still sleeping, I'll bet." Sister pulled the plug in the sink, the water swirling downward. Bubbles floated into the air. She reached up and balanced one on her finger. "Life is a soap opera and we're the bubbles."

"How'd you know it was Aunt Netty?" Valentina finished wiping out a wineglass.

"First that silly brush. Pathetic. Always has been. Then, no one runs like Aunt Netty, she burns the wind."

"Did you get a look at the other fox?" Tootie asked.

"No, but Betty said it was Grace, who lives at Fox-glove. Cindy spoils her with candies."

"As I recall, someone in this room occasionally puts out treats." Gray pushed off with his right foot, the rocker gently rolling.

"Well, it's true. Of course, now that we've got the little gray back in the orchard I'll put out some dog biscuits for her, too."

Tootie hung the sopping-wet dish towel over the drying rack. "Anything else?"

"We've performed heroic labors. Done." Sister wiped her hands.

Valentina walked to the mudroom. Her barn coat hung there. She'd put her iPod in the pocket. Returning to the kitchen, everyone sitting by the fireplace, she handed it to Sister. "I keep forgetting to play this for you."

"Ah, I've wanted to see one of these," Sister said, admiring the small electronic device.

"I recorded this music, uh, I forget the exact name. Something about Henry IV hunting. Henry of France. Anyway, it was written during the French Revolution."

"Off with their heads." Felicity giggled.

"You know, I didn't think anyone wrote music during the Revolution." Sister placed the tiny earpieces in her ears. She blinked and pulled them off.

"Too loud?" Valentina turned down the volume.

"No. No. That tinty sound."

Valentina put the earphones in her ears. "Oh, that." She handed them back to Sister. "Sorry. I didn't erase all of that. The hunting horn will start in a minute."

"Val, play that again." Sister listened intently. "What is that sound?"

"Special effects."

"From what?"

"From the Halloween dance. That's a witch's voice. Well, it's my voice really. I recorded my voice and changed the speed until I got the right sound. We had all these little flying witches and each one had one of our voices. It was so cool."

Putting her arm around Val's waist, Sister walked her over to the wall phone. She dialed the sheriff.

"Ben, listen to this."

It was also a perfect night for Target, the big red. He'd feasted on Thanksgiving leftovers from two different farms. There wasn't a garbage can Target couldn't open. Deer hunters would clean carcasses, leaving behind the offal. He didn't like that but other little creatures did so Target could sometimes grab a quick bite there or even better, the rack hunters would saw off antlers, leaving the entire deer. All that deer meat was getting tedious. The turkey and stuffing leftovers tonight were wonderful.

He stopped, crouched. At the edge of the wildflower meadow lay a blackbird from St. Just's flock. He crept toward it, prepared to pounce, then stopped. The bird was dead. He sniffed it. Nothing smelled unusual. No marks on the crow. It could have dropped from a heart attack, a common enough death among birds given their heart rate. He picked up another odor, human. Ten feet from the crow rested a human finger, relatively fresh, torn at the joint. The simple gold ring had an onyx oval stone, a crest carved into it. The ring was half on, half off the finger. Target pulled it off with one extended claw.

Toys delighted him. He'd steal balls that house dogs

dropped outside. If it rolled or was shiny, he wanted it. He picked up the ring, taking it home.

He knew humans buried or cremated their dead. Their fastidious ways amused him because the body did the earth not a bit of good then. However, every creature has its habits so if humans wanted to render their dead useless to the soil, so be it.

It occurred to him that finding the finger was not a good sign for the humans. One more reason he was glad he was a fox.

CHAPTER 21

Thanksgiving vacation offered quiet but no relief from paperwork. Charlotte and Carter lived on campus in a lovely home, but try as she might, Charlotte couldn't work at home. She needed to leave the familiarity of her needlepoint pillows and her two cats.

As she walked across the main quad she was surprised to see Knute Nilsson, blue cashmere scarf wrapped around his neck, walking toward Old Main.

"Knute, walking off your turkey?"

He smiled wanly, "I'd have to walk to Seattle and back."

"See, if you rode, you'd burn off those calories."

"The horse burns them. I don't know about the human." He fell in alongside her. "But I burn plenty of calories sailing."

"Bill tore his britches yesterday, revealing more of Bill than anyone wanted to see," she said cheerfully.

"Actually, there's a lot of Bill, isn't there? He can't even claim that it's middle-aged spread now that he's on the other side of sixty."

"How was your Thanksgiving?"

"Good, but five children in the house under the age of ten! I thought I would lose my mind or go deaf or both."

"Maybe when we're younger we don't mind it. I don't know."

"Sometimes I look at my children and grandchildren and wish I'd been celibate."

At that they both laughed.

Charlotte chided him, "You wouldn't make a good monk."

"No."

"So coming to the office for peace and quiet?"

"Yes, and to crunch numbers." He opened the large main door, the paned glass on the top half frosted. "Amy wants four new centrifuges. She said what she has is ancient and two are broken. My God, Charlotte, do you know how much a centrifuge costs? I told her she'd better not break any of those microscopes because that's it for this year's budget." He paused. "Really, the security patrol is wreaking havoc with the numbers."

"I know," she commiserated. "What can we do, Knute? We have to have that presence to create confidence."

"I don't think the students are in danger. Whatever happened had to do with Al, himself, not any of the girls."

"Let's hope so. The problem is, we don't know." Her loafer heels clicked on the polished floor as they walked by the artifact case.

"We could reduce the number of security people. Shave two people off the payroll. I'm not sure anyone would notice."

"No."

He frowned. "We've got to do something. And I guarantee you the bill Professor Kennedy submits with her report will be as fat as the report." He stopped when they reached the door to her office. "She didn't give any kind of hint, did she? Like when and how much?"

"She said she'd have the report to us right after New Year's. But she gave no indication of the final cost. She probably doesn't know until she sits down and adds it all up."

"I dread it."

"I do, too, but I dread unrest more. We can't afford that kind of publicity. At least belt-tightening doesn't have to make the news."

"Be sure to tighten Bill's first."

CHAPTER 22

The remnants of the moon, still full enough to cast light through the clouds, revealed low popcorn clouds, sailing in from the west. By eight-thirty they'd turned into low, fleecy gray clouds.

When hounds were cast at nine o'clock at Little Dalby, the temperature leveled off at forty-seven degrees. The moisture in the clouds gave the morning a raw feel. From a foxhunter's point of view, this was good because scent would hold on the ground.

Eighty-four people in formal attire filled the pasture where the trailers had parked this Saturday after Thanksgiving. Holidays brought people out. Many were eager for a foxhunt to sweat off the calories. Then, too, the cold air cleared the head from all the family tension that holidays seem to bring out.

Postcard Thanksgiving dinners so rarely occur. The soup isn't the only thing simmering. Many a person seated atop their sleek hunter inwardly groaned at the thought of Christmas. The expense of it was bad enough; worse, for some, was spending it with their families. Since southerners, especially, put a good face on it, many people thought they were alone in their misery.

People needed a good brisk day out to release their pent-up, silent resentment.

The hounds couldn't wait, charging out of the party wagon. Sybil and Betty dropped the thongs on their whips, calling, "Hold up. Hold up."

Shaker, voice calm, sat atop HoJo. "Settle down. Just relax."

"We're ready!" Delight said.

"And it's a new fixture. I can't wait." Her littermate, Diddy, twirled in a circle.

"If you don't quit babbling, Shaker will put you back on the trailer," Ardent warned with the wisdom of full maturity.

That shut up the two giddy girls.

Once Sister thanked Mrs. Wideman and informed the field that a tailgate would follow they got right down to it. No point wasting a minute on a day as promising as this.

The staff didn't know the foxes on this estate. Little Dalby backed up on Beveridge Hundred, which had been hunted by Jefferson Hunt for over a century. If a fox skedaddled that way, they'd have a better chance of knowing the fox since the animal's home territory might be Beveridge Hundred.

But hounds no sooner put their noses down on the grass than Dasher found a strong line and called the others to him. Before people could tighten their girths they were off, in some cases literally.

No harm done as those who had parted ways from their mounts lurched back up, usually with the help of a friend holding on to their horse. It's difficult for a horse to stand still when the rest of the herd thunders away. However, these pathetic humans couldn't run a lick, so the good horses knew to wait and hope they could catch up without their passenger flying off again.

The fox headed straight south away from Beveridge Hundred, straight as an arrow, too. Within twenty minutes Sister and the first flight cleared six new coops and post-and-rail jumps they'd built. Then, as so often happens, the fox vanished.

Hounds cast themselves looking for the elusive scent. As no creek or river was near, no one knew how he or she did it, but it was as though that fox had never existed.

Sitting at the check, Sister felt the slight drop in the temperature and a cool air current curling out of the forest. The faint rustle of the dried leaves on the oaks filled the air as did the cry of an angry redtail hawk overhead. The hounds spoiled her hunting.

The low series of hills stretched out before them was covered with broomsage. These fields needed care. However, what's bad for grazing may be good for game.

Out of the corner of her eye, Tootie saw a large red fox walking toward the forest. He'd circled them, arranging to ruin his scent where the hounds lost it. She resisted the urge to blurt out "Tally ho," which would have sent the fox on faster as well as brought up the hounds' heads. Every time a hound lifts its head a precious moment may be lost because the scent, nine times out of ten, is on the ground.

Sometimes if scent is breast high the hounds can carry it until it lifts over their heads.

Heart pounding, Tootie turned Iota in the direction the fox was moving. She took off her cap, stretched her right arm out straight, and said nothing.

Sister didn't see her, as Tootie was behind her. A low murmur alerted her; she turned and saw with pride that the young woman did just as she was supposed to do. She also heard at that moment Crawford bellow, "Tally ho."

Shaker, trotting and now close to the field, said in a voice that carried, "Mr. Howard, kindly shut up." Crawford fumed, face cerise, but he did button his lip.

Shaker quietly called the hounds to him, walking them toward the sighting. At that moment, since there was no wind, he didn't have to factor in how far scent would drift. He had to give the fox time to get away. Scent was good today. No reason to gallop about.

He glanced at Tootie, put the hounds on her vector but fifty yards behind. As the hounds passed her, then Shaker, he touched his cap with his crop.

Tootie grinned from ear to ear.

Before her grin faded, Cora, good as gold, called, *"Let's go."*

The fox, full of vigor, feeling loosened up from the first part of the chase, glided into the forest, darted over rotting logs, their pungent aroma detectable to the humans. The fox, inexperienced with hounds, had heard from the Beveridge Hundred foxes how the chase worked.

Confident that he could elude and outrun the pursuers, he merrily ran. He scrambled over huge orange fungus sprouting from the base of trees. His weight broke off pieces, releasing their earthy scent. He skidded across pine needles, the fresher the needles, the stronger the scent.

St. John's lay dead ahead and he shot right for it. He inhaled an enticing aroma from under the church but knew if he ducked in there so would the hounds. Better to allow the marvelous fragrance to throw them off. He'd be long gone by the time they gave that up.

He was right, too, for the hounds swarmed the church.

"Let's dig in here," Doughboy gleefully sang out.

"Yeah, this will be really good." Delight supported her brother.

Cora, tempted by the aroma, ordered, *"No. We've got to stay on our fox."*

"Won't the humans want some of this?" Diddy inquired.

Tinsel, a year older than the "Ds," hunting for the third year, sniffed. *"Look how high they are on their horses. Do you know how long it will take scent to reach them even if the air warms? Diddy, we've got to leave this. And if an exceptionally well-nosed human gets a whiff they won't like it."*

"It smells so good," Delight said with a backward look, and followed Cora.

Shaker called out, "Hark to 'em."

They moved on, catching up with Dragon, Dasher, and Cora.

Running hard, Tinsel said to Diddy, *"Humans don't like that kind of food."*

"No!" Diddy pitied their undeveloped palates.

Scent grew hotter as they moved forward, so conversation stopped.

Galloping past the charming church, Sister noticed that truck tracks indented the road. The Widemans must have come to inspect their little church. She hoped restoration would follow. A faint hint of an abandoned deer carcass or something assailed her nostrils, then disappeared as she hurried on.

A sprinkle hit her cheeks; the raindrops felt cold. She looked up at the sky. The clouds were so low she felt she could touch them as mist filtered down through the forest.

They burst out of the woods, over a stout new coop, still unpainted, which spooked some of the horses.

She felt sorry about that but there just hadn't been time to paint, plus one had to wait for the temperatures to rise above the forties.

Still running straight, the fox fired across the pasture, dipped under an old fence line, and shot into Beveridge Hundred, where he made for an old granary, built of stone. He waited a moment, shook himself, then placidly slipped into his den.

Hounds raced to the granary but were too large to squeeze under the ragged edge of the old wooden door, the once-bright blue faded to a chalky baby blue.

"Let me in!" Dragon howled.

The fox paid no mind to the uproar outside the door.

Shaker chose not to open the door. He knew the fox had to be in his den, but he didn't know if any farm equipment was still in the granary. If so, his hounds could get torn by tines in their excitement or smack into old tools, which would fall on them.

Hound welfare came first for Shaker.

The rain accelerated from a fine mist to a light drizzle.

"Boss?" he asked Sister after he'd blown "gone to ground."

"Time to pick them up, I think."

Walter, back in the field, pulled the collar of his coat up, as did others. The rawness of the weather cut to the bone.

Within fifteen minutes all returned to the trailers. Despite the drizzle increasing in tempo, the tailgate was crowded.

As he put on his Barbour coat in the dressing room of his trailer, Crawford swore. "I will get that son of a bitch huntsman. Who the hell does he think he is? Who is paying his salary? I put more money into this than anyone!" Marty had sense enough not to argue with him.

Anselma Wideman returned in her truck. She'd seen them off.

"Sister, why don't you all come into the house?"

"Thank you, but as you can see, the food's about demolished. Thank you, though."

"Well, if you're worried about the mud, don't be. I've got one of those big standing bootjacks. They can pull off their boots and walk around in their socks."

Sister smiled. "Grab something before it's all gone."

"I just might do that." The pretty forty-year-old cut the motor, slid into her Barbour jacket. As she stepped outside she clapped an oilskin hat on her head. "You must be cold."

Sister walked next to her toward the tailgate. "You get used to it. Where's Harvey today? I was hoping we'd see him to thank him. It's wonderful to be back here. So many memories. All of them happy. It's a beautiful, beautiful place and you all are doing so much to bring it back to life."

"We have Beveridge Hundred as our example."

"The Cullhains never give up." Sister motioned toward the family that had owned Beveridge Hundred for centuries, in flush times and lean. As farming grew tougher and tougher their little profits dwindled, but they struggled to keep the place together, not selling off any land.

"This area is full of remarkable people, people who don't bend to hardship," Anselma said admiringly, her black eyes soft and warm.

"Well, Anselma, all God's chillun' got problems. It's what you do with them."

"True enough."

"Where is Harvey, by the way?"

"I forgot that, didn't I? He's in Baltimore. Family business, so he killed two birds with one stone."

"I saw truck tracks back to St. John's. Thought

maybe he drove back for inspiration."

"He may have. There are so many outbuildings at Little Dalby I'm working my way outward. Eventually I'll get to St. John's myself."

"Well, this place is being reborn."

"You know, Sister, I am, too."

"Every day." Sister smiled.

"Beg pardon?"

"Every day. One is reborn with the sun. And today that fox gave us such a run, I feel like I'm thirty."

They laughed and on reaching the tailgate joined the others.

It wasn't until three days later, Tuesday, that Sister recalled her conversation with Anselma and realized she'd fumbled the ball.

CHAPTER 23

B alls." Bill leaned back in the leather club chair, putting his feet on the leather hassock. "He's so full of it."

Amy shrugged, "That's what he said."

"He's always crying poor. It's a professional hazard." Bill would have none of it. "There's money in the budget for centrifuges. For Christ's sake, Amy, every school budget has a layer of fat in it. Think of it as high cholesterol." He glanced down at his own expanding belly, the corners of his mouth turned down. "When did you see him, anyway?"

"I stopped by his office at eight-thirty. Before my first class."

"I'm sure he was toiling away." Bill's voice dripped sarcasm.

"He was."

Alpha Rawnsley opened the door to the teachers' lounge, inhaling the seasoned oak crackling in the fireplace. "Solace!" She closed the door behind her, took in Amy's face. "Perhaps not."

"Oh, Alpha, I'm just mad at Knute, that's all. He says there isn't money in the budget to replace the four centrifuges that broke."

"Crying poor." Bill nestled farther into the comfortable old chair, made so by decades of teacher bottoms.

"He can be strict," Alpha wryly replied as she poured herself a sherry from the decanter.

As each of them had taught their last class of the day, they repaired to the lounge. It was their version of stopping by the bar to have one with the boys before going home. The difference was the Custis Hall faculty thought of it as collegiality.

"Anal," Bill said.

"That may be so, but Custis Hall remains in the black. You have to give him and Charlotte credit for that. And once the alumnae fund reaches its target, they'll both relax."

"If I have to wait that long for four centrifuges, I'd better leave." Amy decided a spot of sherry would do her a world of good, too.

Outside the paned, leaded-glass windows a few

snowflakes announced more to come.

Alpha smiled. "To the first snow." She handed Bill a sherry.

They toasted the true beginning of winter.

"You know what else he's obsessing about?"

"Amy, he has a laundry list." Bill giggled, which made the two women laugh.

"Professor Kennedy's bill. He must have droned on and on for a good twenty minutes about all the time she was here because she charges by the hour. He anticipates her report, which, his words, 'Will be a pulp novel larger than the Cedars of Lebanon.' He's not exactly sliding into the holiday mood."

"Wonder why he called it a novel?" Alpha, ever the English teacher, queried.

Amy shrugged but Bill piped up, "She'll make it up."

"Bill!" Alpha was surprised. "She hardly seemed like that kind of person, and do you think she would have the recommendation she does or her position at Brown if she were a fraud?"

"I don't know." Bill drained his sherry glass. "I just don't see how anyone can authenticate an iron lock or a pair of dancing pumps. I suppose you can come close, but I know from my work that you wind up with what was most popular. For instance, let's say I'm doing a production of *The Lion in Winter*. Twelfth century and it happened to be a period of clean, quite beautiful designs, especially for women's clothing. But what do I see? Stained-glass windows. A pretty painting in a Book of Hours. There's not a scrap of fabric left. Besides, I'm seeing idealized representations of royalty and nobles. I don't think it's that easy to authenticate certain objects or clothes. It's always an approximation."

"Carbon dating." Amy poured another round for Bill and herself. Alpha waved her off.

"Sure. That will really put Knute over the edge. Do you know how expensive that is? Look, we're doing this to pacify a segment of our student body. It's window dressing."

"I don't think so." Alpha disagreed without being disagreeable. "Once the administration committed to this, it realized that nothing has been done with those items since the day they were given to Custis Hall. No one knows their value. It may be important for insurance."

"Sell off one old ribbon and I'd have my centrifuges," Amy griped.

Bill laughed, "I can see it now, science teacher sentenced to fifteen years for theft of valuable ribbon."

The three laughed.

Alpha lowered her voice slightly. "This is when we need Al Perez. He could jolly Knute along."

Amy struggled, then replied, "I try not to miss him, but I do."

Diplomatically Alpha said, "You were closer to him than we were. He had his faults. Don't we all? However, he worked very hard for Custis Hall and we're close to our alumnae fund goal because of him."

"Fifteen million dollars." Bill inhaled. "That sounds like so much money until you realize that two decades ago Stanford University launched a drive to raise one billion dollars in alumnae contributions. Now the other first-flight," he used the hunting term, "universities have followed suit."

"Pity poor University of Missouri." Alpha kept up with educational news. "Kenneth Lay, a graduate, promised beaucoup dollars. They based their budget on that and, well, we know the rest of that story. I can't imagine doing that to people or to one's alma mater. He doesn't seem to have a smidgen of shame."

"Never steal anything small," Bill replied. "Remember that movie with James Cagney? Wasn't that the title?"

Amy glared at Bill. "How would I know?"

"That's right, Amy. I forgot. You were still in swaddling clothes." Bill let out an uproarious laugh and Alpha couldn't help but laugh with him.

"Bill, you went ugly early." Amy smiled for a change.

"Guess I did." He finished his sherry. "My wife has promised something new and exciting with the turkey leftovers. My curiosity is rising."

"Along with your appetite." Alpha listened to the grandfather clock ticking in the corner. "Snowing a bit harder now. Bill, think you'll foxhunt tomorrow?"

"It's from Beasley Hall. Crawford will have the road plowed out. We'll go unless it's a blizzard. I didn't check the weather this morning. What's the call?"

"Light snow. Not much accumulation, maybe one or two inches. Enough for the highway department to clear the roads," Alpha said.

"With what we pay in state taxes the highway department could do a better job of snowplowing." Amy folded her arms across her chest.

"Budget. See. We come back to Knute. Same drama, different theater." Bill enjoyed his wordplay.

"This is a rich state," Amy said.

"It's a well-managed state," Alpha said, amending Amy's response. "We aren't rich compared to New York or California. We're better managed, and because of that, our taxes are lower."

"We don't have people pouring in across the border using state services and not paying for them." Bill had strong thoughts about that issue.

"True," Alpha simply replied.

"It always comes back to money, doesn't it? I don't see why we can't afford more snowplows and I don't see why I can't have four centrifuges."

"If the state buys more snowplows it's wasteful. Contract out the labor, allow those men who already have the equipment to make some money. The state doesn't have to maintain the equipment, put the gas in the engines, or buy the bulldozer initially. It's a better system. It's up to the contractor to factor in those things when he bids." Alpha believed passionately in reducing the number of people employed by the state government or any level of government. Let the private sector do it.

"So what do you want me to do? Go write a bid and turn it in to Knute?"

"Try an angora sweater that fits, uh, that shows off your assets." Bill felt wonderful, the sherry warming him.

"Works on you, not Knute." Amy knew her compatriots.

Alpha remarked lightly, "You can't blame a man for looking."

"Alpha, you'd be surprised." A sour note crept into Bill's voice. "If our society becomes any more politically correct the only people who will teach, run for office, you name it, will be robots. God help anyone with blood in his or her veins."

"You've got a point there, Bill. I'm glad I'm getting older." She spoke to Amy, "Bill and I will soon retire. You and your generation are going to bear the brunt of this. And you're also going to endure a wicked recession, so my advice, dear, forget the centrifuges for now. Be as helpful as you can and the best teacher you can be. When the pink slips fly, your name won't be on one. Because by the time this economy hits the skids, Knute will be even more powerful."

"Hear, hear." Bill raised his glass and Amy poured him another round.

He was a big man and could absorb it.

"We haven't really talked about this, but Al's murder is certainly going to affect the school. If the person who did it isn't caught soon, parents will get nervous and so will alumnae. Our recession could start before the nation's," Alpha shrewdly noted.

"They'll catch him," Amy confidently said.

"Who knows?" Bill's blue eyes were doubtful. "Murder is a very easy crime to commit. Steal something large, they'll track you down sooner or later. Again, Kenneth Lay. But murder? It makes for good movies, but in real life people get away with it every day."

"That's cynical." Amy wanted Al's murderer caught even if she did cling to her resentment of the way in which the affair ended.

"Going to be more than two inches if it keeps coming down like this. What is there about the first snow? Pristine. Beautiful." Alpha changed the subject. "I'll bid you two adieu. I want to get home before the roads are a slushy mess."

"Sun's setting, too. It'll ice up pretty fast. I guess I'll find out what my dearest has conjured up with the leftovers."

Amy waited alone in the lounge for a few minutes as she watched Alpha and Bill, walking together in the snow. She loved this old lounge. It was where she began her flirtation with Al that turned into something much more. For the first time since his death, the tears came. Lost loves, always emotionally potent, are even more so when death removes all possibility of resolution. Poor thing didn't even know she needed resolution until this grief overtook her.

CHAPTER 24

A light snow, a thin white curtain, continued to fall when the Jefferson hounds cast from Beasley Hall on November 29. Three inches had accumulated overnight as the snowfall abated, then picked up again, but the main roads were easily passable. Crawford plowed the tertiary road to the huge stone pillars announcing the entrance to his estate. The massive, expensive bronze boars atop the pillars had snow on their tusks, in their hackles, which added to their ferocious appearance.

The only dicey part for those braving the weather was the one mile of secondary road before turning off to Crawford's road. Everybody crawled along and arrived to park in front of the hunter stables. Fifteen sturdy souls arose in darkness for the morning's hunt. True foxhunters, they knew today was the kind of day when one could ride on the chase of the season.

And they weren't far wrong, because the hounds cast promptly at nine and by ten minutes after the hour, Asa, wise in his seventh season, caught a whiff of fresh rabbit blood. He flanked the pack, put his nose down, and tracked the scent droplets in the snow to a small covert folded into the land.

"He's in the covert!" Asa called out and the other hounds honored him.

A big red dog fox, hearing the music, bolted out the other end of the small covert.

Betty, on Magellan, who danced about, saw him shoot northeast so the light wind would be at his tail. No fool, this fellow.

"Tally ho!" Betty called out.

Sister slipped and slid as they cantered down the slope. Going up the slight rise proved easy enough, and by the time they crested it, she and the small field could see the beautiful sight of a red fox against white snow in the distance running flat out, the whole pack as one behind him.

The snowflakes stung as they hit Sister's face, caught in her eyelashes. The cold awakened everyone but most especially the horses, who loved days like today. Snow flew off hooves; some large clumps smacked people's chests like hard snowballs.

A black coop, half white on the bottom now, loomed ahead. Shaker soared over it on Gunpowder, white as the snow himself. Sister and Rickyroo popped over but as successive riders took it, the footing grew ever more treacherous. The last four horses over rode straight to the base and popped way up and over.

Against the snow, everyone could see the red figure diminishing up ahead. The snow impeded him but it slowed the hounds, too. As they were heavier, they sank down into it.

A zigzag fence was ahead and the riders took their own line coming back together on the other side of the lovely old snake fencing. The fox sped over the next large field, dashed into a thick woods. His perfect paw prints announced his progress to human eyes because he was harder to see once in the woods. He ducked into underbrush.

Dragon and Trident, fast, nudged ahead of Cora. Both boys closed on the fox. Dragon lunged for him, jaws snapping, and the red jumped up in the air, turned a ninety-degree angle, and again ducked under thick brush that proved tough going for Dragon and Trident, but they persevered.

A crystal-clear deep creek lay ahead, the banks steep, filled with ice, too. He launched into the creek, swimming downstream, scrambling out on the other side. He gained two minutes on his pursuers with this tactic because they all crashed into the creek, then had to pick up his scent on the other side, which took a few moments since they clambered out higher up than he did.

Sister gave Rickyroo a hard squeeze. He soared over the creek, landing cleanly on the other side. He didn't like the reflections from ice but he was learning—he was seven—that the old girl on his back was trustworthy. She didn't ask him to do anything stupid.

A mass of boulders, jumbled together like a giant's discarded building blocks, marked the edge of the heavy woods. The fox dove into his den at the base of the smooth gray rock.

The hounds dug at the rock. Shaker praised them. As he swung his right leg over he glanced down, noticing to his right fresh bear tracks. He put his right foot back in the stirrup. He blew "gone to ground" very briefly from the saddle, then turned the pack in the opposite direction of the tracks.

Sister rarely questioned her huntsman. His abrupt departure keyed up her already heightened senses. She turned and followed, Walter, Crawford, Marty, Gray, Sam, Tedi, Edward, and others behind her.

No sooner had they moved into the rolling white field on the other side of the woods than the hounds struck again. This scent was older but strong enough to give another ripping twenty-minute run. Miraculously no one slipped and went down. At least going down in snow is better than on hard-baked earth.

By the time they returned to the trailers, wiped down their horses, and threw blankets over them, everyone was exhilarated and exhausted.

Marty had her cook prepare a hot breakfast at the long hunt table. The luxury of sitting at a table instead of balancing a plate on one's lap couldn't have come at a better time.

Sausages, bacon, hot flaky biscuits, eggs, steaming steel-cut oatmeal, pancakes, waffles, pastries as well as the ubiquitous ham biscuits covered the table. Marty even had the cook fill the tureen with bubbling chipped beef gravy.

Crawford sat at the head of the table with Sister at his right. Marty commanded the other end, Walter at her right.

Once the warm food hit everyone's stomach as well as some bracing coffee or tea, a few coffees laced with bourbon, the volume of conversation in the room rose.

Shaker was usually reluctant to join a breakfast for he had many chores, but once he knew the hounds were snuggling down in deep straw and had plenty of fresh water, and Marty had Rory give everyone biscuits, he came to the table. His presence delighted everyone and he was peppered with questions. This hard-core group truly wanted to know about hound work. Even Crawford, not a hound man, feigned interest.

"Let the poor man eat first," Marty good-naturedly ordered.

As the merriment continued, Crawford addressed Sister. "You know, Saturday, when we rode past St. John's of the Cross, I thought what a good thing, to have a chapel of one's own."

Knowing him, she replied, "When are you going to start and are you using clapboard, brick, or stone?"

He smiled at her as he nibbled a piece of Canadian bacon. He put it on his plate. "Well, stone is impressive."

"Your stone pillars certainly are."

"I was thinking the same type of stone."

"You know you place the altar facing south." She ate her oatmeal laced with orange blossom honey. She didn't know what she liked more, oatmeal or honey.

"No."

"Always."

Tedi, on Crawford's left, gleefully told him, "Crawford, as you know, my father's family was from Connecticut, so you might say I have double vision. I can see both sides of the Mason-Dixon line. When one is south of the line, the altar is south because no true southerner will worship with his face to the north."

"Good God," Crawford exploded genially, "doesn't anyone ever forget?"

"No" was said in unison.

"Gray, Sam, doesn't all this worship of the Confederacy worry you?" Crawford asked.

Sam deferred to his brother.

"Those who do not know their past are doomed to repeat it," Gray stated.

This set off a lively conversation, which delighted Crawford. He considered himself a Renaissance man even if he appeared nouveau riche to others. Better nouveau riche than nouveau pauvre.

"What shall you name your church?" Sister returned to his building project.

"I was thinking of St. Swithun, a good English saint."

Tedi wrinkled her brow. "Oh, dear, all I remember is if it rains on St. Swithun's Day it will rain for forty days following. July 15. So much for my catechism studies."

"We think of you as St. Tedi." Sister laughed at her old friend.

"Lots of St. Theodores, but they're men." Crawford read history constantly and since saint days and the ecclesiastical calendar bound Western culture for close to two thousand years, he was a font of information on such subjects, as was Sister.

"We'll make a new saint, then," Sister said as she ate a second bowl of oatmeal.

"There's a St. Teath, a woman of Cornwall, thirteenth century. Nothing is known of her," Crawford expounded.

"Why St. Swithun? Is there another reason apart from his being English? I mean, you could have picked St. George. Who's more English than the dragon-slayer?" Tedi was curious.

"Swithun had healing power. He was bishop of Winchester. Died in 862. I admire those people in the so-called Dark Ages. Think of what they accomplished and with so little, with such personal hardship."

The breakfast broke up after an hour. More snow had fallen, and the drive home took longer.

Sister and Gray crept along in his Land Cruiser. Betty was driving the gooseneck loaded with horses. Sister liked hauling to the meets with Betty but Gray wanted Sister with him so they could talk and he adored showing off what his Land Cruiser could do. At a base price of $55,000 his sold for almost $60,000 since Gray couldn't resist any gadget.

She had to admit, the vehicle could probably double as an armored car and it plowed through everything.

"Wonder how much Crawford will spend on his chapel? St. Swithun. I like that he's naming it that," she mused.

"He'll use the best stonemason in the county so that's forty dollars a cubic foot right there; he's lucky because that price represents a bargain."

"My God."

"Sobering."

"I keep forgetting how rich he is."

"You're the only one." Gray laughed at her. "Hey, have I told you how much I love riding behind you?"

"Tell me again."

"You're bold, you know what the hounds are doing, but mostly I like seeing your little butt over the fences. Your butt is so little it's like a boy's."

"More."

"Your breasts aren't bad either. Of course, I can't see those when you're leading the field."

"Gray." She just ate this up. Suddenly she sat upright out of the comfortable seat. "Honey, can I use your cell phone?"

"Sure, it's wired through the car. All you have to do is push these buttons and the phone icon. When you want to hang up, push the icon where the phone is level." He pointed to a green button, then a red button. "Forget something?"

"No, no, I've had a terrible thought." She dialed the Widemans. "Henry, hello, we missed you Saturday."

Sister's voice was distinctive, so he knew immediately who it was. In fact, Sister rarely had to identify herself.

"Wish I could have been there. Heard that fox ran you clean to the old granary at Beveridge Hundred."

"Did and thumbed his nose at us, too. How was your trip to Baltimore?"

"Good." He paused. "City's changing. Guess they all are. I worry that all this renewal will throw the baby out with the bathwater."

"Excuse me for being nosy, but I was wondering if you'd gone out to St. John's before you left for Baltimore."

"I'll get in there sooner or later."

"Would you mind if Gray and I drove to it? We're in the Land Cruiser so we'll get in. I think I lost something there," she half-fibbed.

"No, not at all. Anything I can do to save you the trip?"

"Thank you, no. Letting us come back and hunt Little Dalby is the best thing to happen to our club in years. I can't thank you enough, and you know, we stand ready to make good on gates or if you have a project that takes strong backs, call. In fact, I'm sitting next to Samson here."

After a few more pleasantries she disconnected.

"What are you up to? What have you gotten me into?" He shook his head.

"Honey, won't take too long. You know the way."

Gray, a good driver, was particularly alert if another vehicle was on the road. So many people, deluded by technology, would fly down a snowy road only to soar off into a bank, a ditch, or flip over. It was as though two generations of Americans had lost all sense of nature's power.

Within twenty minutes they were at St. John's of the Cross.

Sister stood before the doors. She opened them. Cold. No sign of change since she and Betty were there. A disturbed *"Hoo"* let her know who else was in there.

"What are you searching for?"

"Gray," she rested her gloved hand on his chest, "Betty and I were here marking jumps and trails. We walked on back here and I guess I took a trip down Memory Lane. Anyway, it was apparent no one had been here in years. But when we hunted Saturday I noticed tire tracks, covered now, obviously, and the hounds went straight to the chapel rear. Shaker called them off. I didn't pay attention. The chase was too good. But I did note somewhere in the back of my mind that the tracks didn't pass over tracks coming from the other direction. Whoever came here came to the chapel. And I smelled rot."

"It's deer season, Jane. No reason a hunter wouldn't park here and go deeper into the woods. Can't drive into the brush. And you know as well as I that some hunters will leave the carcass or parts of it."

"Got a flashlight in that tank of yours?"

"I do."

Within seconds they were walking around the chapel.

"I'm looking for any recent disturbance."

"Why?"

"Well, I don't rightly know, except that I trust my hounds. Shaker called them from here in short order but they were highly interested. Of course it's below

226

freezing now so I can't smell a thing."

"Fox under the chapel?"

"Could be and if it is, I need to worm him or her. If I'm lucky maybe I can lure him into a humane trap and get one rabies and distemper shot in."

They walked around to the back. The old stone foundation had some gaps in it large enough for a hound to crawl in, or a human for that matter.

With the biting cold the decaying leaf smell was not discernible, although a pleasant odor to the human nose.

She crouched down, shining the beam into the opening. She handed the flashlight to Gray as he hunched down next to her.

"Jesus H. Christ on a raft!" He dropped the flashlight and sprinted for the Land Cruiser.

CHAPTER 25

The snow, still falling, drifted, creating waves that looked like Cool Whip. Ben Sidel, Ty Banks, and three other officers patiently worked in the cold. Although only three in the afternoon, the deep gray clouds hung low; visibility wasn't too good.

On the one hand, the cold had preserved what remained of the body under the church. But the snow obscured any tracks or other bits of evidence that might have been there. Ben knew, when this snow melted, evidence would melt with it.

Ty rubbed his gloved hands together as he stood up. He shook his legs for circulation. "Sheriff, how long do you think she's been under there?"

"Maybe a week. And we're lucky. The animals that got to her didn't take the head. We've got the teeth."

"Looks like a big dog or something pawed away at the stones."

"Yeah. Sticking her under the church was a hurry-up job but not such a stupid one. People rarely come back here. Whoever killed her shoved her under the church as far back as he could crawl, piled up leaves over her, then put some stones back in the foundation. Don't know if he opened up the foundation or if the stones crumbled away. Not all of these," he pointed to snow-covered stones, "match."

"Guess there's not enough for a visual I.D."

Ben shook his head. "Been tore up pretty good. Nature's recycling." He grunted softly. "The teeth. We'll get a positive I.D."

Ty jammed his hands in his pockets as two men in orange hazard suits slid back out on their stomachs, body pieces in plastic bags.

Ty asked, "Do you think Mrs. Arnold knew who that was under there?"

"She probably has an idea despite the condition of the body. Sister's uncanny. She said she should have trusted her hounds when they went to the chapel."

"Do you want to call Mrs. Norton? I can if you—" Ty didn't finish, for Ben interrupted.

"I'll call. She knows it's coming."

"Because Brown University called her yesterday."

Ben shrugged, "Well, she's a bright woman. They asked her if she had seen Professor Kennedy, who has never missed a class. The conclusion has to be dismal. Now we have the evidence." Ben rolled his eyes toward the slightly waving treetops. "Ty, we're in the fog, but it's about to lift."

"Why?"

"Because our killer had to hurry. People who hurry make mistakes."

"When are you going to give a statement to the press?" Ty considered what Ben had just said.

"Tomorrow. I need tonight to think." He lifted his foot, shaking the cold out of his toes, snow spraying. "And I want to call on a few people."

"Long night?" Ty's expression was dolorous.

"Not for you. Tomorrow I want you to see if you can find Professor Kennedy's backup system. Someone as meticulous as she had to be in her line of work wouldn't have had only one copy of her data. It's possible that whatever she found, whether it had to do with those artifacts or with something else at Custis Hall, might be encoded in that data."

"Okay."

"The other thing is this: My statement will simply be that the remains of an unidentified woman were found. I'll give an estimate of age and race and say we won't have any more information until the dental records are checked, which may take some time."

"Okay. Anything else?"

"Find the killer."

Ty's eyebrows furrowed. "Sister said he knows the territory."

"After this, there can't be any doubt about that."

CHAPTER 26

Soft golden light flooded the snow-covered campus. Tracks crisscrossed the quads. The lovely diffuse December light somewhat made up for the long, black, cold nights. Last night the mercury had dipped to twenty-one degrees, but at eleven in the morning it shot up to forty-six with promise of further rising.

Tootie, Valentina, and Felicity, in riding clothes, walked toward their dorm.

"Did I bump Money? I swear I didn't. Bunny's in a mood. She always takes it out on me." Valentina loved the look of the school after a snow.

"Didn't see. I was in front of you," Tootie said.

"Me, too." Felicity noticed a determined squirrel stuffing acorns into her fat cheeks from a chinquapin oak.

Tootie noticed as well. "Mrs. Childers said chinquapins grow where the soil is alkaline. Sure are a lot of kinds of oaks."

"I like water oaks. Don't see them this far west." Felicity liked botany. "There's something romantic about water oaks."

Valentina's blue eyes narrowed. "You're talking

about oaks and I got my ass chewed by Bunny, the bitch."

"One dollar," Felicity grinned. "No, two."

"Oh, pulease!" Valentina rolled her eyes. "Ass is a body part."

Tootie stopped, holding up her hands. "I'll make the call on this. Otherwise you two will go on for days. Val, you owe one dollar. I accept your explanation for 'ass.' Okay, F.?"

"Okay." Felicity kept grinning as Valentina dug into her britches for a dollar.

"You're such an accountant. How boring."

"It won't be boring when we throw our end-of-the-year party, funded mostly by your mouth." Felicity laughed, her features relaxing from her normal strained visage.

"Did anyone ask for early acceptance?" Tootie wondered about college.

"No," said Valentina as she shook her head. "We'll get in to wherever we apply. We've got good grades and lots of extracurricular activities."

"Don't be so sure." Felicity's worried expression returned. "Places like Stanford and Yale, Smith, those places, the best of the best."

"Well, I don't know about you, but I'm going to Princeton and they'll be lucky to have me," Valentina said with lightheartedness.

"Be funny if we wound up at the same college." Felicity wanted the comfort of her dear friends even if they did bicker.

"Never happen," Valentina pronounced. "What are the odds of the three of us getting in to Princeton?"

"Pretty good according to your analysis," Tootie replied.

"Jennifer and Sari both got in to Colby." Felicity liked the two college freshmen, having ridden with them many times.

"Colby isn't Princeton," Tootie remarked. "It's a good school and all, but how many people want to go to Maine? Too cold."

"If that was the criterion then no one would apply to Wisconsin or Michigan or Vermont." Valentina saw the door of the dorm swing open and Pamela Rene emerge. "Chicago's dream girl, in her own estimation," she said under her breath.

"Okay, we all applied to Princeton. Tootie and I applied to Duke. You and I applied to Colgate. You and Tootie applied to Bucknell. At least two of us might make it." Felicity kept on track.

"And I applied to Virginia Tech," Tootie added.

"Yale," Valentina said.

"Northwestern," Felicity chimed in.

As Pamela approached them, Valentina asked, nicely, "Pamela, where'd you apply to college?"

Fingering her red scarf, Pamela stopped. "UVA, Tufts, Ole Miss."

"Ole Miss?" Tootie's eyebrows shot upward. "A Chicago girl like you at Ole Miss. Pamela, that surprises me."

"I did it to piss off my mother." She laughed. "She

wanted me to apply to Radcliffe, Mt. Holyoke, Bard, and Vassar. If I get in to all three, I think I'll go to Ole Miss anyway. But I put in a late application to Brown because I liked Professor Kennedy. Did it over Thanksgiving."

"Did you have a good one?" Felicity didn't like Pamela either but she tried to like her. Felicity tried to like everyone.

"No. But it was good to see my friends. What'd you guys do?"

"Stayed at Sister Jane's. We hunted with her and she took us to other hunts. We hunted almost every day," Tootie bubbled.

"Yeah, we cleaned the kennels with Shaker and we learned all the hounds' names." Felicity's eyes sparkled.

"Cleaned all the tack, too." Valentina's stomach rumbled. Time for lunch.

"I like cleaning tack." Felicity heard Valentina's stomach, reminding her that she was hungry, too. "It's therapeutic and Sister cleaned with us so she told us stories about hunting when she was our age. It was really cool. Back then people stayed out so long they brought two horses," she enthused.

This happiness weighed on Pamela. "Guess you all are the favorites."

"If you'd stayed here, Sister would have invited you, too." Pamela knew Sister was evenhanded. "You're a good rider, Pam."

This caught Pamela off guard. "You think?"

"Yeah," Valentina backed Tootie up.

"You couldn't hunt your horses every day." Pamela was curious as to what she missed.

"Sister let us ride hers!" Felicity boasted.

"She said, 'Light hands, keep out of his mouth, and be still,'" Tootie added.

"Wish I'd been there." Pamela told the truth.

This struck all three friends because they knew enough about Pamela to know she went to great pains to hide her emotions. What you saw was not what you got.

"Maybe she'll let us have a sleepover some weekend after Christmas," Felicity suggested.

"Sister might but I don't know if my adviser will let me go. They're all mad at me. The administration and the faculty, too." Pamela overstated the case.

"Maybe some are, but Mrs. Norton isn't like that. If your grades are good and Bunny says 'okay,' Mrs. Norton will flash you the green light." Valentina liked the headmistress.

"Dad says I'm costing Custis Hall money. He says I'm right to raise the issue but wrong the way I did it. And he said I should never have gone behind Mrs. Norton's back to find Professor Kennedy." The usual defiance wasn't in Pamela's voice.

"What'd your mother say?" Tootie asked.

"She didn't care. I'm overweight. Okay, maybe I'm ten pounds overweight but I'm not Queen Latifah. She doesn't care what I think or what I do. She cares about how I look and that I meet 'the right people.'"

Pamela's voice dripped with sarcasm.

"You are meeting the right people." Valentina smiled her politician's smile. "Hey, you're with us, aren't you?"

"You're so modest, Val." Pamela listened as the bells chimed noon. "Lunch. I'm starved."

"Me, too," Valentina and Felicity said in unison.

They fell in step, walking to the dining hall.

Pamela remarked, "I can't wait for Professor Kennedy's report."

"You missed the point, Pamela." Val sounded as though she were talking to a child. "The stuff in those cases is just stuff. What matters is how Professor Kennedy interprets it, and I still don't see how she can be sure who made what."

Felicity countered Valentina. "If a bit was made by slaves she'll know. That's her field, Val. It is evidence, not interpretation."

"Oh, come on, F." Valentina was impatient, an impatience intensified by hunger. "She can identify some things, sure, but most of it? No one will ever know. And face it, what's a piece of old plate to us?"

Pamela's face darkened. "That's just like you, Valentina."

"What? You're going to pitch a fit over a broken teacup? The stuff is junk. It just happens to be two-hundred-year-old junk, that's all."

"My dad said the real reason this junk, as you call it, is going to cost Custis Hall so much money is once Professor Kennedy's report is delivered, the school will realize the whole security system is inadequate to protect it. He said some items might even be worth hundreds of thousands of dollars."

"So you'd rather have the school raise money to save broken teacups than build a new gym?" Valentina stepped toward Pamela.

"You're so white," Pamela fired right at her.

"And you are so fucked up."

"One dollar."

"Felicity, not now!" Tootie stepped between the two antagonists. "Pamela, it's our heritage, white and black. It's important. Valentina doesn't care about history and it wouldn't matter what color she was. She thinks the world began the day she entered it."

"Tootie!" Valentina raised her voice.

"Hey, Val, that's the truth, but in a sense, you're right. The world began for you, anyway." Tootie returned to Pamela. "But if you're as political as you say you are, then maybe you need to think about the right use of resources. Do you preserve the past or prepare for the future? If you have tons of money, great, do both. If you don't, then I guess I'm with Val, build the gym."

"I knew you'd stick together." Pamela brushed by Valentina with her shoulder as she stomped toward the dining hall, the archway crowded with students hurrying to get in.

"I can't believe you said that about me." Valentina turned on Tootie.

"Look, Val, self-esteem isn't your problem. Do I

care about what's in those cases? I do. Let's eat."

"If we go in riding clothes, Mrs. Childers will give us demerits," Felicity warned.

"Mrs. Childers can stuff it." Valentina's face reddened. "It's a stupid rule."

"Come on, F., what's two demerits?" Tootie cajoled the normally placid Felicity. "We don't have time to change. I'm starved."

"All right." Felicity hated getting demerits.

As they walked toward the graceful archway, Valentina asked Tootie, "Why'd you apply to Virginia Tech?"

"If I don't get into Princeton, Bucknell, or Duke, I'll go to Virginia Tech and stay there. That's where I want to go to veterinary school once I get my B.A."

"Your father isn't going to like that," Felicity said as she shook her head. "He told you he wouldn't pay for it."

"How come I don't know all this?" Val threw up her hands in exasperation. She hated feeling left out.

"Because I only had this discussion with my dad last night and I didn't see you until now. Dad says I'm too smart to be an equine vet; he wants me to be an investment banker. He's being a real shit."

"One dollar." Felicity commiserated but stuck to her mission.

"I owe you one, too." Valentina paid up, as did Tootie.

"Sorry." Valentina was, too. She was blessed with parents who felt she needed to make her own choices, even bad ones. Sometimes a person learns more from a bad choice than a good one, but the important thing was that Valentina's parents trusted her and loved her.

Tootie's father loved her, too, but he pushed her. Her mother, more sympathetic, had ideas about one's place in the world that weren't too dissimilar from Pamela's mother's, although Tootie's mother wasn't quite the snob that Mrs. Rene was.

Felicity's parents, like Valentina's, were one hundred percent supportive. However, if Felicity wanted to do something unusual like take a year off before college and walk through Europe, she would have to earn the money for it. They were very firm that they would pay for her education and only her education.

They walked in silence. Then Felicity piped up, "I think your father is a shit, Tootie." She then took a dollar from her right pocket and put it in her left with the other money.

The administration and the faculty convened at their own tables, which faced the students' tables. Dining under the watchful eye of the adults usually ensured good behavior. The girls would sing but at least there were no food fights, and the singing was quite spirited.

Charlotte knew from Ben Sidel that the corpse was most likely that of Professor Kennedy. He told Charlotte not to reveal this until the tests proved conclusively that it was Professor Kennedy. This would give them both an opportunity to try to pick up the scent.

Charlotte asked if she herself was a suspect. Ben had replied that she shouldn't worry about it. Of course, everyone must be questioned, the answers examined and compared to those of others. That was police work, lots and lots of tiny bits of information pieced together.

She then asked if she or the students were in danger. He said he didn't think the students were but if she came across whatever or whoever was behind this, yes, she was.

Charlotte struggled to act as though all was well. She didn't even confide in her husband because she was told to just wait until the I.D. was confirmed. However, the strain in her face made her look tired, older.

Alpha, sitting next to her today, regaled her with stories about the junior class reading *Twelfth Night.*

". . . they get it."

"It does take some time to adjust to the language. That's a wonderful play to read at this time of year," Charlotte responded as she pushed a spear of asparagus with her fork.

Knute sat on Charlotte's left, Bill on Alpha's right. They tried to keep to the old rule of man, woman, man, woman, but it depended on who came to lunch or dinner that day.

"Any time of year is the right time to read the Bard." Bill stuffed his mouth with gusto.

As Tootie, Valentina, and Felicity walked by, Charlotte called to them, "Girls, come up here when you're finished."

"Are we in trouble?" Valentina was racking her brain to think of what they could have done wrong, apart from wearing riding clothes.

"We're sorry about coming into the hall in our riding clothes, Mrs. Norton," Felicity apologized.

"Sometimes it can't be helped and you're in luck because Mrs. Childers isn't here for lunch." Charlotte smiled at them.

"You mean you aren't going to give us demerits?" Felicity balanced her overflowing plate.

"No." Charlotte shook her head.

"Great!" Valentina breathed deeply.

"If you girls would like a demerit, I'll arrange one or two," Bill teased them.

"No, thank you, Mr. Wheatley." Tootie took this opportunity to head toward a table.

As the girls followed her, Alpha said, "The Three Musketeers."

"Who's d'Artagnan?" Knute loved the Alexandre Dumas novel, but then who didn't.

"Valentina, but a seasoned one, she's past the girl-from-the-country stage," Alpha smiled.

"Well, Tootie's the brains of the bunch," Bill said, pouring more hollandaise sauce on the asparagus, which was quite good for institutional food.

"Let's get her in the administration," Knute laughed.

The holiday season picked up everyone's spirits.

The kids burst with energy and the faculty and administration were looking forward to their vacation as much as the students. The only person not bubbling was Charlotte, but she was trying.

After dessert the three girls came up to Charlotte.

"Ladies, did you keep any notes from your work with Professor Kennedy?"

"Yes, ma'am," they chimed.

"Bring them to me after classes. How about four?"

"Yes, ma'am."

Then Felicity said, "Mrs. Norton, mine are in a notebook."

"That's fine. I want you to sit down and go over your notes with me. And if Pamela has notes, bring her. On second thought, I'll talk to her." She smiled, realizing these three did not get along with Pamela. "What I want to do is review what you found, what you learned, and then when Professor Kennedy's report comes in, we can compare. I think it will be very interesting."

"Yes, ma'am."

"And as my Christmas present to you, you can hunt with Sister Jane this Thursday. The field will be small and you can get up front to see the hounds work."

"Thank you!" Their faces flushed with their good fortune.

"That means you are missing my class," Alpha remarked with sternness.

"Well, Mrs. Rawnsley, I am the culprit," said Charlotte. "Will you accept this absence if they write a book report on Siegfried Sassoon's *Memoirs of a Hunting Man*?"

Alpha's eyes lit up, "Marvelous book. All right, ladies, you have your assignment."

After more thank-yous, the three hurried out of the dining room to the library to check out copies of Sassoon's book. The library boasted extensive hunting titles as well as a vast equine collection. Some of these books were worth hundreds of dollars and could only be read in the rare book room.

Knute watched them hurry out while trying not to run. "You made them happy. I can't imagine their notes will be much."

"At the least there should be descriptions of the items each girl had to handle." Alpha was all for training young people to use their powers of observation and then accurately describe what they saw, heard, felt, tasted, touched.

"I think we're lucky some of it didn't disintegrate in their fingers," Bill added, stifling a laugh.

"Bill, it's not that bad," Knute replied.

"Not that good."

Alpha shrugged, "Mixed blessing."

"Why do you say that?" Charlotte's senses were keen. She looked for anything out of line.

"Custis Hall has a long, dramatic history. Our founder, our benefactors, truly have given so much to this school, but what do we do with it? And Pamela may be a troubled child, an unhappy child, but I think she's hit the nail on the head."

Knute snapped, "By calling us racist pigs, in so many words."

"She was pretty direct." Bill again had to stifle a laugh.

"No." Alpha was accustomed to her male colleagues' flares of ideological passion, or of plain old ego. "She's forcing us to look anew. Her motives are scrambled but then is there anyone on the planet with pure motives? In a way, I think she's done Custis Hall a favor."

Charlotte thought a moment. "Alpha, I think you're right."

"Well, I don't. Whatever this report turns out to be it's going to cost us money." Knute put his right hand on the table, quietly, palm down. "Obviously, some of those pieces have to be worth money. And even if they aren't, they are important to Custis Hall. We're going to have to wire the cases, put up new locks, and who knows what else?"

Bill grimaced. "Nothing has been right since Al was killed."

Knute nodded in agreement. "We'll never find another Al."

"No progress." Alpha's eyebrows raised quizzically.

"Not that I know of," Knute replied.

"It will take time, but you know Sheriff Sidel will keep at it; he's a dedicated man." Charlotte liked Ben Sidel a lot.

"Small-time," Knute simply dismissed Ben.

"Back to the objets d'art or whatever you'd like to

call them." Bill felt expansive after his delicious lunch. "You can't rewire those old cases. You'll have to rebuild everything in there, which means the whole damned hall gets torn up. And the contractors will probably find old horsehair stuffing in the walls, which someone will declare a health hazard. People used horsehair for insulation for centuries and seemed to live quite normal lives, but trust me, it will all be ripped out. And then the old plaster will crumble and that will come out, too. You'll rebuild the interior of the whole damn hall, I'm telling you, and the electrical costs alone will fry you, forgive the pun."

"You're full of Christmas cheer," Knute sourly replied.

"It's the truth. Your worry about security costs is scratching the surface. The security costs will be a pittance compared to the rest of it."

Alpha asked Bill, "Isn't there another way? Does it have to be that extensive?"

Bill laughed, a true belly laugh. "Well, I can make it look like it's wired, like we have a security system. Hell, I can even set up infrared beams. It won't cost the school more than two thousand dollars because I'll throw in my labor for free."

"Bill, that is completely irresponsible!" Knute raised his voice. Those left in the dining hall looked at him. He immediately shut up.

"Why don't we wait for the report?" Charlotte smoothly said as she rose, her folded napkin on the side of the plate.

244

CHAPTER 27

Even in summer's sunshine, Hangman's Ridge exerted a brooding presence. On a cold December night, with clouds piling up on top of the Blue Ridge Mountains, the place reverberated with accumulated sufferings, no matter how well-deserved.

Georgia, exploring her territory, climbed up to the ridge, beheld one murderer's ghost jibbering, and shot down through the underbrush.

She ran up on her mother, Inky, strolling to the kennels.

"I'm not going back up there again!"

"Dead humans," Inky simply said.

"Why don't they go away? Where do they go?" Georgia hadn't considered the human soul.

"Depends on the human, I guess. Some believe they go up to the sky and play harps."

"How strange." Georgia thought that version of an afterlife quite tepid.

"Others think they go to paradise and have forty virgins if they die a martyr's death," Inky wryly commented. *"Exhausting, I should think. And others think they don't go anywhere. And then there are those who think they come back in some other form at some other time."*

"We could have been humans?" Georgia thought out loud.

"I don't know. They call it reincarnation, and if it's true and a human comes back as a fox, it would be a step up," Inky confidently replied.

"Be on four legs. That's a whole lot better right there." Georgia marveled at how humans kept their balance. "How happy they'd be. They could run and jump and turn in midair. They could see at night, too. I hope reincarnation is right."

"I don't know." Inky inhaled the tang of oncoming moisture. "Snow in a few hours. Light, I think."

"My den is warm. I'm glad Sister moved me. Shaker, too. They set out treats."

"They're good that way."

"Where are you going?"

Inky heard a faint complaint in one of the trees as a wren awakened. "Kennels. Thought I'd see if Diana would be out for a walk. She likes to sit still at night and listen. She's very enjoyable."

"May I join you?"

"Yes, that's a good idea. It's time you got to know the hounds and they you."

As the two foxes passed Shaker's cottage they inhaled cinnamon. Lorraine's car was parked in the drive, a light sheen of frost forming on the windshield.

A pair of headlights just missed them, turning left toward the main house.

"I'd like to ride in a car," Inky mused, as she reached the outdoor gyp run.

Cora, also out for a walk, heard her. "It's fun unless you ate too much. Makes you sick."

"Cora, this is Georgia, one of my daughters. The other one made a den at Mill Ruins. Georgia, this is Cora, she's the strike hound. That means she usually finds the scent first and runs up front."

"You're the young one Sister and Shaker put in the apple orchard," Cora noted as Diana came alongside.

More introductions followed.

"Diana is the anchor hound. She is the leader, she tells the others what to do if they need it."

"You'll learn how to foil your scent, how to double back. There's a lot you can do to throw us off or slow us down. If we get too close, duck into a den, anybody's den," Cora advised.

"You're only half-grown, Georgia. Don't go too far from your den this year. There's a lot to eat right here around the kennel and stables. Learn all you can before going out on long runs." Diana also gave sensible advice.

"Will you kill me?" Georgia worried.

"I'd roll you first." Cora told the truth. "Blast off sideways. Whatever you do, don't reverse your direction, because you'll run smack into the entire pack since I'm usually first. Just go sideways and run like hell. If you can't find a den, climb. But this year, really, don't go far from home. Dragon, especially, can't be trusted. He's out to kill."

"That's one of my brothers," Diana informed her. "The other one, Dasher, is fast, too, but he has a lot more sense."

"You should stick close to home, anyway, honey. It's

247

one thing if a pack of foxhounds do their job. It's another if a hound that's been left out by deer hunters or one that's lost comes around. They'll eat anything, and that includes you. You need to learn the ropes," Inky said firmly.

"I will," Georgia promised. "Why would a human turn out a hound?"

"Cheap," Diana replied.

"Pardon me?" Georgia was a polite young fox.

"Too cheap to feed them once deer season is over. Now, the coon hunters will rarely turn out a hound. Bear hunters, too, but there are many, many more deer hunters than those other kinds. Some of them are bottom-feeders." Cora did not mince words.

"And Sister gets blamed for any problem with any hound. Someone sees a hound, they think it's one of ours. Doesn't even look like a foxhound but most people don't know the different types of hounds. Once deer season ends, Sister, Shaker, Betty, Walter, and Sybil are out picking up starving hounds. The SPCA can't adopt them out very easily because people think hounds are dumb. It's pretty awful." Diana loved Sister and worried when her dear old human friend became worried.

"What happens to the hounds?" Georgia asked.

"Well, whoever picks one up has to get him healthy once again. Once the animal is okay they housebreak him and then call all their friends to see if someone will take a stray. Most foxhunters will help a hound, if they can. But it's sure a lot of work." Cora lifted her fur. The cold was settling in.

"Why would a human be so . . . so . . . horrible to a hound? To let an animal starve and in the winter, too?" Georgia was shocked.

"Georgia, they let their own children starve, some of them. They even abandon their children," Inky told her.

"How can an animal abandon her cubs?" Georgia just couldn't believe it.

"They do." Cora lifted her head straight up to the sky. *"And they kill other people's children."*

"They walk up to the den and kill them?" Georgia was bowed under the weight of this news.

"Let's put this in order," Diana, always thinking, said. *"No, they don't walk up to a human den and shoot their children. It usually is some sick human. He'll snatch them off the streets—in big cities mostly. You don't have much of that in the country, but humans will kill other humans' children in wars, by the millions. It's very hard for a hound or a fox to imagine that kind of bloodlust. But really, Georgia, millions die in wars."*

"I don't know what a million is," Georgia soberly replied.

"They don't either. They just think they do." Inky laughed.

"Would Sister kill children?" Georgia was perturbed.

"No," Cora and Diana replied in unison.

"Do a lot of them do this?" Georgia wondered.

"Enough for it to be a problem, apart from war, I mean," Diana said. *"War is different. They can kill and it's all right. I can't explain why, but they truly believe this. You can kill anyone you want as long as they are on the other side. Men, women, children, it doesn't matter. They call them an enemy so it's not like killing your neighbor. They don't have to think about it."*

"Do they eat what they kill?"

"No, Georgia, they aren't allowed to do that," Inky flatly replied. *"That's forbidden."*

"Unless they are starving. But even then, it's a terrible taboo. If they eat another human sometimes they lose their minds because it's so horrible to them," Cora interjected.

"Let me understand, a human being can kill millions of other human beings if it's called war and that's okay. But a human being can't eat another human being?" Georgia paused. *"It doesn't make sense."*

"No one ever suggested it did. But that's humans for you," Diana said. *"There was a dead human under St. John's of the Cross, but we couldn't pull it out. Now, that is kind of unusual. Even if they kill, and kill in numbers, they do their best to bury or burn."*

"Couldn't a human have crawled under there to die?" Georgia already knew how some animals chose to die.

"They don't die like that. They flop down and croak." Cora giggled. *"I mean they just flop around like a chicken. It's because they don't listen to their*

bodies so they don't know when they're going to die. They deny it and then they just die in front of everyone unless they're in a hospital or something. We've been talking, those of us who hunted that day, about the body at St. John's. We didn't see it. Smelled it. The humans couldn't."

"*Is it a bad thing?*" Georgia asked.

"*It is,*" and Diana fretted over this. "*And Target has a ring. We're pretty sure it came from that body because he said it was on a finger. He doesn't have the finger anymore. He's been bragging to everyone about the ring. He hoards stuff.*"

"*He even has a Day-Glo Frisbee.*" Inky laughed.

"*Charlene made him find his own den.*" Cora mentioned Target's mate. "*She said she couldn't stand the clutter. He won't give up anything.*"

"*Are all dog foxes like that?*" Georgia really was a youngster.

"*We'll talk about males some other time,*" Inky replied as Cora and Diana laughed.

"*I heard that,*" Ardent called from the boys' run, which made them all laugh more.

CHAPTER 28

All living things, plants and animals, have optimum living conditions. Even plants have patterns; in their case it's when they pollinate, bloom, and bear fruit. For the higher vertebrates the patterns center on food, shelter, mating, and rearing the young.

Sister rested her hands on Keepsake's withers. Her white string gloves warded off the cold. The snow rested in crevices of rocks, down in the crease of ravines, and on the north side of those hills that received little sun because of the winter angle of the sun. Winds had blown off some of the snow; bald patches of ground dotted the meadows.

The sky, crystal clear, brilliant blue, heralded one of those high-pressure systems that delight the eye but make scenting difficult.

Knowing her quarry, Sister searched for evidence of last night's hunting, a tuft of feathers here, a hank of cottontail fur, sweet little berries, dried now, nibbled off lower branches of bushes and scrubs. If hunting had been spectacularly good, whole pieces of the kill would be strewn around as the fox ate the best parts and took other delicacies home to stash. Foxes, like humans, believed in bank accounts.

She caught her breath, for they'd had a fifteen-minute burst at top speed and they were lucky to have it considering the day. The hounds threw up, which is to say they lost the line, and Diana as well as Shaker were trying to figure out if they overran the line or simply zigged when they should have zagged.

When a high-pressure system is in place, the air is dry, almost light. Sound carries true to origin whereas in heavy moisture the ear can be fooled by the horn, the cry, or even the chatter of birds. It sounds as though it's coming from one direction, but in fact it's coming from another. Even on a high-pressure day, sound ricochets off mountains, hillocks.

Sister was a good field master. She kept the huntsman and the hounds in sight most times. Sometimes, though, she couldn't. St. Hubert himself would fall behind. On those days, she used her ears and her knowledge of quarry.

She knew the fox was close by. She also knew the luxurious trail of scent wouldn't hold on this bright meadow, which was the very reason the fox bolted from the covert only to cross the meadow. Sybil gave out a "Tally ho," but by the time hounds were set on the line, the saucy red devil scurried a healthy seven minutes ahead of the hounds.

Sister thought of the meeting the previous night with Charlotte and Ben, who joined them later. She was especially glad that Gray was with her as he possessed a logical mind.

Ben suggested the meeting. Since Sister and Gray had discovered the body, there was no point in pretending to them that it wasn't Professor Kennedy. While they couldn't identify the body given the leaves and such covering it, they could see enough to know the corpse was slight, perhaps female.

She knew that Ben, waiting for conclusive lab evidence in making an I.D. before relating more information, was trying to figure out the pattern of his quarry.

Charlotte, on the other hand, wanted to see if there was a connection between Al Perez and Professor

Kennedy. She couldn't find one. They may not have known each other, but she believed the second death was related to the first.

Gray took in all the conversation, then laid out what they knew and what they didn't know like the excellent tax lawyer he was. Trained to look for loopholes, he found an oddity, perhaps not a loophole. The first death had been staged. The second death had been hidden.

They batted around the possible meanings of that but could go no further than the seemingly obvious, which was the first death was a gaudy warning before an entire audience. The second removed a person who somehow got in the way.

Gray suggested there could be more than one type of irregularity. The artifacts could house illegal drugs, or pharmaceutical drugs from Canada here to be resold at cheaper prices than American prices. Smuggled diamonds might be on certain clothes or items like sword hilts without arousing suspicion. Hide it out in the open.

Ben wanted to keep the artifacts intact. He didn't want to go through them just yet. He asked Charlotte to check each night, then each morning, to see if anything had been disturbed.

"We're in a waiting game" was all he said.

It gave them all a lot to think about.

Diana loped on a diagonal and the pack fanned out. Shaker liked for them to cast themselves. This nurtured their self-confidence. Not all huntsmen do that.

Some direct their hounds, lifting them, setting them down in another covert, directing their every move. This was a matter of personality as well as the type of hound.

Both Sister and Shaker believed the American hound would figure it out faster without their interference.

As she watched her hounds work, she remembered it was December 8, one of the principal feast days of the Blessed Virgin Mother. Today was the Feast of the Immaculate Conception of Mary in the womb of her mother, St. Anne. She mused about these immaculate conceptions, a bizarre twist in a patriarchal religion. She thought it an odd manifestation of male self-hate as well as a perverse nod to female power, to the remnants of matriarchy that even a religion as violently antiwoman as Islam can't quite eradicate.

Sister did not think of herself as a religious woman, although she attended the Episcopal church. Her deepest belief was that religion is in the service of political power. Spirituality is not. She couldn't imagine foxes dying for their version of God or blowing themselves up among the Infidel, believing they would immediately ascend to paradise and be rewarded with forty fat chickens.

The longer she lived, the more she pitied the human animal and admired the fox.

These ruminations evaporated as Diana, with an assist from the steady Asa, found the line again. Barely perceptible it was, but as the two determined hounds trotted across the meadow, down the hillside, frost visible on the bare patches, the aroma of fox intensified. They opened, the others honored, and off they ran.

By the time the intrepid band returned to the trailers they'd been rewarded with some excellent hound work and three bracing runs in the bargain.

Sister felt these were the days that make your pack. Any pack looks great on a good day. It's the trying days that reveal how they work together, how much drive and intelligence they display. She loved her pack of hounds beyond measure.

Valentina, Tootie, and Felicity, wreathed in smiles, walked by Sister before they dismounted.

"Good evening, Master."

"Good evening, girls."

"Thank you for the day."

"You know I'm happy when you hunt with me." She smiled as they rode to the big Custis Hall van where Bunny, her horse untacked, waited.

Pleased that the three young women correctly addressed her, saying "Good evening, Master" even though it was twelve noon, she made a note to give them each a different classic hunting book for Christmas.

Betty rode up. "I was in the back of the beyond."

As she dismounted Sister said, "How was it?"

"Cold. Heard Sybil viewed the fox away."

She's improving so much as a whipper-in. It's good to see that, isn't it, considering the ups and downs of her life."

"Hell, Jane, in this group anyone over thirty is riding the roller coaster." Betty undid the noseband of Outlaw's bridle, slipping off the martingale.

"Make it forty. Some of our group are slow learners." Sister laughed.

"And some don't learn at all." Betty looped the martingale through the breastplate.

"Scary, isn't it?" Sister considered Betty one of her best friends. She wanted to talk to her about Professor Kennedy's murder because Betty had a good mind, but Ben told her to keep quiet until he released the I. D., which would most likely be next Monday or Tuesday.

"Well, it is until you consider it makes the rest of us look smart." She tossed the cooler over Outlaw's back, keeping the saddle on although loosening the girth.

Both Sister and Betty kept their saddles on until the horses were back to the barn. They thought it kept their backs warm. Once in the wash stall they'd be cleaned with warm water, wiped down, put in a stall to eat without pinning their ears at another horse in the field. When dry, on would go the winter rugs and they'd be turned out to walk around, visit with friends, and be horses. The closer a creature can be to its natural state, the happier it is. Unfortunately people haven't learned this about horses, but then, they haven't learned it about themselves. At least Sister and Betty agreed on that and had many a deep conversation on the neurosis, self-inflicted, of the human animal.

As the two friends reviewed the day's hunt, the three girls returned to Sister's trailer, having taken care of their own horses.

"Sister," Valentina said, "we'll miss you over Christmas vacation. But we'll be back in time for New Year's Hunt."

"You'll be here for the hunt ball?"

"I will," Tootie smiled.

"Me, too," Valentina agreed. "Then I fly home."

"Ditto," Felicity said.

"Well, you know if anything goes wrong and you're stuck at the airport, call; Shaker or I will pick you up. I don't want you all stranded. The school shuts down on Christmas so you can't go back to the dorm."

"Me, too, kids." Betty scribbled down her cell number on the back of her business card. "You never know with that small airport. The weather can turn in a heartbeat."

"Thanks." They really were glad.

Tootie hung back as the other two walked away. "Sister, if my parents will let me, can I stay with you after the hunt ball? Until Thursday, then I'll fly home, too." She waited a minute. "I, well, I'm happier here than home but I'll go home. I know I have to do it."

"Honey, of course you can. You ask your parents and then if you'll give me their number, I'll talk to them. You know, parents always want the best for their children, but sometimes they can forget that you have to find your own way. Is it something like that?"

Tootie nodded. "Dad wants me to be an investment banker," she said in a rare burst of emotion. "I'd die."

"Don't do that. I'll invite your parents to come stay here if they'd like, sometime when it's convenient. I'd like to get to know them, and maybe, Tootie, if they see what you love, they'll begin to understand."

Tootie threw her arms around the tall woman. "You are the best!"

After she walked away, Betty said, "I can see both sides of the story, can't you?"

"H-m-m."

"That girl is brilliant. Her father translates that into money, prestige, comfort. She belongs in the country even though she wasn't raised in the country. She belongs with animals just like you and I do. We're born that way, you know."

"I do. You're a good mother, Betty, you never pushed your kids. Yes, you made them do homework and all that, but you allowed them to be themselves."

"Christmas is hard, Janie."

"Betty, you *are* a good mother. Cody blew up her life. You didn't. As for Jennifer, she's a fabulous kid and having her and Sari back for Christmas vacation will be a joy. I love having kids in the house. I expect Sari and Lorraine will be here more than they'll be at Alice's. Well, they'll spend some time with Alice."

"Wonder if Shaker will marry Lorraine?"

"He will, but he has to approach this in his own way. He's so cautious now." Sister patted Keepsake on the neck as she led him first into the trailer.

259

The tailgate was light since Thursday's field was small.

Soon, Sister and Betty followed the hound party wagon down the winding dirt road to the paved road on the way home.

"What's wrong?" Betty flatly asked.

"Preoccupied."

"Jane Arnold."

Sister glanced at Betty, then back at the road since she was driving the rig. "Betty, Ben Sidel has asked me to keep quiet until Monday, as in not speak to anyone. And I will talk to you then, but I have to honor my promise. I am preoccupied. Something is very, very wrong at Custis Hall. Al Perez's death will lead us to something, if I only knew what."

"You think other people will be killed?"

"I do."

Betty grimaced. "Good God. What's worth killing over?"

"Motive, means, opportunity. We know the means. We know the window of opportunity for Al's murder. We lack the motive."

"Money or sex."

"Betty, that sounds good, but as I get older I think there are a lot more motives."

"Like what?"

"Prestige, not losing one's status. Religious fanaticism or political fanaticism. Even economic fanaticism. People will kill when a new technology displaces them or if they think a current one is evil. I mean what about that American physician in 2004 going over to England and encouraging the antivivisectionists to kill the doctors engaging in experiments? People will kill for anything that makes sense to them. Doesn't have to make sense to us."

"Vivisection is wrong. Just flat wrong."

"I totally agree, but I'm not going to a lab and blowing up people in white lab coats. You can make change out of the barrel of a gun—thank you, Chairman Mao, another fat hypocrite for you—but it doesn't stick. Sooner or later, when the people have the ability, they sabotage or organize against the change. Or they try to turn back the clock. The only way change can work is with consensus, and that takes time, talking to people, listening to people, respecting the differences. It's the longer route, the seemingly harder route, but, ultimately, the successful route, and Betty, there is no other way. We have all of history to prove that point."

"Well," Betty thought a long time, "you're right. But who is going to listen to two middle-aged country women?"

"One middle-aged country woman. This girl is old."

"Bullshit."

"You say the nicest things to me."

They laughed, then Betty returned to the murder. "I'm glad Christmas vacation is coming. I'm glad those girls will be out of here."

"Me, too. This thing isn't finished."

CHAPTER 29

Her heels clicking on the highly polished floor, Charlotte walked through the Main Hall on her way to her office.

Bill Wheatley and Knute Nilsson stood in front of the case containing Washington's epaulettes.

"Knute, you look mournful," Charlotte said.

"I was thinking about the lemonade stand I had when I was six. I made two dollars and I thought I was rich. Well, I was. I went home and that night I bragged to my father how much lemonade I sold. He seemed proud of me, but he warned me, 'Now that you have assets, you have to protect them.' I look at all this stuff and I see assets." He waved his hand as if this was boring. "You've heard it all before. I don't know what we're going to do."

Bill, his usual ebullient self, put his arm around Knute's shoulder. "You don't have to figure it out before Christmas vacation. You don't even have to figure it out when Professor Kennedy's report comes in. You are perfectly within your rights to ask the board of directors for suggestions and help. Doesn't do you any good to carry the weight of the world, or at least Custis Hall, on your shoulders. Besides, Knute, there's Christmas to celebrate."

"An excuse to waste money."

"Knute, stuff cloves in oranges and give them as

gifts. Won't cost more than twenty dollars and they smell wonderful," Charlotte suggested with a hint of merriment.

"I know, I know, you two think I'm Scrooge."

"We think no such thing." Bill let his arm slide off Knute's back. "We know! Except for your sailing hobby you are tighter than the bark on a tree."

"All right. I'm leaving." Knute half-smiled and headed toward the hall containing the offices.

Bill turned to Charlotte. "He'll worry himself into a heart attack. There is such a thing as being too conscientious."

"Perhaps, but that's why we depend on you, Bill, to lighten the mood."

"I'll take that as a compliment."

"Do. I hear that you and some of the students in your department have come up with a fantastic theme for the hunt ball. Marty Howard told me the best thing she ever did was get you all involved."

"You just wait and see." He winked. "Silver and white. Crawford and Marty appear to have a limitless budget. Even Knute and Yvonne are going to come, and you know how hard it is to get him in a tuxedo."

"That puzzles me. If a gentleman wears scarlet, that's tails. So why aren't hunt balls white tie?"

"Technically, they should be, but I guess allowing men to wear tuxedos is a nod to the wallet. More men own a tuxedo than black tails. Of course, if they would wear white tie the effect would be smashing." He glowed; he loved costumes and staging. "You'll be in white or black?"

"I surprised myself and my husband. I bought a white gown from Nordstrom. I am sick of wearing black."

"You'll look beautiful no matter what."

"Bill, you flatter me and I am grateful. Okay, I have one more question since you study these things. Since Jane Arnold is master, why can't she wear scarlet?"

"Well, that's a good one. If she wanted to upset the applecart, she could. She's the master, right? Who could stop her? But convention and unwritten laws are stronger than the written ones. A hunt ball decrees that women wear white or black. That's it and you know as well as I do that Sister is a slave to tradition. She doesn't wear scarlet in the hunt field, and many American lady masters do."

"Actually, Bill, given our recent uproar here, I'd not use the word 'slave.'" The corners of her mouth turned upward. She knew how much Bill devoured a tête-à-tête and this little comment would delight him.

He lowered his head, whispering in her ear, "A servant to fashion."

She whispered back, "I look forward to all of us being servants to fashion." She gazed into the display case. "Those epaulettes look brighter than I remember."

"When Professor Kennedy took everything out to examine and photocopy, she had the girls clean them. Pamela, wearing surgical gloves, began to repent of her protest when all that dust and mold shot up her nose." He laughed.

"Well, maybe we won't have to clean for another few decades." She paused. "Guess not, huh?"

"Hey, for all I know, Knute will install a system where the air circulates and the objets d'art or d'histoire clean themselves. Actually, I shouldn't poke fun at him; it really has become one hell of a burden."

"I guess it's like his father said, protect your assets. Bill, back to my desk, though I'd much rather talk to you. I really do look forward to seeing what you all do for the ball."

"You'll never forget it."

CHAPTER 30

Nine more days," Marty fretted as she twirled her pencil around in her fingers.

Sorrel, sitting across from her at the table in Marty's opulent kitchen, checked her yellow notepad. "We're sold out. At least we don't have to get on the horn and push for RSVPs. People don't RSVP like they used to do. I can't decide if it's because they don't know any better or everyone's on overload."

"A little of both, maybe." Marty peered down at her own notebook, a lavender-paged stenographer's notebook, pages covered with names, numbers, arrows pointing up, down, right, and left and some squiggling along the margins.

"Bill says he and the girls will be at the Great Hall at seven A.M. I'll be there, too."

"That's a good idea. It's probably also a good idea to just let him run the show. If he needs more bodies, we can supply them, but Bill can do this in his sleep." Marty thought snagging Bill Wheatley was one of her biggest coups.

"You've checked the silent auction list?"

"Yes. We still need more high-ticket items. We've got caps from other hunts, always a nice idea. We've got framed prints, a weekend at Grand Cayman Island, another weekend with theater tickets in New York. Patricia Kluge and Bill Moses have donated a case of their wine. Jay Tomlinson donated one free shoeing. Nothing like a good blacksmith to keep your horse right." Marty tapped the pencil on her frosted lipstick. "I know we need things that are affordable for most people but we need one or two very spectacular items like the weekend in New York."

"I've racked my brain." Sorrel leaned back in the ladderback chair—not an easy thing to do, so she tipped on the back legs.

"What about jewelry? A gorgeous antique pair of studs, you know, gold foxhead studs with ruby eyes for a gentleman and maybe a brooch with a fox-hunting theme. What about those painted crystals from England? You know, the round things, oh, they can be earrings or pins or even cuff links."

"Marty, you can't find antique ones. No one gives them up until death, and a new pair of cuff links might cost $2,500. We can't even buy them wholesale to put them in the auction." She read down the list again. "The Lionel Edwards prints ought to fetch at least $2,500, don't you think?"

"I hope so. Those," she read her own notes, "were donated by Henry Xavier, God bless him."

"Riding lessons from Sam Lorillard." Marty smiled. "I didn't have to lean on him. He wanted to do it."

"What about a tax review by Gray?" Sorrel wondered.

"Well, he'd do it, but that's not exactly a festive item. He's already donated a white vest; how many of those do you see?" Marty thought she might bid on it for her husband, then realized that Gray was more fit and slender than Crawford, who was fighting the battle of the bulge.

"I guess we can't ask Bill to take on a decorating job, you know, someone's den?" Sorrel didn't want to go to the well too often.

"No, maybe Dolly Buswell would give a consultation. Now, that's pretty appealing." Marty cited a local interior decorator.

"I'll call her."

They sat there, then Marty said, "It's a good list. You've done a great job." Then she paused. "It's that one spectacular item that eludes us."

"Free breeding to Salem Drive and Tom Newton also donated a breeding to Harbor Man." Sorrel thought that was pretty good as both Thoroughbreds had useful bloodlines for foxhunters.

"Sure, that appeals to horsepeople, but I'm thinking of a spectacular piece of jewelry, an antique car, or a carriage or buggy. Now, the sculpture Crawford donated is good. I'm thinking along those lines. Big-ticket items."

"Do we have any pals at Tiffany's?" Sorrel lusted after a pair of pearl-and-diamond earrings priced at $16,500. Not that she could afford them.

"Not good enough to donate the earrings," Marty said with a sigh.

Sorrel sighed, too. "We have nine days. Maybe I can find a pal at Tiffany's. Well, we've got to keep pushing."

They double-checked the menu; the open bar would last for an hour, then switch to a paying bar. Finally they settled into an exchange of news and views over hot chocolate.

"She's so drawn. I hope she's not sick." Marty was referring to Charlotte Norton.

"I expect she's worried half to death. Until Ben Sidel nails Al's murderer, she has to feel vulnerable. You know parents will have long talks with their kids over Christmas vacation, and I'm sure some won't return to Custis Hall. I'm surprised more weren't yanked out of here."

"Charlotte's a brilliant headmaster. She's contained the damage as much as she can, reassured students and parents as much as she can."

"Sorrel, isn't it funny how people respond to things? Sister says little, keeps going, but since she saw that hanging and it was on Hangman's Ridge, you know that brain is whirring at high speed. And she won't rest until the killer is found either. Then there's Bill Wheatley. Cried about Al's death, then bounced right back, his old jolly self. As for Ben, it's his business. Can't expect him to be emotionally involved. Crawford says the board meetings are strained, everyone is worried, but at least no one is blaming anyone else or fighting out of frustration. But he said they are all affected by this."

"Someone stands to gain something. Hard to imagine, though." Sorrel reflected on her own experiences. "I still wonder if this doesn't lead to sex. You just never know."

"No, you don't."

The back door opened. Crawford stepped into the kitchen—all marble tops, recessed lighting, a Sub-Zero refrigerator, and an Aga stove. The cost of the kitchen exceeded the cost of most homes. The heart pine flooring provided what visual warmth there was, that and the huge step-down fireplace, a nod to Sister's fireplace, except this one was all gorgeous veined white marble that echoed the marble on the counters.

"Hello, Sorrel, how are you?"

"Fine, and yourself?"

"Cold."

"Sit down, honey, I'll make you a hot chocolate." Marty rose as Crawford removed his coat.

"Oh, hey." He reached into the pocket as he hung it

up. "Here. Put that in the auction since I see you've got out your lists." He dropped a ring into Sorrel's hands.

"That's pretty."

"Might get a hundred dollars."

Marty walked over to inspect it. "Good gold. The onyx is lovely. Where'd you buy that? I thought you were out with Sister today fixing jumps. X crashed into that timber jump," she hastened to add. "Wasn't his fault. By the time he reached it the footing was horrendous."

"We fixed that first and then you know Sister. She always kills two birds with one stone. She had buckets of feed on the back of the pickup. I mean she had the entire bed filled with fifty-pound bags. We used them. Anyway, this was outside a den at Tedi and Edward's. Sister said it was Target's den. She remembers every fox. Don't know how she does it. They look red or gray to me." He was in a good mood.

"Isn't that odd?" Marty poured the milk onto the cocoa.

"She said some foxes are pack rats. They can't resist shiny things, toys. I peeked into his den and there was a baseball in there. She said he'll take any toy the dogs leave out and so will Uncle Yancy, another of her foxes. But she said Uncle Yancy prefers clothing more than toys. He'll steal hats, T-shirts, barn rags." He shook his head. "She loves these animals. I think she loves them almost as much as her hounds."

"Hey, why don't we put, 'donated by Target, red fox

living at After All.'" Sorrel sat up straight, eyes bright.

Crawford shrugged. "Might bring another hundred dollars."

CHAPTER 31

M ill Ruins, so named because of the massive stone gristmill, and the huge waterwheel still turning the gears inside, had been the estate of Peter Wheeler. Given Peter's penchant for losing money, the word "estate" was used loosely. To the now-deceased Peter's credit, he hung on, never selling one acre of land. He thought the mill would be a tourist attraction and he ground grain there. This provided enough cash to feed his horses, though not himself. Peter finally hired himself out as a lawyer, a profession he hated despite his training at the University of Virginia.

Christmas Hunt had been held at the Wheeler place—Peter was the seventh-generation Wheeler to live at the mill—since 1887. The hunt was usually held on the Saturday before Christmas unless that Saturday happened to be Christmas Eve. This year Saturday was December 24, so Christmas Hunt was December 17. Many clubs did go out on Christmas Eve, but long ago prior masters at the Jefferson Hunt determined it was too busy a day for most people to braid horses and spend four hours, more or less, in the saddle.

The "ruins" referred to the rest of the place as it began to fall into rack and ruin. Although he made a decent living at the prestigious law firm eager to have the Wheeler name attached to it, he spent only on his mill, his horses, his fencing, and his feed. At the end of his life, he lived mostly in the kitchen, with its fierce wood-burning stove, and a bed he put in the large pantry off the kitchen. He drove his 454 Chevy pickup proudly down to the office. His turnout, at work and in the hunt field, was always correct—he just didn't care about the rest of it.

He fought daily with his neighbor, Alice Ramy. He knew foxhunting and he loved true foxhunters, which meant he loved Jane Arnold best of all. Their affair lasted for close to twenty-five years. A big, booming, rugged man with refined manners, Peter kept his looks way into his seventies. He loved Sister because she was strong, smart, and thought like a fox. Each was the other's grand passion as far as people were concerned. Their true grand passion was foxhunting.

When Peter died peacefully sitting in his kitchen chair, he had willed Mill Ruins to Jefferson Hunt as well as the Chevy 454. Rooster, his young harrier, he personally willed to Sister.

As she sat atop Aztec gazing over the large field on this nippy Saturday morning, she thought of how fortunate she'd been with the men in her life. They were real men, accustomed to physical exertion; no task was too dirty or too difficult. Sister never could warm to soft men. Then again, she scared the bejesus out of them, so it worked out just fine.

The last Christmas of Peter's life, he drove his truck—he could no longer ride as his hips had been shattered once too often—in full regalia: black weazlebelly, top hat, the works. She fought back the tears then and she fought back the tears now.

Walter lived at Mill Ruins, renting it from the hunt club. He had a long-term lease, which helped the coffers grow. He poured money into the place. Slowly, Mill Ruins returned to its former glory. It needed a wife, children, chickens, dogs, and cats running about to be absolutely perfect. Walter, however, did have a pet fox with one paw that had been amputated and a sweet little Welsh terrier.

Sister thought of Peter as Walter welcomed the crowd to his place on this, the third of the High Holy Days. She refocused on the present. Ninety-eight people sat on braided horses, puffs of condensed air escaping from their nostrils.

The Custis Hall girls with the exception of Tootie and Valentina, not big into the theater program, were decorating the Great Hall under Bill Wheatley's direction. Apart from their absence most of the riding membership was present.

Aztec fidgeted. This was his first High Holy Day. He could feel the excitement from humans and horses.

Finally the formalities were over, Sister called "Hounds, please," and off they walked down toward the great three-story mill, the millrace running hard and fast to the wheel. An arched stone bridge carried

273

them over the millrace. As the wheel turned, flumes of water slid off the paddles, spraying thousands of rainbows into the air. The smell of water, of grain, of the damp stone foundation filled everyone's nostrils. As they passed the mill, they came onto a wide farm road that ran through a small pasture and then into a heavy woods.

It wasn't until he reached the woods that Shaker realized Lorraine was on a horse. He was so intense when hunting, in this case when he was holding the hounds, that he barely noticed the people. He glanced up once or twice but it only now registered. A grin crossed his face and he regretted that he couldn't ride back to the Hilltoppers and give her the biggest kiss.

Heavy frost silvered the pastures, the low shrubs in the woods, some with bright red berries, a contrast to the world of silver, gray, brown, and black.

Delight whispered to Diddy, *"What do you think?"*

"Need the temperature to come up five degrees. Then even a human could put his nose to the ground and get it."

"We can get something off the frost." Trident also whispered because talking on the way to a cast is considered babbling.

None of the hounds wanted to be censured.

"Have to hit it right and be careful not to overrun. It's not as hard as people make it out to be." Ardent, older and wiser, quietly encouraged the younger hounds. *"Go a little slower until you're sure. You have a long nose to warm the air you inhale, so you'll pick*

it up. Just be more deliberate."

"Why didn't Shaker cast us at the mill? All the foxes go there." Diddy liked learning.

"Not sure." Dreamboat wondered why, as well.

"Better to pick up a fox on the way to the mill than one on the way out. If he's eaten any grain he'll just turn around and go into the mill. This way we might get a longer run," Ardent again explained. *"There's an art to it, kids. Shaker's got it. Trust your huntsman."*

"What happens if you get a stupid huntsman?" Diddy wondered.

"Hounds ignore him and do what they want." Ardent laughed. *"Never been one at Jefferson Hunt. Never will be, not as long as Sister's the human anchor hound."*

"Getting a little loose, kids," Shaker quietly reprimanded them.

They continued walking, as he didn't cast until they reached the edge of the woods and jumped over the lovely stone fencing into the pasture. He swung the hounds crosswind, then turned Gunpowder's nose toward the woods. The hounds fanned out over the middle of the pasture but kept in mind the direction of Gunpowder. They'd work a big half circle before moving into the woods, where they would be directly into the light wind.

Dasher found a stale line. He kept with it, hoping it would freshen. It didn't. So Cora, after checking that line, moved twenty yards away. Although mid-

December, sometimes the grays will begin courting. Courting time varies greatly with how the foxes interpret the coming spring's food supply. Somehow, they know. If it's going to be an early, fecund spring, the grays will start in December in Virginia. The reds usually follow suit two to three weeks later.

Cora wanted to hit early. On a day like today, the fox had most of the advantages, but the sun washing over the pasture would warm the scent if a fox had crossed over.

Old lines continued to tantalize them but not enough to open. No point boohooing on a stale line. It might sound great to the humans but mostly you'd walk your fox to death if hounds even got close to him. If a Jefferson hound was going to open, it would open on a strong, fresh line. Therefore, they had to work together very well and possess great drive. Colder-nosed hounds don't need all that much drive because they'll always find something to talk about. The Jefferson hounds had good noses but they weren't what's called cold-nosed, as some other types of foxhounds are. Each type of foxhound has its devotee, and always for good reasons.

"Let's go into the woods," Cora commanded.

"Be colder in there." Trinity questioned Cora's judgment, not a good idea.

"Yes, it will, you impertinent pup! And the fox knows that, too. He'll be a little more lax traveling through the underbrush. Don't you ever question me again or I'll roll you in front of everyone, humans included."

"Yes, ma'am."

Cora trotted ahead, leapt over the stone wall, landing on soft, moist earth. These woods, mostly hardwoods, carried a different scent than evergreen woods. The scent of pine could be overwhelming in those woods, beautiful though they were.

She put her nose down. The rest of the pack crawled or leapt over. On landing they moved forward like the front line of a football team. To anyone loving hound work, this was an impressive sight. Not one hound lagged behind or skirted off.

For twenty minutes they worked in silence, total dedication.

"I got it!" Trudy, thrilled to be the first, shouted.

Cora noted the direction of Trudy's travel, ran ahead of her by ten yards, put her nose down, and honored the third-year bitch's finding. The rest of the pack fell on the line so quickly that Shaker didn't have to blow the tripled notes in succession. He went right to one long note, tripled notes, repeating this three times. Betty and Sybil, on either side of the pack but about a quarter mile out, heard and knew it was time to press on.

Sister patted Aztec's neck, held him a moment so Shaker could get far enough ahead of her that she wouldn't crowd him, then she squeezed the six-year-old Thoroughbred and he answered with a smooth surge of power like the acceleration of a Mercedes 500S.

Sister reached the farm road in the woods. When the

hounds turned hard left, she picked up the deer trail that Shaker, too, had picked up.

She emerged on the other side of the woods, where a twenty-acre field of Alamo switchgrass waved in the wind. This was one of Walter's forage experiments. Turned out to be useful for cattle but not much good for horses. The mice, ground nesters, and foxes sure liked it, though.

The hounds were in the switchgrass. Sister could see the long slender grasses bending as the hounds moved through. She usually rode around the outside of any planted field, but Walter yelled up, "Go on. I don't care."

Heeding her joint master's advice, she plunged into the tall grasses, some swishing up over her feet, tickling Aztec's belly.

The music filled the air, a crescendo as sweet as Bach to a musician. Deep voices, middle voices, and the odd high notes of younger hounds blended into a chorus that had thrilled mankind since before the pyramids were built.

Artemis smiled on the hounds today. The mercury crept up to forty-two degrees, the air moist, low, the sky various shades of gray. Scenting was perfect.

Sister and Aztec blew through the twenty acres in a few heartbeats to soar over a tiger trap jump in the new fence line Walter built himself. They galloped down into a crevice in the next meadow, a tiny rivulet feeding a larger creek some half mile off, bisecting this whole meadow, which was in redbud clover.

Aztec, beautifully balanced, powered over the frosty pasture. Then over an imposing hog's back jump, two strides, and a drop jump from the bank onto another low farm road heading at a ninety-degree right angle straight west.

The fox followed the shady part of the road, tiny ice crystals jutting out of the earth. This slowed the hounds down slightly, but the minute he crossed over another frosty redbud clover meadow, they picked up speed.

They flew through Mill Ruins in half an hour, soon finding themselves on a pre–Revolutionary War farm called Cocked Hat. Fortunately, the owners allowed the hunt to pass through. After being slowed by some old barbed-wire fences, Sister and the field were soon on their way but had to press to catch up with the hounds.

The fox turned back east. They had to stop again, throw coats over the old barbed-wire fences, jump over, and go. Whoever left their coat on the wire could either stop to pick it up or leave it, returning for it later. The pace was so good that Walter, who had dismounted to put his coat on the wire, thought "the hell with it," and chose to ride in his vest and shirt. He was sweating. He also made note to finally panel Cocked Hat. It was last on everyone's list because the foxes rarely came this way.

If the fox was tiring he gave no evidence, for Betty, keen-eyed, caught sight of him vaulting over a fallen tree, serenely running on toward the hundred-acre enclosure called Shootrough, the very back of Mill Ruins. Peter had set up his clay pigeons here and Walter, sensibly, worked from close to the house out. It would be another three years before he cleaned up this field and fixed the fences; although the old snake fencing held, a few places sagged.

The fox leapt onto the top of the snake fencing and nimbly loped along, jumping over the places where the split rails crossed. He then jumped off, ran straight and true down to the strong creek that fed, finally, the millrace. He didn't use the creek at that point but ran alongside it, neatly stepping on stones or anything to foil his scent.

Betty, keeping him in sight and riding hard on Magellan, marveled at this big red's sangfroid.

Finally, he launched into the creek, swimming downstream, letting the current do most of the work. He clambered out two hundred yards later, shook himself, then trotted to his den, the main entrance being under the exposed roots of an enormous willow twenty yards from the stream but high up, for the ground rose up. Betty could see other holes in the ground from where she stopped, some cleverly concealed and others out in the open.

She breathed deeply, as did Magellan. They waited. The hounds sounded fabulous as they drew closer. She saw Cora and Dragon running neck and neck, the rest of the pack behind them by a few paces. Dragon flung himself into the main entrance. Cora followed.

As Shaker galloped up, Betty moved to him, wordlessly taking his reins as he dismounted.

He blew "gone to ground," then patted each hound, praising them by name.

He mounted up, gathered the pack, turned toward the field.

"Big night tonight," Sister said, glowing with happiness for the morning's run. "Let's go in."

"Right you are," he said, then rode alongside the field, stopping at the Hilltoppers, where Bobby Franklin doffed his hunt cap in appreciation of the excellent sport.

Shaker touched his cap with his crop, rode right up alongside Lorraine. He took off his cap, leaned over, and kissed her.

"Merry Christmas," she whispered.

He kissed her again, smiled bigger than anyone remembered seeing him smile, put his cap back on, and rode back to the trailers at the mill. He whistled and sang to himself the whole way.

The hounds just thought it was the best.

CHAPTER 32

The Great Hall, swathed in silver and white, dazzled the celebrants as they passed through the massive wooden doors. In the middle of the room, Bill Wheatley and his theater crew fashioned an enormous silver fox, seven feet high. This beautiful creature sat looking out over the crowd, her tail wrapped around her hind feet. Around her cavorted a litter of gray foxes with one black fox, in honor of Inky. Forming a circle around this family was a delicately interwoven garland of grapevines and holly, the berries red against the silver. A placard, black with silver script, rested at the base of the fox. It read: "In honor of our own silver fox, Sister Jane, MFH."

Beyond the tables and the great fox was the dance floor, the raised dais behind that would hold the band when they made their appearance after dessert.

A separate room housed the silent auction. Sorrel, Marty, and the other ladies of the hunt spent the afternoon arranging the tables, carefully placing each item to good effect.

Marty did come through with one huge item—a nineteenth-century wicker cart, two big, graceful wheels at the side. Even if a guest was not a horseman, it would be sensational in the garden or used in decoration.

As the girls decorated they sang Christmas carols, which the ladies would then pick up and sing along. This progressed to where each room took turns selecting a carol. It was a lovely way to spend a December day, the light fading so quickly darkness engulfed the late afternoon.

The Jefferson Hunt ladies wisely brought their ball gowns with them. Charlotte arranged for them to use the various guest houses that dotted the campus. The ladies, in turn, gave generously to Custis Hall for this honor.

As classes had ended December 16, most of the girls had gone home for the holidays. But as was the custom since 1887, the best riders stayed on for Christmas Hunt and the hunt ball if they so desired. It was considered a singular honor to be asked to stay. And a few girls were chosen to stand in the receiving line, a tie of the younger generation to the older. No Custis Hall student so selected was required to pay for the ball, and if they wished, they could bring an escort. His fee would also be waived. Some girls asked Miller School boys, others headed straight for UVA. Valentina and Tootie, always fending off male attentions, wanted to go stag. Felicity surprised everyone by asking a boy from Woodberry Forest, Howard Lindquist, the quarterback on the football team.

Bill Wheatley wore scarlet tails as did Gray, since both men had their colors. The evening attire for a male foxhunter, while expensive, is breathtaking. Sister, in an off-the-shoulder white Balenciaga gown, a three-stand pearl choker at her neck, with two single pearl earrings, flanked on top by diamonds like teardrop leaves, her silver hair brilliant, was a show-stopper herself.

Most women wore black. It was always easier to find a black ball gown. Marty's had black bugle beads, and her ruby necklace, bracelet, and earrings were worth a king's ransom. No one could fault Crawford for not properly honoring his wife as far as jewelry was concerned. And no matter how much a lady might tell the man in her life that jewels didn't count, they did. Jewelry is the woman's version of battle ribbons.

The Custis Hall girls wore no major jewelry. Even Valentina's parents knew better than to give her important stones. Young women should not wear large diamonds, rubies, or sapphires. They are not yet ready to carry such responsibility, for jewelry, in its way, determines a woman's place. Much is expected of a woman perceived as wealthy. Then, too, few young women understand the value of those stones. One has to live to understand both money and value, which are separate. Valentina wore a simple platinum necklace with a solitaire diamond nestled in the hollow of her beautiful throat.

Pamela Rene, proud of her work on the silver fox, wore beaten-silver earrings that her mother had sent by FedEx for the occasion, along with a black dress that looked quite good on Pamela.

Tootie wore no jewelry at all. Felicity wore a single strand of pearls that had been her grandmother's.

The girls had had no time to investigate the silent auction but each was hoping there might be some pin or bracelet there that would be appropriate. Felicity desperately wanted one of the nineteenth-century painted crystal pins that she heard had made it into the auction thanks to Mrs. August, a member now in her nineties. This was Sorrel's coup just as the wicker cart was Marty's.

The girls stood in the receiving line along with Charlotte, Sister, and Walter. A four-piece combo played until the dance band showed up.

By six-thirty the room was packed. The girls were amazed at how handsome Knute Nilsson was in white tie. As for Bill, they knew he'd be the peacock and he was, for with his scarlet he wore silk breeches, white silk hose, and the dancing pumps of the eighteenth century. The other men wore patent-leather dancing shoes, but they stuck to pants. It had to be admitted that Bill looked good because he had good legs.

Dorothy and the food service did a marvelous job on the food. The open bar in its hour of glory was used well. The wine and champagne flowed and by the time the couples hit the dance floor, everyone was in exceedingly good cheer, including Shaker, who didn't drink but was intoxicated by Lorraine's effort to please him by hunting.

As the gyrations on the dance floor intensified, Crawford was bumped hard in the rear by Bill Wheatley, which sent Crawford straight into Lorraine's cleavage. As he reached out to balance himself he had the misfortune to grasp the front of Lorraine's dress, which freed her bosoms to the light. Beautiful as they were, this was not what Lorraine had ever intended. She screamed and crossed her arms over her breasts as Shaker manfully pressed himself to her until she could hike up her gown. Once this was accomplished, Shaker whirled to an ogling Crawford, hit him with a straight right, and decked him.

Sister couldn't reach her huntsman fast enough to prevent what she feared would happen. Gray escorted Shaker off the dance floor.

"He's always wanted Lorraine! I'll kill him if he touches her."

Lorraine, hanging on to Shaker's free arm, tried to placate him. "Honey, he didn't mean it."

"They all want you."

Gray said in a soothing voice, "She's a beautiful woman, Shaker. You're right to protect her, but in this case Crawford was pushed by Bill Wheatley."

"Did you see the way he looked at her!" Shaker wanted to kill Crawford.

As Bill pushed his way through the dancers to apologize, leaving his wife high and dry, Crawford was being lifted to his feet by Walter and Sam Lorillard. Marty kept patting her husband's jaw. He held his hand over the red mark and as he was coming back into focus he was rip-shit mad.

The girls watched with fascination. The others watched as they danced. The music was too good to stop.

Gray and Lorraine walked Shaker outside, now bitterly cold. Lorraine was shivering. Shaker wrapped her in his scarlet tails. Bill Wheatley sprinted out.

"Shaker, I'm so sorry. This is my fault."

"It's Crawford's damned fault and don't make excuses for him."

Gray said, "Bill, the silent auction will close in half an hour. Why don't you make an announcement after the next dance for people to go in there and close out the bids? Your voice will carry over the noise."

Bill assented and left.

"I know he's a big landowner. I know he's paid for this ball and pumps money into the club, but he better never put a hand on Lorraine again or I will kill him."

Lorraine, still shivering, said, "Honey, if he values his teeth he won't even look at me."

This brightened Shaker up a bit. "Here I am blowing off steam and you're shivering. Come on. Let's go back inside."

As Gray was steering Shaker and Lorraine in a direction where he hoped they would not run into Crawford or Marty, Crawford, white-lipped with rage, stormed out of the Great Hall, leaving Marty in the lurch.

He was so mad he was deaf to his wife's entreaties.

Walter put his arm through Marty's as she started after Crawford. "Let him walk it off."

"You don't know Crawford. When he gets like this nothing good can come of it." Concern shone on her face. "He's unpredictable."

"Would you like me to talk to him?"

"No." She shook her head. "Let me find him."

"Then let me go with you. And get your coat. No point freezing as we search the grounds."

By the time they emerged, sufficiently bundled up, Crawford was roaring down the road to the kennels, eight miles away. Marty threw up her hands, as she was left in the lurch again.

A hired hand hit him. That was bad enough. But this hired hand thought he was a fool, couldn't ride, and knew nothing about hounds. He'd show that arrogant son of a bitch huntsman that he could handle hounds as well as Shaker.

It wasn't rocket science. It's a bunch of dogs.

He screeched to a halt by the kennels. He knew the party wagon would be parked by the draw run.

He backed the trailer to the gates, got out, slid them open, then closed them on either side of the trailer so hounds couldn't scoot out.

That wasn't so hard.

Then he walked to the dog run, opened the gate, walked to the bitch run, opened the gate, and watched as the hounds, a bit confused but willing, walked down the large kennel aisle. He opened the door to the draw run. They filed in, then walked onto the party wagon. He shut the doors to the trailer, closed the runs. Then he walked into the office and took Shaker's walking-out horn and placed it through his white vest buttons.

He double-checked the back trailer door when he pulled away from the gates. Soon he was on his way back to Custis Hall.

"Anyone can handle hounds," he said to himself, his jaw still aching.

In a way he was right. The Jefferson Hunt hounds were easy to handle because Sister and Shaker poured their love and life into their pack.

Meanwhile, Bill Wheatley announced the silent auction had but a half hour to run. The band took a break so people walked back into the room to bid anew. Valentina, Tootie, and Pamela finally got into the room as they'd had no time up until now. Felicity and Howard also walked in.

The girls admired the saddle from Horse Country in Warrenton. There was even a bridle of English leather with the bit, English steel, the best, sewn in, which Jim Meads, the famous photographer, had sent over from England. As they slowly walked down the long rows of tables they marveled at the items.

They stopped dead in front of the gold ring with the oval onyx stone. The script on a white card read, "Ring donated by Target, the red fox living at After All Farm."

For a moment no one said a word. Knute Nilsson, also getting into the room for the first time, was moving toward them. He didn't want to buy anything, but knew he had to put his name on some small item and hope someone would soon outbid him.

He stopped at the ring, too, noticing the stunned expressions on the girls' faces.

"Girls, are you unwell?" Then his eyes took in the ring, a flicker of the eyelids.

"Mr. Nilsson, this is Professor Kennedy's ring."

"Well, perhaps she donated it," he replied.

"No, it says Target the fox," Pamela answered.

"Professor Kennedy wasn't a foxhunter," Valentina said.

"She knew everyone here was and this is a hunt ball." He shrugged, seeing Bill walk toward him out of the corner of his eye.

"Professor Kennedy had no sense of humor." Tootie

felt her stomach sink, a nameless dread overtaking her, but she kept her wits. "It must be some mistake. Come on, gang." She smiled brightly at Knute and Bill, who now reached him, and dragged the girls with her. "Shut up. Just shut up," she hissed under her breath.

As the girls walked away, Sam Lorillard noticed a heated, whispered conversation between Knute and Bill, both men's faces red as fire.

Tootie dragged Valentina, Pamela, Felicity, and Howard to Sister, luckily talking to Charlotte during the break in the music.

"Hello, girls," Sister smiled. "This is the best ball we've ever had, thanks to your efforts."

"Sister, Mrs. Norton, something's really wrong." Tootie kept her voice low, her breath in short gasps.

"What is it?" Charlotte instinctively put her arm around Tootie's shoulders as the others looked on.

"Professor Kennedy's ring is in the auction." Valentina supplied the answer.

The release of the identity of the corpse would be made Monday. The girls did not know that Professor Kennedy was dead. Only Charlotte, Sister, Gray, and Ben Sidel knew that. Even Walter didn't know.

"Oh, God!" Charlotte blurted out.

Very calmly Sister said, "Girls, not a word. Not yet." She almost said "Your life may depend on it," but figured they were upset enough.

She motioned to Gray, who came over. The little group walked back to the silent auction.

The ring, not a hot item, had garnered few bidders, but Knute Nilsson was one. He bid $100.

"It's Professor Kennedy's ring," Tootie declared.

Charlotte nodded, "Yes, it is."

"Mrs. Norton, she wouldn't part with her ring," Tootie said.

"What are you saying, Tootie?" Pamela began to feel Tootie's fear.

"She's dead," Tootie barely whispered.

"Why? And wouldn't we know?" Pamela resisted this.

Sister stepped in. "Girls, come with me."

Sister, Gray, Charlotte, Tootie, Valentina, Pamela, and Felicity followed, as did Howard. Sister and Charlotte spoke low to each other.

Charlotte quietly told the girls that Professor Kennedy was the corpse under St. John's of the Cross. The positive I.D. would be released Monday. Until the lab in Richmond verified the remains, she wouldn't announce Professor Kennedy's death.

"Where's the sheriff?" Felicity asked.

"On duty. That's why he's not here tonight," Charlotte said.

"Shouldn't he see the ring?" Tootie asked.

"Yes," Charlotte answered.

"I'll call him. Honey, do you have your cell phone stuck somewhere?" Sister asked Gray, who pulled the tiniest, flattest phone out from his inside breast pocket.

As she was calling, Pamela said to Charlotte, "This

is about the slave work, isn't it?"

"I don't know," Charlotte honestly replied. "But I believe it certainly has something to do with whatever is in those cases."

Before anyone could respond to that a hell of a commotion erupted in the Great Hall.

Crawford let loose the hounds, horn to lips, and he was bearing down on Shaker, stunned at this perfidy.

"You dumb son of a bitch!" Crawford bellowed. "I can hunt these hounds."

Sister, Gray, Charlotte, the girls, and Howard ran into the room as fast as their finery would allow them.

Tootie, wearing not high heels but dancing slippers, lifted her skirts, ran up the steps to the bandstand, then jumped off. She reached Crawford before Shaker did. The hounds milled around causing havoc, eating leftovers on plates. Tootie put her body in front of Crawford's as Shaker reached them.

Shaker pushed through the crowd toward Crawford. He had the presence of mind to say to the hounds, "Steady, steady."

"Don't, Mr. Crown, don't," she said quite calmly, but with true command.

The sight of this slip of a girl, ravishingly beautiful, in front of a man he couldn't abide, made him realize Crawford wasn't worth hitting. He snatched the horn from Crawford's vest.

Hounds gobbled leftovers, gleefully pulling plates off tables or getting on the tables.

Valentina looked over the astonished crowd and saw

Knute, knife in hand, pursuing Bill. Both men crashed through the double doors.

"Sister! Sister! It's Knute and he's got a knife, chasing Bill."

Sister walked up to Crawford and slapped him hard across the face. "I will see you rot in Hell."

This stunned the onlookers more than the hounds filling the Great Hall.

Shaker put the horn to his lips, blowing three long notes.

Cora, Diana, Ardent, the Ds, the Ts, all came, although they hated to leave the feast.

That fast, Sister, holding up her own long skirts, hurried out of the building. "Come on, huntsman, come on."

There was not a moment to load the hounds, much as Sister wanted to put them up. In fact, there wasn't a moment to lose.

Shaker, Gray, Charlotte, Sam, Walter, Valentina, Tootie, Pamela, Felicity, and Howard followed.

Rarely had Shaker seen that urgency in his master. He trusted her completely and followed her with the pack.

Betty yelled over to Sybil, "Whip in, Sybil. You take the right. I'll take the left."

Holding up their skirts, they plunged outside into the deep cold, caught up with the hounds, and, shivering, running along, ensured order.

In the distance they could see Knute, a fitter, faster man, gaining on Bill Wheatley, who was heading for the theater department. He made it, slamming the door in Knute's face, but Knute got it open before Bill could lock it.

The hounds and humans ran faster, Gray up front with Shaker. "Hurry, man, hurry!"

By now, the rest of the celebrants spilled out onto the quad to watch in fascination and wonder at the sight.

Gray hurled open the door, hounds moving ahead of him.

"Get 'em up," Shaker called, as he was beginning to get the picture.

Naturally, they looked for foxes, and there were some tatty old furs in the costume storage room. The hounds heard the human feet ahead, running, as Bill bolted into the costume room, hoping he could somehow hide from Knute.

Knute was quickly in the room, brushing costumes aside, tearing them off hangers in a silent, efficient rage.

Bill tiptoed through the rows of costumes until he came to the back of the room where the fake guns, battle-axes, and swords were stored. He flipped open a cabinet and pulled out Zorro's sword, sharp enough to cut rope and ribbon, which the play demanded. He waited.

Gray and Shaker opened the door. They could hear the costumes being pulled off hangers. The hounds were silent. As the men moved forward so did the hounds.

Sister, Charlotte, and the girls were right behind the hounds, as were Betty and Sybil. Howard had moved up with the men. He was young, strong, and confident.

"I know you're here." Knute was oblivious to the hounds and humans moving through the costumes.

Bill waited, listening intently for Knute's footfall. He was coming from the right.

Knute pulled aside the last row of costumes and saw Bill, who hid the sword behind his back.

"Knute, fancy meeting you here." He smiled genially.

"You son of a bitch!" Knute flung himself forward, knife in the air.

That fast, Bill Wheatley ran him through.

The hounds reached the twitching figure first, blood oozing from Knute's mouth.

"It's a kill!" Dasher declared.

"Leave it," Cora ordered.

The hounds surrounded Knute and Bill, who said, as the humans reached him, "Mad as a hatter."

CHAPTER 33

D id we do something wrong?" Little Diddy asked Ardent as they were being loaded on the party wagon.

"No," Ardent stated authoritatively.

"Crawford did wrong." Asa's gravelly voice carried

in the bitterly cold night air. *"That's why Sister slapped him."*

Sister, a floor-length mink over her white Balenciaga, was loading hounds with Gray, Sam, and Shaker.

Shaken as they were by what had happened, they had to take care of the hounds, their first responsibility.

Charlotte, Carter, Walter, and the other men of the club remained with Bill Wheatley as Ben Sidel's squad car siren screamed in the distance.

The revelers, by twos, walked to their cars. This surely had been an unforgettable hunt ball.

Sorrel, frantically, made sure those who won their bids took their items, as she didn't want anything of value left in the Great Hall. Marty couldn't help since she was ministering to her husband. Marty loved him but knew he was wrong and feared Sister's wrath. She guided him out of the hall to the parking lot. He was shouting and cursing but she managed to get him in the car.

The decorations needed to come down, but at that moment they couldn't think about it. No one in the hall knew of Knute's murder for twenty minutes until Felicity and Howard, sent back by Charlotte, informed them they should go home. When asked why, the two young people told the truth.

Tootie and Valentina, Betty and Sybil, stayed with Sister, helping to load hounds.

Lorraine, aghast at the turn of events, silently

watched as Shaker calmly praised the hounds, loading them into the trailer.

"Good food!" Dragon enthused.

"Roast beef," Trudy dreamily said, her belly full of it.

When the door was closed and latched, Shaker headed for the driver's door.

"Shaker, I wouldn't complain if you killed him," Betty said.

"This isn't over. You go. I'll stay." Sister half-closed her eyes for a minute.

"I'll stay, too. You're in danger." He put his arms around his boss's broad shoulders.

"No, honey, go. Hounds first. Gray and Walter are here." She then opened the passenger door, opened the glove compartment, and removed the .38. She took out the box of shells, clicked open the chamber, filling the six holes with bullets. She put the box of shells in her left pocket, the .38 in her right. Usually Shaker or Walter rode with a .38 under his coat. If a deer had not been finished off by a hunter one of the men completed the unenviable but humane task.

Shaker looked at her. "Boss, for God's sake, be careful."

A broad smile crossed her face; she was energized by the danger. She said, "I'm a tough old bird. Go on."

Tootie, shivering—her coat wasn't heavy enough—said, "We should go to the cases."

"Yes. Can you collect the girls who worked with

Professor Kennedy to meet me at the Main Hall? Get Mrs. Norton, too."

Shaker, Lorraine in the truck cab with him, fired up the motor and slowly pulled out, worried sick about Sister.

Gray put his hand on Sister's shoulder. She turned to him; they started the long walk to Old Main Hall.

"I will kill Crawford myself. The point is a pack of hounds, any kind of hounds, has been bred, trained, developed, and loved for one purpose and one purpose only: to chase the quarry. I don't believe in demonstrations before crowds. I don't believe in marching hounds in parades on hot pavement. I don't believe in taking hounds to county fairs so children can pet them. If we want to promote foxhunting in a positive light then the first thing we do is honor our hounds. Make videos if you must, but do not use your hounds for any frivolous purpose. I know I'm conservative on this but that's what I believe and as long as I am master of Jefferson Hunt, these hounds will not be trifled with, and I know once Crawford's rage passes he will find a way to make himself right and Shaker and myself wrong." Her heel slipped on a bit of icy sidewalk. He grabbed her elbow. "Sorry, Gray, I didn't mean to pontificate." She took a deep breath, the frigid air hitting her lungs. "And I'm worried. We've got to find what's in those cases. We aren't going to like it."

As the hounds were driven out, Ben Sidel pulled up to the theater building, an ambulance behind him.

Charlotte gave him what details she could. Ben whispered something to Ty Banks as the rescue squad removed Knute's body.

Charlotte, Ben, Walter, and Carter walked Bill Wheatley to Old Main Hall. He professed to know nothing about the cases. As for why Knute Nilsson would suddenly turn on him with a knife, he accounted for it by the tremendous financial strain Knute was under.

"What strain?" Charlotte asked as they headed across the oldest quad, Old Main straight ahead.

"He bought that schooner. Do you know how much one of those things costs?"

"I don't," Charlotte said.

"He paid $575,000 for that thing. It has a navigation system, a galley, sleeps people. It's incredible. He just lost his head. Midlife crisis, I guess."

"Why would he take it out on you?" Ben asked, voice level as though this were a coffee-break conversation.

"Don't you usually lash out at the people closest to you? Knute and I have been friends ever since I moved here. I told him he was losing it. Told him not to be impulsive. He wouldn't listen. The bills mounted up and I think he just snapped. Even his wife didn't know how bad it was."

Charlotte, Carter, Walter, and Ben considered this as they walked up the long steps to the front doors of Old Main Hall, lights blazing inside.

Felicity, Howard, and Pamela Rene had joined

Sister, Tootie, Valentina, and the others.

Sister greeted Ben, then said, "Whatever this is about, starting with the hanging of Al Perez, is in these cases."

Ben's eyes took in the artifacts. He turned to Tootie, Valentina, Felicity, and Pamela. "You worked with Professor Kennedy more than the other students, didn't you?"

"Yes, sir," they replied.

"When she handled these objects, did she say anything that aroused your interest?"

"No. We gave Mrs. Norton our notes," Pamela replied.

"They did. I reviewed them briefly. Seemed like a dry description to me."

"What about the photographs?" Ben persisted.

"No," Valentina answered. "She made us shoot every side or angle of the objects. But she didn't say anything."

Tootie thought a long time, then said, "The only thing she did that I noticed was sometimes when she was writing up her description she'd put a star by an item."

"Did you put that in your notes?" Sister asked, her intuition about Tootie's intelligence and plain good sense again confirmed.

"This ring a bell with any of you other girls?" Ben corrected himself, "Young ladies?"

"Well, I saw her do it, but I didn't think anything of it. I didn't put a star in my notes. But my notes aren't very good," Pamela confessed.

Valentina shrugged, "I didn't pay much attention. Sorry."

Felicity chimed in, "Sometimes when I'd photograph an object—that was my job—I didn't take too many notes, but Professor Kennedy would come over and pick up some things, not others."

"What's unusual about that?" Bill was curious.

"At first I didn't think anything, but then I began to see that what she picked up was usually in good shape. She didn't touch other things at all and some things no one touched. They were too delicate. She had me photograph them in the cases."

"Charlotte, would you get Tootie's notes?" Ben asked the headmistress.

"Of course."

As Charlotte left for her office, Ben said, "Why don't you first show me what she wouldn't touch?"

"Sure." Pamela walked right over and pointed to a large basket made of soaked strips of wood. Small bits of yarn, the balls long ago removed, remained inside along with a pair of horn knitting needles.

"Was the area underneath, around these kinds of things, clean?" Ben asked.

"Depends." Valentina led him to the case next to the one where Pamela had pointed out the basket. "See this baby's bonnet? It's been dusted around it but we were afraid to pick it up because it's disintegrating."

"I see."

"But most of the stuff is clean, shelves, too." Valentina wondered what they'd find.

"Are the jewels real?" Ben asked, just as Charlotte returned with Tootie's handwritten notes as well as the ones she'd typed into her computer. She also had the key to the cases.

"She didn't say anything about that. I mean, Professor Kennedy didn't say if the jewelry was expensive." Felicity studied a fancy brooch as Charlotte returned.

"Charlotte, have any items ever been removed from these cases with your knowledge?"

"The only time I know anything has even been taken out of these cases is during Professor Kennedy's investigation."

"Tootie, point out from your notes anything Professor Kennedy starred."

As Tootie's eye ran down her lists, Sister asked Bill, "Would it be possible to sew diamonds onto dresses without anyone noticing?"

"You mean noticing that they were real diamonds?"

"Yes."

"It's possible." He shrugged. "Seems like a lot of work. Wouldn't it be easier to put them in a safe-deposit box?"

"Old Main Hall is always open, right?" Gray asked.

"No, it's locked at night," Charlotte answered.

"So who could get in?" Ben raised an eyebrow.

"Any member of the school's administration or Jake Walford, in charge of buildings and grounds."

"You could unlock the doors?" Ben asked.

"I could. My secretary could. Knute. The entire

administration is housed in Old Main."

"Al Perez?" Sister was beginning to get an idea of how the crimes were committed but she still didn't know what it was—was it diamonds, was it drugs?

"Yes," Charlotte answered.

"Could Bill get in?" Sister persisted.

"No, not without one of us." Charlotte, too, was seeing the pattern.

"But Bill, you could come in the middle of the night with Al or Knute?" Sister focused on Bill, who was calm.

"I could. I didn't, but I could."

"Were Al and Knute close?" Ben asked. "I didn't think they were. If they were, it didn't come out when Custis Hall people were questioned."

"They had a good working relationship," Bill offered. "I wouldn't say they were close."

Charlotte nodded in assent.

Tootie quietly asked the sheriff, "Do you want me to point out the items?"

"I do, in one minute, Tootie. Charlotte, who knows about the key to the cases?" Ben could feel his own excitement rising.

"Teresa, my assistant. Knute, the treasurer. I think that's it."

"Did you ever notice the key had been moved?"

"No," she answered Ben.

"Is it locked up, the key, I mean?"

She blushed. "Well, no."

"Do you have it now?"

"Yes." Charlotte opened her hand, a key on a wide, dark blue ribbon nesting within.

"Charlotte, if you have no objection, I'd like you to open these cases and for Tootie to remove those items that Professor Kennedy starred."

"Of course."

Bill interjected, "Charlotte, what if something falls apart in your hands?"

"I'll take full responsibility. Under the circumstances, I think harming an item is the lesser of two evils."

Bill said nothing, but his disapproval was apparent.

"Carry them over here to this table," Ben instructed.

Tootie removed a gold snuff box with a small ruby in the center. She took out General Washington's epaulettes, his dress sword, shoe buckles, and a beautiful brocade vest.

Sister, Charlotte, Ben, Pamela, Felicity, Howard, Gray, and Valentina crowded around the table. Bill stood just behind this group as did Walter and Carter.

"May I touch this?" Ben pointed to the snuff box.

"Of course," Charlotte assented.

Delicately, Ben picked up the snuff box, examined it, flicked open the lid. He sniffed the inside; no hint of tobacco remained. He replaced it.

As he reached for the epaulettes, Sister remarked, "Aren't they in remarkable condition?" It hit her. "Ben, too remarkable."

A collective intake of breath followed. Sister pulled the .38 from her coat pocket.

Bill took a step back, turned.

Walter grabbed his arm but Bill shook him off.

"Bill!" Charlotte called.

"Bill, stop or I'll shoot," Sister also called.

"Ty's outside the door. You won't need to exercise your marksmanship." Ben's dry sense of humor somehow fitted the rigors of his profession.

Bill flew through the front doors, only to be brought back in a matter of minutes, hands handcuffed behind him.

Ty marched him to Ben and the gathering. "He thought he'd rather live."

"Bill, what have you done!" The enormity of his betrayal was seeping into Charlotte's consciousness.

"You might as well tell us, Bill. If you cooperate, things will go easier for you."

"Sheriff, that's what you guys always say," Bill said, his lips pressed together.

"I'll say this for you, Bill Wheatley. You're a fabulous costume and set designer. You've obviously stolen the original items and faked these"—Sister picked up the epaulettes—"under our noses."

Bill remained silent.

"You killed for this?" Tootie asked her teacher.

"Tootie," Bill smiled sardonically, "there are six and a half billion people in the world. What's one more or less?"

CHAPTER 34

Tuesday's hunt, December 20, was well attended. College students were home for the holidays. Jennifer and Sari were there and Sari was thrilled that her mother rode with the Hilltoppers. People took off work. Tootie, Valentina, Felicity, and even Pamela, who begged her parents, stayed with Sister and would be there until December 22, when they'd all go home.

Charlotte, also on school break, hunted with Bunny. Everyone needed a physical release from the strain and the extraordinary events.

Sister had had a long talk with Shaker and Walter. They all agreed that Crawford must be asked to leave the hunt. Still, there were many details to be ironed out. They expected him to hit back and hit hard. They'd just have to deal with it, although they knew one of his weapons would be money.

The good news was the hunt ball made Shaker realize that he couldn't live without Lorraine and he loved Sari, her daughter, as his own. He had asked Lorraine to marry him yesterday so she wouldn't think he'd done this in the upheaval of the ball or the arrest of Bill Wheatley. She had said yes.

"Guess you asked her when she experienced a weak moment," Sister teased, then hugged him.

The hunt, down at Chapel Cross, proved wonderful. The grays began traveling in twos early so they picked up a courting gentleman fox. After they ran him to ground, they picked up two others. What a lovely day.

Once back at the trailers, Ben Sidel joined them. He could rarely take off a Tuesday, usually hunting only on Saturdays.

They gathered around the tailgate as Ben told them Bill finally confessed.

"How did it all fit together?" Sister asked Ben for all of them.

"You know, it was ingenious. I'll give them that. Knute, Bill, and Al all wanted and needed money. Not that Custis Hall doesn't pay a fair wage, but academic salaries are slim by comparison to other professions. Write it down to greed. Al would sound out those alumnae, or usually their husbands, who would pay big bucks for a sword of Washington. Some people want to own things. We've begun questioning those alumnae who bought things from Al and Knute. Knute had a wide net of contacts but quite different from Al's. Some knew the items were purloined, others did not. Knute's contacts were people in business who wanted Washington's epaulettes on their desk or in a display case. An ego thing. They even sold the sword to a museum in Oregon and they faked a document of agreement from Custis Hall. They did this for two years. At night, Al and Knute would unlock a case, after Bill had made a replica, take the original item; Bill would replace it with the fake."

"And there'd be nothing unusual about Al or Knute

working in the evening if anyone passed Old Main," Charlotte remarked.

"They split the money evenly three ways," Ben continued. "But Al got shaky after a time and wanted out. Neither Knute nor Bill trusted him not to turn on them to save his own hide should any of this come to light. Knute wore the second Zorro costume. Bill arranged that. And before killing Al, Bill showed Knute Hangman's Ridge, where the den was. When Halloween came, according to Bill, it was a piece of cake. Knute sprinted to his car, parked away from the Great Hall, drove back, and lured Al out of his car by saying they could have some fun with the kids, seeing double, scare the hell out of them. Bill said he wasn't there, obviously, being in the school bus, but Al willingly went along with Knute's 'gag,' including putting his head in a noose because Knute said he had another fake corpse. He just wanted an idea how high to lift it or something like that. Bill embellishes."

"Why so public an execution?" Charlotte thought it way too grisly.

"Theatrical. Make a show. Draw everyone away from the real issue, which was the artifacts in the cases. All was going well until Pamela staged her protest. Al lost his composure after that. He wanted out anyway, that put him right over the edge. It worked for a while. The hanging diverted our attention."

"Then Professor Kennedy showed up and they both

knew time was running out." Sister felt sorry for the tiny lady, whom she liked.

"Knute did his best to keep current with Charlotte's plans about responding to the protestors' issues, which, of course, involved the artifacts. He thought they could make it through the middle of the next semester—wrap things up, as it were. Bill could feign an illness. Knute, if it got too close, would just vanish, but they'd be out of here before the theft of the items was discovered."

"Yes, we were going to appoint a search committee for an expert in this time period and in slave life," said Charlotte. "but Pamela beat us to it. When I investigated Professor Kennedy's credentials, I thought, 'Why not just get this over with in this fiscal year?' Knute harped on the budget so I thought we might as well take the hit now in hopes our treasury report for next year would be better. I didn't see any point in spreading out the pain."

"Both men showed great self-possession," Walter said, wondering how they could do it. He'd be ravaged by guilt.

"That they did, until the hunt ball." Gray also thought their ability to act almost admirable. "Who called Sister?"

"Bill," Ben replied. "He couldn't resist adding to the drama. And maybe he was beginning to fear Knute."

In Bill's case, they might expect it, but for Knute to keep cool, that was something.

"When I asked for the girls' notes at lunch both Bill

and Knute were at the table. That must have sent a bolt of fear through them."

"It did," Ben answered Charlotte. "They had no way of knowing how extensive those notes were. They didn't think Professor Kennedy had told you of her findings because she was the type to make a complete presentation. She wouldn't have wanted to upset you or Custis Hall without a thorough documentation. Bill met her at the airport before her flight, and learned that she had mentioned irregularities."

"He killed her?" Betty thought this all dreadful.

"He offered to help with her bags. Said he was flying out, too, but the flight was delayed, which it was as it turned out. Luck played him a good hand. He talked her into a quick lunch, drove down a back road close to the airport, opened the passenger window, shot her in the left temple before she knew what hit her. Most of the debris flew out the window and he cleaned up the rest, dumped her at St. John's of the Cross. Before he shot her he pulled the gun on her, asking if she'd told Charlotte that items were bogus. She told the truth, hoping to save her life."

"How much money did they make?" Gray asked.

"Six and a half million dollars. They also sold forged signatures of George Washington. Bill is a man of many talents." Ben reached for a chocolate chip cookie.

"And a good actor," Walter said.

"This is terrible for Custis Hall. It will be public record," Charlotte honestly stated.

"They were clever. They might have gotten away with it for several more years if Pamela hadn't thrown a monkey wrench into the works. There's no way anyone could have foreseen this," Gray said soothingly.

"No, but it might have been prevented if there had been better security on those cases," Charlotte said, admitting her failing.

"Knute would still have been able to get into the cases. He was treasurer of the school. You trusted him. We all trusted him," Sister said.

They talked, ate, considered why some people break the social contract and others don't.

As people returned to their trailers to head for home, Walter asked Tootie why she stepped in front of Crawford at the hunt ball.

"I owed him one, Mr. Lungrun." Tootie smiled sweetly. "He helped us when we were lost in the fog."

"A debt of honor." Walter, towering over her, dropped his arm over her shoulder.

While Tootie was with Walter, Pamela, Felicity, and Valentina had seen to the horses, even cleaning the tack using the five-gallon water carrier in the trailer tack room.

Sister double-checked the hound list at the party wagon with Shaker. "Good day, huntsman. Good day, hounds." She called out to Betty and Sybil, "Thank you. Good work."

"It was a good day, wasn't it?" Betty beamed.

Sister gazed at the four girls, all together now at her

trailer. "Shaker, it's wonderful to have children in the house. Today is the feast day of Dominic of Silos. He was born around A.D. 1000. He's credited with healing powers, especially about pregnancies."

"Thinking of throwing a litter?" Shaker laughed.

"Ah," she smiled, "my time has passed, but if I could, I would. Well, you can make up for me."

"I don't know." His face turned red. "Funny how we hunt Chapel Cross and there's St. John's of the Cross at Little Dalby. And so many times the foxes will run to the little country churches. Guess they're getting religion since those churches are full of dens."

"Crawford has already broken ground for St. Swithun. The foxes at Beasley Hall can now worship. It will cost a bloody fortune." Betty now stood with Shaker and Sister. "We haven't talked, but Jane, I know what you have to do. I think most of the members will understand. He'll go down swinging."

"Well, we'll get through it, Betty. We always do." Sister paused a long time. "Funny thing about getting older. You realize every relationship you ever had, on every level, is always with you. The people who hate you. The people who love you. The people whose love turned to hate. And the people who didn't think much of you and over time learned you were worth your salt. And then you think of the ghosts. Their feelings about you. I sometimes think RayRay is near."

Shaker nodded, "And Archie."

"Always Archie." Sister named the great anchor hound they lost to a bear years back. "I loved that hound with all my heart and soul." She sighed. "Well, if everyone is building chapels, churches, or cathedrals, I suppose we could build one."

"St. Archie?"

"There isn't one, a human one anyway. We could build a little one, would have to be clapboard, to St. Hubert. That would be in keeping."

"Sister, I've got it. We build one to St. Rita, the saint of impossible causes," he laughed.

Sister laughed with him, glad that life goes on, no matter what, and foxes will always run.

SOME USEFUL TERMS

Away—A fox has "gone away" when he has left the covert. Hounds are "away" when they have left the covert on the line of the fox.

Brush—The fox's tail.

Burning scent—Scent so strong or hot that hounds pursue the line without hesitation.

Bye day—A day not regularly on the fixture card.

Cap—The fee nonmembers pay to a hunt for that day's sport.

Carry a good head—When hounds run well together to a good scent, a scent spread wide enough for the whole pack to feel it.

Carry a line—When hounds follow the scent. This is also called "working a line."

Cast—Hounds spread out in search of scent. They may cast themselves or be cast by the huntsman.

Charlie—A term for a fox. A fox may also be called Reynard.

Check—When hounds lose the scent and stop. The field must wait quietly while the hounds search for the scent.

Colors—A distinguishing color—usually worn on the collar but sometimes on the facings of a coat—that identifies a hunt. Colors can be awarded only by the master and can be won only in the field.

Couple straps—Two-strap hound collars connected by a swivel link. Some members of staff will carry these on the right rear of the saddle. Since the Middle Ages hounds had been brought to the meets coupled. Hounds are always spoken of, counted, in couples. Today hounds walk or are driven to the meets. Rarely, if ever, are they coupled, but a whipper-in still carries couple straps should a hound need assistance.

Covert—A patch of woods or bushes where a fox might hide. Pronounced *cover.*

Cry—How one hound tells another what is happening. The sound will differ according to the various stages of the chase. It's also called "giving tongue" and should occur when a hound is working a line.

Cub hunting—The informal hunting of young foxes in the late summer and early fall, before formal hunting. The main purpose is to enter young hounds into the pack. Until recently only the most knowledgeable members were invited to cub hunt since they would not interfere with young hounds.

Dog fox—The male fox.

Dog hound—The male hound.

Double—A series of short, sharp notes blown on the horn to alert all that a fox is afoot. The "gone away" series of notes is a form of doubling the horn.

Draft—To acquire hounds from another hunt is to accept a draft.

Draw—The plan by which a fox is hunted or searched for in a certain area, like a covert.

Drive—The desire to push the fox, to get up with the line. It's a very desirable trait in hounds, so long as they remain obedient.

Dwell—To hunt without getting forward. A hound who dwells is a bit of a putterer.

Enter—Hounds are entered into the pack when they first hunt, usually during cubbing season.

Field—The group of people riding to hounds, exclusive of the master and hunt staff.

Field master—The person appointed by the master to control the field. Often it is the master him- or herself.

Fixture—A card sent to all dues-paying members, stating when and where the hounds will meet. A fixture card properly received is an invitation to hunt. This means the card would be mailed or handed to you by the master.

Gone away—The call on the horn when the fox leaves the covert.

Gone to ground—A fox who has ducked into his den or some other refuge has gone to ground.

Good night—The traditional farewell to the master after the hunt, regardless of the time of day.

Hilltopper—A rider who follows the hunt but does not jump. Hilltoppers are also called the "second field." The jumpers are called the "first flight."

Hoick—The huntsman's cheer to the hounds. It is derived from the Latin *hic haec hoc,* which means "here."

Hold hard—To stop immediately.

Huntsman—The person in charge of the hounds in the field and in the kennel.

Kennelman—A hunt staff member who feeds the hounds and cleans the kennels. In wealthy hunts there may be a number of kennelmen. In hunts with a modest budget, the huntsman or even the master cleans the kennels and feeds hounds.

Lark—To jump fences unnecessarily when hounds aren't running. Masters frown on this since it is often an invitation to an accident.

Lift—To take the hounds from a lost scent in the hopes of finding a better scent farther on.

Line—The scent trail of the fox.

Livery—The uniform worn by the professional members of the hunt staff. Usually it is scarlet, but blue, yellow, brown, and gray are also used. The recent dominance of scarlet has to do with people buying coats off the rack as opposed to having tailors cut them. (When anything is mass-produced, the choices usually dwindle, and such is the case with livery.)

Mask—The fox's head.

Meet—The site where the day's hunting begins.

MFH—The master of foxhounds; the individual in charge of the hunt: hiring, firing, landowner relations, opening territory (in large hunts this is the job of the hunt secretary), developing the pack of hounds, determining the first cast of each meet. As in any leadership position, the master is also the lightning rod for criticism. The master may hunt the hounds, although this is usually done by a professional huntsman, who is also responsible for the hounds in the field and at the kennels. A long relationship between a master and a huntsman allows the hunt to develop and grow.

Nose—The scenting ability of a hound.

Override—To press hounds too closely.

Overrun—When hounds shoot past the line of scent. Often the scent has been diverted or foiled by a clever fox.

Ratcatcher—The informal dress worn during cubbing season and bye days.

Stern—A hound's tail.

Stiff-necked fox—One who runs in a straight line.

Strike hounds—Those hounds who through keenness, nose, and often higher intelligence find the scent first and press it.

Tail hounds—Those hounds running at the rear of the pack. This is not necessarily because they aren't keen; they may be older hounds.

Tally ho—The cheer when the fox is viewed. Derived from the Norman *ty a hillaut,* thus coming into the English language in 1066.

Tongue—To vocally pursue the fox.

View halloo (Halloa)—The cry given by a staff member who views a fox. Staff may also say tally ho or tally back should the fox turn back. One reason a different cry may be used by staff, especially in territory where the huntsman can't see the staff, is that the field in their enthusiasm may cheer something other than a fox.

Vixen—The female fox.

Walk—Puppies are "walked out" in the summer and fall of their first year. It's part of their education and a delight for puppies and staff.

Whippers-in—Also called whips, these are the staff members who assist the huntsman, who make sure the hounds "do right."

Center Point Publishing
600 Brooks Road ● PO Box 1
Thorndike ME 04986-0001 USA

(207) 568-3717

US & Canada:
1 800 929-9108